T0106628

Affairs of the Heart

ANIL GOEL

iUniverse, Inc.
New York   Bloomington

Affairs of the heart

Copyright © 2009 Anil Goel

This is a work of fiction. All of the characters, names, incidents,
organizations, and dialogue in this novel are either the products
of the author's imagination or are used fictitiously.

iUniverse books may be ordered through booksellers or by contacting:

iUniverse
1663 Liberty Drive
Bloomington, IN 47403
www.iuniverse.com
1-800-Authors (1-800-288-4677)

ISBN: 978-1-4401-6155-1 (pbk)
ISBN: 978-1-4401-6154-4 (ebook)

Printed in the United States of America

iUniverse rev. date: 7/29/09

1

Anant made up his mind to ask Sheila for a divorce. From her perspective, she had a man to take care of her, to take her out to lunches, dinners, and parties. A divorce would leave her single and lonely, and her family would be on her case to get married again. But he had suffered enough, and was at the end of his rope. Also, he felt that he was getting a raw deal; staying married to her was really useless as far as he was concerned. He had wanted to talk to her in September but didn't want to upset her near her birthday. Then she sprained her ankle stepping down into the garage, and he felt bad and waited for her to recover. Pretty soon, it was Christmas and then New Year's Day, and he didn't have the heart to spoil her mood during the holiday season.

Finally, after the second week in January, he said, "Sheila, I would like to talk to you."

She looked at him. "What about?"

"Well, I have been thinking about us and this marriage."

"What were you thinking?"

"I think we should get a divorce. This marriage is not working."

"I don't understand, Anant. I'm okay with the marriage. Aren't we friends? Don't we live together and do stuff, watch movies, go out to eat?"

"Yes, we do all that. But you know what I mean. There is more to a marriage than watching movies and eating at restaurants."

"You mean we don't have sex anymore?"

"You know what I want, Sheila. I have decided that I can't live like a monk anymore. Please give me my freedom. I don't want us to have a contentious divorce. You take whatever you want. I will leave the house for you and go stay in an apartment."

"Do you want to have a divorce just so you can fuck other women?"

"Not just sex, Sheila. You know that whenever I made love to you, I always approached you with love. No, Sheila, it's not just sex. It's also lack of communication, and frankly, I am tired of your mood swings and your depression and crying because we can't have children. There are a lot of women out there who can't have kids, but not all of them lose their marbles."

How could he explain to her his feelings of loneliness and despair in the evenings and the long nights? The lack of companionship, physical as well as emotional, was turning him into an angry and bitter man. She completely shut him out of her life. They lived like roommates, rather than husband and wife. Hugs, kisses, and quickies were things of the past. He had waited all those years for her to understand how he felt. He missed her affectionate touch and the look of love in her sparkling eyes when she drove off to work in the mornings. He missed their evening tea, sitting close together on the couch, comparing notes about their days. He missed her eager kisses and passionate embraces in the evenings, when they were reunited after a separation of many hours at work.

Sheila started crying and yelled at him, "So now you are saying that I am a madwoman?"

"No, I am not saying anything. I really want this parting to be amicable. Please don't torture me anymore."

"Okay, do what you want. I am leaving this house. You can have everything. I don't need anything. Just find an attorney and get it over with."

She ran upstairs to her room and shut the door with a bang.

The next day, when she was recovered and calm, he convinced her to stay in the house until the divorce was finalized. "Sheila, please don't leave the house. I want you to have the house. I will find an apartment."

"Anant, I came to Kansas only because of you. Now that you have decided that you no longer want me in your life, I will move back to the East Coast as soon as the divorce is finalized. I think it is best if I move into an apartment until we get a divorce."

"That's not necessary, Sheila. Please stay in this house. We are still friends, and we can live under the same roof for a few more months. Anyway, we have been sleeping in separate rooms for years. There is no point in your spending money on an apartment if you have decided to move back to the East Coast."

She smiled. "You have always been a penny-pincher, and you will never change. I will stay here until the divorce is finalized."

The day after their divorce was settled, she wanted to drive from Kansas City to her parents' home in Maryland. It was a long drive, about twenty hours, and Anant wasn't happy with her decision. Notwithstanding the divorce, he still cared for her and even loved her.

He told her, "I don't think you should drive that far all by yourself. We will ship the car to your parents' house, and you can fly to Washington, D.C. Your parents can pick you up at the airport."

But she was stubborn. "I can stop at Columbus, Ohio, and stay with my friend. I haven't seen her recently; the last time was at a meeting in San Francisco a couple years ago. I can spend a day or two with her and then drive on to Maryland. My car is in a good shape, don't worry."

In the end, he had no choice but to let her drive. But he made sure that her car was serviced, all the fluids were topped off, the tires had the right amount of pressure, and the car washed and vacuumed inside. He charged her cell phone so that she would have a working phone in case of an emergency. He also made sure that her AAA membership was current.

She decided not to take anything with her except her clothes. "I don't care for all the other stuff. It will only remind me of our life together, and I want to move on."

Anant said, "Sheila, all your clothes and shoes may not fit in your car. We may have to ship some by UPS. Why don't you take what you can, and the rest I will ship to your parents' house."

She was leaving for Maryland on a Saturday morning, and Anant helped her load her car on Friday evening after she came home from her last day at work. He was glad that she was leaving a week after the clocks sprung forward, as she would reach Ohio while there was still some daylight. Anant told her that it was better if she left first thing in the morning so that she could be in Ohio before dark. For once she didn't argue with him and said, "Fine, but you'll have to wake me up."

It was his habit, on weekdays, during those ten years of their marriage, to get up when the alarm clock by his side went off around five in the morning, brush his teeth, do his exercises for thirty minutes and then wake her up. She always complained bitterly about getting out of bed and was in a bad mood until she had her first cup of coffee. She never ate breakfast as she wasn't hungry so early in the morning. She had two cups of strong coffee with cream and sugar and was out of the house before seven. Anant had the luxury of eating his breakfast in a leisurely manner, watching Joan Lunden on *Good Morning America*. After a few cups of coffee, he went to his office. The university campus was only a five-minute drive from his house, and his lectures started at nine. Only when he had a grant deadline or a manuscript to complete, did he go to his lab early in the morning.

On the morning of Sheila's departure, after a sleepless night and with a heavy heart, Anant got out of his bed around six in the morning, went downstairs, turned on the coffee machine, and went back up to wake her. Her eyes were red and swollen, her face puffy and blotched, as though she had been crying all night. Since it was a Saturday, he didn't exercise, just sat in the den with his coffee while she got ready upstairs. After a few minutes, she came down, dressed in jeans and a T-shirt with a light jacket and had a cup of coffee with him. Neither dared to say a single word, as it might betray their emotions. They both knew that after that day they may never see each other again. They were both on the verge of tears but kept their emotions in check lest it affect the other person. She got up, "Anant, take care of yourself, I am off." She got into her car and drove away. After she left, he broke down and cried his heart out. He hated himself for what he had done to her, all because of his selfishness and his desire to fulfill his needs.

He moved from room to room, remembering the good times as well as the bad ones he had had with Sheila. On full-moon nights, they had stood on the landing of the stairway and kissed; they had made love in the guest bathroom, with her sitting on the vanity. He lost count of the number of times they made out in the living room, as that was the room they used most. He remembered how Sheila, on an occasional day when she stayed home just to rest, yearningly watched the schoolchildren in the playground across the street.

In the spring, with so much pollen around she had

suffered from severe allergies, sometimes with big welts and flares on her face, arms and legs. Her lips would become swollen and her eyes itchy and watery, and she was miserable unless she took some antihistamines. On those days she suffered from allergies, she was difficult to live with. Everything bothered her, and she would say, "It's all your fault that I am having these allergies. I never had them on the East Coast. You brought me to the Midwest, and look at the result. Every spring I have to go through this, and I have to swallow so many pills to keep my allergies in check. Let's move back to North Carolina or Maryland. I will get a job there quickly. You can get something too."

"But, Sheila, I might get tenure here, and if we move somewhere else, I have to start from scratch again."

"What's the big deal? You can teach anywhere. What's the use of tenure when you make so little money? And you teach the same damn course every year and go to your lab and shake some test tubes and call it research."

While Anant sympathized with Sheila and did everything possible to make her feel comfortable when she had those allergic episodes, he didn't like it when she reproached him for moving to Kansas. When she drove him up the wall with her comments about his job, he had difficulty in maintaining his composure and occasionally gave it back to her. "You can move anywhere you want. I will stay here and get my tenure and work until I can retire."

It was an amicable divorce, and the attorney who was helping them said, "You guys agree on everything. Why in the world are you going through with this divorce?" They gave the attorney a list of the property and how they had decided to divide it between them. Sheila relinquished her rights to the house, and in turn she got half of what they put down on it. They cashed their mutual funds and savings account and divided the sizeable total in half. They decided to leave their individual retirement plans as they were. The attorney pointed out that Anant and Sheila were entitled to half of each other's retirement account. If they did that, Anant would benefit, since Sheila's retirement money was greater than his. But Anant did not want to go through the hassle of moving funds out of the retirement accounts. Sheila kept her three-year-old car, and Anant's car was sixteen years old and worth almost nothing. Anant was aware that he was being generous to Sheila, as he felt that was the least he could do for her. After all, she had suffered a lot and gone through a lot of mental anguish. Even though it was not his fault, he felt responsible in some way for her situation. He was the one who wanted the divorce. He knew that she still loved him, and she also knew that he loved her. But she was unable to fulfill one of her duties as a wife. Even the thought of sex was repugnant to her, and however much she loved him, she couldn't bring herself to sleep with him. In the beginning of their relationship, before they got married, she never could keep her hands off him. The moment he came into her apartment, she would grab him, kiss him passionately and make love to him. Even after their marriage, her fervor for him continued unabated for several years and came to an end only when she realized that she couldn't attain the most important thing she cherished—motherhood.

After Sheila's departure, Anant had to make a few adjustments in order to live on his salary alone, which was about a third of Sheila's. When he first joined the University of Kansas as an assistant professor, his salary was about forty-thousand-dollars per year, and during the next several years, his pay went up to about seventy-thousand-dollars. Once she got well-established in her career, Sheila had wanted to purchase a bigger house. Anant had resisted the impulse to splurge and convinced her to stay put in their house. Now, he was glad that the mortgage payments were within his means. He was able pay all his bills, live frugally, and even save a little. Of course, he had to forgo some of the luxuries that he had gotten used to when living with Sheila. He got rid of maid service, lawn service, pest control, magazine subscriptions, and cable TV, and he stopped eating out at expensive restaurants.

But after the dust had settled, he began to feel lonely in the evenings and wondered if he should find another woman. In the Kansas City area, where he worked and lived, there were not many opportunities to meet Indian women his age. He was a handsome fellow, fair-skinned (which he inherited from his paternal grandfather), almost six feet tall, slim, and well-dressed. He took two showers every day, one in the morning and the other in the evening. He shaved every day and kept his curly hair short and combed with a part in the middle. With chiseled features, sensuous lips, a high forehead, and a small straight nose, he looked like one of those models in *Esquire* magazine and was attractive to women. To work, he wore cotton pants and starched cotton shirts and dress shoes. He wore a jacket and tie whenever necessary. When he worked in the laboratory, he never forgot to wear a crisp, starched white laboratory coat.

With his good looks, he could have found a suitable American woman in the area. But he decided to look for an Indian woman who might be able to share his interests in reading, music and politics. He felt that he might not be comfortable with women from other cultures, as he might have to explain his background and beliefs. Although he had lived in the U.S. for about fifteen years and become a naturalized citizen, most Americans still perceived him as a foreigner, regardless of their own race. He felt that he might be more readily accepted by a woman of Indian origin, and he wouldn't have to start from scratch. However, the Indian women in town were either married or students much too young for him.

He posted his profile on an Indian website that helped people find suitable partners. He also advertised in *India Abroad*, a weekly newspaper about the Indian Diaspora. In addition to news about India and Indians living in North America, this newspaper had an extensive classified section where people could find properties for sale, cooks, domestic help, husbands, or wives. A typical matrimonial advertisement read:

> Parents looking for a suitable groom for their 28-years-old, beautiful, Ivy League-educated daughter earning 6-figure salary. Groom should be in his early thirties, tall, handsome, well- educated. No divorcees please. Reply to Box # 2417.

In the beginning, Anant was perplexed, reading some of those ads. First of all, he had no intention of dealing with a woman's parents. If a girl, educated at an Ivy League school, was dependent on her parents to find a suitable husband, good luck to her. He wanted to find women who were independent, successful, and confident. He wanted direct contact with women, without any intermediaries.

In the past, he didn't have to resort to personal ads to find a woman. When he met Heather, it was a chance meeting, and they hit it off. Then there was Sheila, who dashed into his life and stole his heart and swept him off his feet. Entering an alien world of marketing himself felt corny and uncomfortable. But anything was better than spending the rest of his life alone. He wasn't sure how to frame his ad, whether to give more details or just be brief. Finally, after a lot thought, in his advertisement he described himself as highly-educated, good-looking, well-groomed, divorced with no children. He said he was seeking suitable women. He deliberately left out what he was actually seeking because he thought that by not mentioning any requirements, he might get a larger pool of applicants.

He was pleasantly surprised when got close to fifty replies to his advertisement, and another fifty or so responses to his profile on the Indian website. He heard from many accomplished women—physicians, nurses, chemists, scientists, professors and others. Although the criteria he chose to create a short list of candidates were rather arbitrary, he decided not to include physicians as he had had such a terrible experience being married to one for many years. Sheila was constantly preoccupied with her patients, always making notes for herself about some patient or other. She worked, on the average, about fourteen hours per day. During the beginning of their marriage, as she was not that busy, they had time to go out to watch movies, eat out, and make love whenever they had an opportunity. As her practice became progressively busier, their time together diminished drastically, and those romantic dinners and spontaneous sexual encounters were things of the past. They made love once or twice during the weekend, when she was not on call. Romantic interludes were completely out of the question on weekdays because she came home late, and there was just enough time to eat something and go to bed. If she was on a weekend call, there was no action at all as she had to answer pages and go to the hospital to admit patients under her service. This time around, he was determined to find a woman who did not have such a demanding job. Ideally, he preferred someone who worked eight to five, with weekends completely off.

Although he wanted to deal with the women directly, this proved to be hard, as after an initial contact, some of the women wanted their parents or brothers or sisters involved in the process. He got calls from different parts of the country asking him about his parents, where they were in India, what his father did for a living, whether they were vegetarian or not. In spite of their education and well-paid jobs, Indians clung to their traditions and customs.

He got a call from a woman who lived in Ohio. After exchanging pleasantries, she got down to business.

She said, "Hi, I am calling on behalf of my daughter. I saw your ad and I wanted to talk to you."

He didn't want to talk to her but was polite. "Sure."

She asked, "Are you a vegetarian?"

"Vegetarian" was a euphemism for a so called "higher" caste member. The members of the higher caste did not eat meat, and in fact, some of them did not even eat eggs, onions or garlic. So when people asked whether one was a vegetarian or a non-vegetarian, they might in fact be asking one's caste. Anant knew what she was up to, but he didn't want to give her a straight answer.

So he replied, "I was brought up in a household where eggs and meat were completely banned."

She was happy to learn that and asked him more pointedly, "Now, do you eat eggs or meat at home?"

"I eat eggs at home. Whenever I go out, I eat meat. You know, after coming to USA I started eating meat just to survive. It is difficult to be a vegetarian in this country, particularly when I don't know how to cook."

Although this was received with a grudging approval from the lady, she never bothered to call him back.

He selected women who wrote good English or whose professional accomplishments appealed to him. Anant thanked them for their replies to his advertisement and said that he would like to get to know them. He also provided additional details about himself, informing them that he was a chemistry professor, teaching and doing research, and that he liked to swim, jog, read, watch movies, and listen to music. Those women who were bent upon involving their family members in the process were removed from his short list, as he felt that they were not independent enough. Most of the women replied to his e-mails, and the process of getting to know each other began. In the evenings, after returning home from work, he logged on and attended to all his personal e-mails. After exchanging a few e-mails, the number of women he regularly corresponded with dwindled to less than a few. In some cases, the women, having more information about him, decided that he was not suited to their life-style. In others, he was the one who did not want to proceed further, after finding out that one candidate smoked, another didn't like to cook or eat meat at home. These kinds of small but important pieces of information helped the women as well as Anant to make an informed decision about further action.

There were four "finalists"—Rosy, Payal, Chitra, and Sara. All the four women were in their thirties, accomplished in their respective fields, and all of them lived in the U.S.. It was a challenge to correspond with four women simultaneously. In the first few e-mails, since the information he gave about himself was identical, he did a lot of cutting and pasting to save time. But once the messages became more involved, he took the time to write more personal e-mails, addressing their individual concerns. He sent them the chemistry department website where his picture, his qualifications, his publications and details about his research and laboratory personnel were posted.

Rosy, a Kerala Christian, had an interesting life and career. Her family had moved from Kerala to California when Rosy was little. She went to the best schools and did reasonably well, and was admitted to Notre Dame on the strength of her religion. She got a college degree and decided to become an air hostess. She worked for an American airline for about five years, had numerous affairs, married a pilot many years her senior, and they had two children. She enjoyed being married but was restless and somehow not satisfied by being with just one man. Even after bearing two kids, she retained (or one should say, regained) her sexy shape and was still attractive to men; when a woman gives a hint that she is available, there are very few men who won't rise to the occasion. Unfortunately, her husband caught her with another man and divorced her. That he was also having an extramarital affair was immaterial at that point. She took revenge and got the custody of the children after a bitter court battle. The pilot did not dare to bring up the small matter of her infidelity in court, as he was equally guilty. Consequently, she got a nice alimony along with child-support payments. She ended her career as an air hostess and decided to pursue a course in health-care management, and after completing the program in a few years, secured a good job in a health-insurance company. It was at this stage that Rosy decided to remarry and contacted Anant.

While she learnt all about Anant quickly, she gave him her details bit by bit. In spite of his repeated requests for her picture, she never sent him one. He was talking to her by e-mail and phone for more than a month and still he was not sure whether he should continue to keep her in his "active" file. She was witty and had a sexy voice and all kinds of anecdotes that made him laugh. She was also raunchy, and everything had a sexual connotation to her. When he said that he had to change his position while talking to her on his cell phone (in order to get better reception), she asked him what position in the *Kama Sutra*. Another day, she called him on his cell phone to tell him that she was doing Kegels while working in her office. He knew what those were in a vague manner but had never bothered to learn more. She explained that it was an exercise to strengthen her vaginal muscles for better control during intercourse. She felt that she should always be ready for it as she could never tell when the right man might come along. Another time, she told him that she made love to a guy twenty-seven times in a single day. When he told her that he drank only decaffeinated tea or coffee, she said that was like making love with a condom on.

All this talk made him curious to meet her and see whether he would still find her attractive. It happened that she had a free voucher on an airline, and she flew in for a weekend. As he didn't see her picture, he was wondering how he could recognize her at the airport, but it turned out that she spotted him first. Anant was a little disappointed when he saw her in the flesh, as he expected someone more beautiful. Her height was slightly above average, and she was a little overweight. She was wearing high heels and a short white cotton dress, revealing shapely legs. She was dark brown, without any makeup, not even lipstick. But she had a pleasant face with deep-set eyes and flat eyebrows, a good set of white teeth and full lips. She had a bob cut, straight black hair covering her ears. He gave her a bouquet of roses and took her bags and led her to his car. Once they reached his house, they started kissing in the living room and slowly went up the stairs to the master bedroom and made love. Although they both enjoyed the coupling, it was not an earth-shattering experience. She was wet and willing, and he was hard and horny, and it was a simple act of sex between two needy people, nothing more. He took her out for lunch at the best seafood place in town.

Rosy complained about the food. "I can cook better

food than these fellows, they don't know anything about cooking fish. Everything is so bland and tasteless. I will make you a spicy fish curry tomorrow; let's go to the grocery store and get all the stuff this evening."

So they went grocery shopping, and on the way he took her around the town to show her the downtown area and other spots of interest. Back at home, he opened a bottle of wine, and since both of them were not very hungry after their late lunch, he made an omelet with mushrooms and habanera cheese, and talked about various things. That was when she told him about herself and her family. Her two kids, a ten-year-old boy and an eight-year-old girl, were now at their grandma's house.

He asked, "Supposing we decide to get married, are you willing to move to the Kansas City?"

"I really haven't thought that far. If I move here, I need to find a suitable job, and then proper schools for my kids and all that."

"Do you think that your kids will be comfortable with a new guy in the family?"

"I don't know all that. Why worry about those things now? Let's have fun."

Anant was surprised that Rosy could drink large quantities of wine; they were already on their way to finishing a second bottle. In his limited experience with women, this was the first time he had seen one drink so much and so fast. He wondered whether she indulged herself daily or it was just a weekend thing.

He asked her as diplomatically as possible, "Do you have wine every day with your dinner?"

He could tell that she was offended at his question. "You must think I am an alcoholic, asking such stupid questions. So what if I drink some wine with my evening meal? In our family, wine at the table is a must at dinnertime. Everybody drinks except the kids. My father has a large whiskey as soon as he comes home in the evening from work, and with dinner he has one or two glasses of wine and a nightcap before sleeping. I guess you don't drink wine every day."

"Yeah, you are right. I grew up in a family where alcohol was completely banned in the house."

Anant's father had an occasional drink with friends at his club, but he never drank alcoholic beverages at home. And though he was a smoker, he never smoked in the house either. Anant had had his first beer when he was eighteen at some sleazy bar in Hyderabad. A bunch of his friends got together and someone suggested they go to a bar as they were in a celebratory mood, having completed their undergraduate degree. Anant and Ramu, his best friend, were a little worried about what their parents might say when they found out about their experiment with alcoholic beverages. One of the fellows offered them cigarettes, and they smoked for the first time. It was awful, all that smoke going into their throats and nostrils, and they both started coughing. Then the beer came with some chicken *tikkas*. Eating non-vegetarian food was another first, and the friends enjoyed that evening. At the end of the evening, Anant and Ramu and were concerned about their breath as it might give away their little secret. One of the guys suggested that they eat a slice of raw onion to suppress the beer breath. After that first time, Anant and Ramu went back to that bar, and soon it became their weekend adventure. But they never smoked cigarettes

every day. Then Anant had to leave for Agra to do his
M.S., and Ramu took up a job at a bank in Hyderabad. In
Agra, Anant took up smoking a pipe under the misguided
notion that it was the paper in the cigarettes that was
harmful, not the pure tobacco. So he went about the
campus smoking a pipe, and pretty soon he was known
as the pipe-smoking intellectual snob. But after Anant
moved to the U.S., he gave up smoking altogether as his
girlfriend couldn't stand the stale smell of tobacco. It was
funny, she enjoyed the aroma from the pipe, but she wasn't
happy kissing him afterwards. It didn't even help that, after
smoking, he brushed his teeth and chewed gum. She was
completely turned off by the lingering smell of tobacco on
his clothes and hands.

The next day, Rosy worked hard in the evening, cooking
cauliflower and potato curry and salmon in a spicy Thai
sauce. Anant's offer to help was peremptorily refused, and
she told him to sit and watch. He never saw anybody cook
cauliflower like she did. She mixed the florets with boiled
potato cubes in a teaspoon of olive oil in a deep baking
dish. Then she added chopped onions, sliced green chilies,
ginger, garlic, turmeric, and salt, and baked it in the oven
for about thirty to forty minutes. By the time she got to
the salmon, he lost interest in watching her cook. He went
into his study to catch up on his work, but he was too tired
and dozed off on the couch. He woke up after a few hours
when Rosy came into the room and turned on the light.
She looked sexy in a black halter dress that reached down
to her ankles. "Dinner is ready. Are you hungry?"

"I am sorry, I dozed off. It was rude of me to leave you
all alone in the kitchen."

"That's fine. When I cook, I want to be left alone. Come on, do you want to have a shower and join me?"

He went upstairs, had a quick shower, put on a nice shirt and tie, and came down to the living room where she already had two glasses of red wine on the coffee table. For a minute he wondered how easily she made herself so comfortable in his house. He must admit that, while temperamental, she was very adaptable. She was a great cook; everything was delicious. They enjoyed the dinner, the wine, and each other's company.

Since she was to leave the next morning, he thought he could try again to discuss their future plans. "If we decide to get married, will you move out here?"

"No, never. I love California, and I will live there forever. With your qualifications, you shouldn't have any problem finding a job there."

"That may be true. But here in this university, I have tenure, and I like teaching here. I may get a teaching job in California, but they won't give me tenure right away. That means I would have to struggle again for a few more years. Here in this job, once I teach my assigned classes, I can do what I want. The teaching is easy because I teach the same thing every year."

"I may be able to find you a cushy job in our organization. I know the director of our outfit, and I might persuade him to hire you. I know that he wants to fuck me, so if I let him have some fun, he will listen to me."

She said it so casually that it completely shocked Anant. He understood casual sex and one-night stands between friends, but using sex to gain favors was reprehensible in his book. The very thought of paying for sex turned him off. But he kept his thoughts to himself and said in an even tone, "You don't have to do any such thing for my sake. If I decide to move to California, I am sure I can find a job without anybody's help." The next morning he dropped her off at the airport, and after coming home he thought about her. He took a pad and a pen and wrote down all the relevant points:

Pros	Cons
Well-educated	Loose morals, can't guarantee her fidelity
Good looking, dresses well	
Good figure	Two kids might complicate matters
Good in bed, knows how to please a man	
Marvelous cook	

He thought about the matter for a few days and came to the conclusion that he could not deal with her. When she called him from California, he told her that he was unwilling to quit his secure job and start all over again in a different place.

Of the four women, Chitra was the most open and easiest to deal with. From the very beginning, he was impressed with her detailed e-mails about herself and her family. Her forefathers were originally from Andhra but were settled in the then Mysore state (now called Karnataka). Chitra's family had fertile agricultural lands and huge mansions in Bangalore and Mysore. Chitra was the eldest, followed by two daughters and a son. Although Chitra's father had a good education, went to good schools and got his Masters degree in English, he was not ambitious and chose to teach at a local college. Since money was not an issue, he never demanded any salary for his services to the school; he simply enjoyed teaching, and his students loved him. In his spare time he went to the Bangalore Club to play billiards and bridge and drink with his friends. Chitra was born and brought up in Bangalore. She and her two sisters were sent to the best convent school for girls and afterwards to Mount Carmel College. In spite of being smart, Chitra did not excel in her studies, barely managing to get by. She somehow graduated with a degree in sociology and philosophy. During college, she developed an interest in fashion and modeling and participated in fashion shows in the city, modeling saris and other apparel for some big showrooms. She became well known in the Bangalore fashion industry and was sought after by many companies. Her voluptuous figure and graceful posture enhanced her appeal, and she would have become one of the top models but for her marriage to Suresh.

She was just twenty-two when the family arranged her marriage to a boy from Hyderabad. Suresh was thirty-three, tall, handsome and highly-educated. He had degrees from the Indian Institute of Technology/Madras, the Indian Institute of Management/Ahmedabad, and the Wharton School of Business. He was making megabucks working for a big firm in Manhattan. Chitra wasn't ready to get married as she wanted to have some fun modeling and doing other things that interested her. When Suresh came to see her for the first time, everybody in her family, her parents, siblings, aunts and uncles, were impressed with Suresh's credentials and his demeanor. He was so suave, even the married aunts were swooning. In the face of such a unanimous approval from all her relatives, Chitra couldn't object to the marriage. Even though Suresh's parents were also quite rich, they demanded a huge dowry befitting their son's accomplishments. Chitra's father didn't argue about the amount as he wanted his daughter to be happy, and he thought bargaining about the dowry with the groom's parents might jeopardize her future. After the wedding and reception, the newlyweds were sent off to Ooty for a brief honeymoon. Her first day with Suresh was a nightmare. The man who was so polished and pleasant in public was a demon in private. On their drive from Bangalore to Ooty, Suresh didn't talk much as he was dozing intermittently and reading a magazine. Chitra was apprehensive about being alone with Suresh because it would be her first time with a man. Once they reached the hotel room, after closing the door, he grabbed her and, without any preliminaries, had his way with her. He was extremely rough and didn't listen when she told him that she was hurting, and the more she cried the rougher he got. After he was done with her, he called up room service for some food and whiskey, and when the food came he ate and had two double shots of whiskey and slept. She was very sore and scared and didn't have any appetite for food. In the middle of the night he woke her up and again abused her, and this continued for the next four days. He never had a kind word for her, never treated her decently. She was his property and he used her whenever he felt like it. From Ooty, they went to Madras (now Chennai) to file for her visa papers. Since Suresh was a U.S. citizen, Chitra would be admitted into the U.S. with a green card. He dropped her off in Bangalore at her parents' house and flew back to the U.S.. When she returned to Bangalore, she was tired, sleepless, and terribly sore all over. She couldn't share her ordeal with anyone, as what she had to go through was demeaning. She hoped that with time her husband would be kind to her and treat her better. She managed a smile for everyone in the house and spent time with her parents and siblings until her visa papers arrived.

When she arrived at JFK airport, Suresh received her and, after dropping her off at his house in White Plains, went back to his office. She was tired from the long flight and slept for about twelve hours. She saw Suresh the next evening and was nice to him and told him all the news from Bangalore. He wasn't interested in listening to her and went on reading his office files. During the next few months, her torture in the bedroom continued almost every night. Suresh worked long hours; he left the house by seven and returned home late at night, sometimes after eleven or midnight. No matter what time he came home, his need for alcohol and sex was unabated, and he used her ruthlessly. She bore it with fortitude, thinking that she was his wife and must do whatever he wanted. When Suresh traveled on business, it was like a vacation for her. She could sleep as long as she wanted, watch TV, talk to her folks in Bangalore, go to the shopping malls, and generally relax without dreading her night duty. She was careful not to say anything about her situation to her parents. Her mom had only one question whenever they spoke: "Are you pregnant yet?" Chitra couldn't bring herself to inform her mom that Suresh asked her to take the pill as he felt that it was too soon to have kids.

When he returned from his trips, Suresh was more

demanding and brutal with her than usual, and sometimes when she didn't come to the bedroom fast enough he would hit her and drag her to the bedroom. Many times she was black and blue all over. She never understood why Suresh was so cruel to her; she didn't do him any harm, and she was always pliant and acceded to his demands, however outrageous they may be. It almost seemed like he got some perverse satisfaction from demeaning her. One night after a lot of drinking, he couldn't function and blamed her for his failure, flew into a rage and called her obscene names and slapped her and beat her savagely. She was bleeding, and somehow she walked out of the room and locked herself in the guest bedroom. He went on beating on the door asking her to come out, but when she wouldn't open the door, he got tired, and after consuming more whiskey went to sleep. The next day, he left for work without even bothering to see how she was doing. After he left, she slowly got up and called her neighbor, a friendly American lady, and asked her to come quickly. The lady was bewildered at this early morning call, but came in immediately, and was shocked to see the state Chitra was in. Immediately, she took her to the emergency room, and they found a few broken ribs and a dislocated shoulder. The shoulder had to be set under anesthesia. She also needed some stitches on her chin, eyebrows, and lips. When the doctor asked her how she was injured, she was embarrassed to tell him the truth and lied that she fell down the stairs. Nobody believed her story, but everyone understood her agony.

Chitra never went back to Suresh. She moved into an apartment, found a job in a department store, and got a divorce. She enrolled in evening courses in business management, and in a few years got an MBA and now she was a marketing manager at a reputable cosmetics company in Dallas, TX. She was just thirty, and Anant wondered if he was a bit too old for her, but she said in one of her e-mails, "Men are like wine, the older the better." How could he argue with that? When he asked for her picture, she attached a bunch of pictures to an e-mail. Pictures of her wearing saris, *salwar kameez*, jeans and T-shirt, dresses, and pant suits. He was amazed at the wide array of clothes she wore, and in every one of them her hair was arranged to suit that particular outfit.

He flew to Dallas for a weekend to meet her. He was dazzled when he saw her at the airport. In person, she appeared more attractive, and he felt that her pictures did not do her justice. As soon as she saw him, she walked towards him in a gait reminiscent of the runway models, slow and elegant. She was wearing a stylish red pantsuit and gold-colored high-heeled sandals. Her gleaming black hair was arranged in a loose bun and her dark brown eyes accentuated with a subtle touch of mascara. She took him to a hotel near her apartment. After he checked into his room, she drove him around the city and showed him the Kennedy Memorial in the downtown area. In the evening she invited him to her apartment for dinner and cooked spicy chicken and egg curry with rice and green vegetables. He was amazed at her ability to put her painful past behind her and move on with her life. That she invited him to her apartment and trusted him enough to be alone with him showed that she didn't lose faith in men. After dinner, they watched a Hindi movie that she rented from an Indian store. Although there were ample opportunities for him to touch her, hold her and kiss her, he refrained from doing anything physical, as he wasn't sure of her emotional status.

She dropped him off at his hotel, saying, "I will pick you up in the morning. We will go the temple and then for lunch at a Chinese place. They cook Chinese in the Indian style, spicy and very tasty."

The next evening, after dinner at a North Indian restaurant, she took him to her apartment. They sat on the couch chatting. He wasn't sure how it happened, but sometime during the evening she pleasantly surprised him by kissing him.

She said, "I bet you wanted to kiss me but you were afraid of making the move. Don't worry, I am not all that fragile."

He liked kissing her, holding her in his arms, smelling her lustrous hair, and the feel of her smooth brown skin. He desperately wanted to make love to her but restrained himself, thinking that they would have plenty of it when they got married. Although they had just met for the first time, they knew a lot about each other, thanks to e-mails and telephone calls, and meeting only reinforced their liking for each other.

Anant proposed to her that evening. "When I came here, I didn't know how this weekend would turn out. Talking to you during the past few months was great, and I know so much about you, and now that I have met you in person, my feelings for you have become more intense. I hope you will agree to marry me."

Chitra had tears in her eyes. "Of course I will marry you. You are a very sweet man, so decent and considerate."

She asked him to go to Bangalore with her to meet

her parents sometime in the next few months. He was not interested in involving either her parents or his parents in their marriage. But he saw no harm in meeting her parents, and he agreed to check his calendar and make plans for their trip to India.

After Anant returned to Kansas City, he continued to keep in touch with Chitra. In one of their phone conversations, she said, "My parents are very thrilled about us and they want to meet your parents. Do you mind if they go to Hyderabad to meet your folks?"

He was vehemently opposed to involving his parents in his affairs, as he knew what kind of objections they would raise. He hadn't even informed them yet of his divorce from Sheila; he thought he would tell them about everything after he got married to a woman of his choice. Chitra's request put him in a tight spot, and he tried to explain her about his position. She was astonished that his parents didn't know about his divorce. "I tell my parents everything. They are happy that I found you, they liked your picture and your academic credentials, but they want this alliance to be arranged in a proper way, and they strongly feel that your parents should be involved in this process."

Anant was caught between his feelings for Chitra and his disinclination to deal with his parents. He agonized about it for a few days and told Chitra, "I can go to India with you after we get married here. Then we can meet everyone, and if your parents want to meet mine it can be arranged. But at this stage, this is just between you and me."

Chitra was crying. "Why are you so obstinate? What do you lose by pleasing my parents?"

But Anant was resolute and stood his ground, effectively ending the relationship. He felt bad about it for a few days but decided to plod along with his search for a suitable bride.

He couldn't tell Chitra why he didn't want his parents involved in his affairs, as he felt the issue was too complicated and private. His parents were domineering, demanding, and always critical of their children's behavior. Most parents who wanted their children to excel academically spent time with their kids, encouraging them and helping them in every possible way. But Anant's parents were way too involved with their own busy schedules and never had time for the children. Given their attitude, it was strange that they produced two kids. They never bothered to take interest in their children's upbringing; this was left to the servants and nannies. When he started going to school, his parents wanted him to do well, get good grades, and make them proud. It was as if his accomplishments gave them some sort of vicarious pleasure. Anant, being the eldest, bore the brunt of his parents' relentless prodding. His father wanted him to become an engineer and his mother wanted him to be a doctor. Between the two of them, he never knew what to focus on, and in the end he neglected his studies and completed each class with average grades.

Unfortunately, average grades were not enough to admit Anant to engineering or medical schools, and to his parents' bitter disappointment, Anant had to join an M.S. program. They gave up on him and turned their attention to his younger sister, hoping that by supervising her more closely they might make something of her. Even though Anant was living in his parents' house, he barely spoke to them and managed to stay clear of them most of the time. As there were always guests in house, relatives from all over Andhra visiting Hyderabad, it was not too difficult to avoid his parents. The guests came unannounced, by bus or train at all hours. When they came, they expected to be fed and given a bed to sleep in. Some of them even demanded that the driver take them here and there in the family car. All this led to too much disruption of the family's daily routine, and invariably there was no privacy for anybody in the house. In the midst of this choultry-like atmosphere, Anant somehow got ready in the morning and went to college, returned home in the evening, and then pushed off to his evening rounds with his friend Ramu.

Both of the friends managed to complete their B.S. with average grades. Ramu's father, a pragmatist, understood his son's limitations and found him a job at a bank. Seeing this, Anant also wanted to get a bank job. But his father didn't want Anant working as a clerk at a bank. He pulled some strings and got Anant into an M.S. program in chemistry at Agra University. Anant had to spend two years in the city where The Taj Mahal was built by Shah Jahan in memory of his lovely wife, Mumtaz. In spite of it being the home of one of the Seven Wonders of the World, Agra was horrible, dusty, badly maintained, and the roads barely passable. The college was primitive, the professors terribly crude, the dormitories located in dilapidated buildings, and the food atrocious. Anant was spoiled by the family cook at his parents' house in Hyderabad. She used to prepare Anant's favorite dishes and keep him well-fed. Now in Agra at the tender age of eighteen, he was not only deprived of those delicious dishes, but also felt abandoned.

Even though he understood that his father meant well by sending him to this awful place for higher studies, he felt that he would have been happier working at a bank, doing a routine job. He was embittered and always grumpy, and consequently made no friends during that difficult period. In those two years he went to Hyderabad only once, and he stayed in his parents' house for only a few days. He completed his M.S. course with honors, maybe because the other students were much worse than him. Being the best of a lousy lot didn't give him any joy. He managed to get into a Ph.D. program at Delhi University. Thus, he was on his way to become a scientist, albeit a reluctant one. His experience in Agra made him resolve that he would never, never let his parents decide anything about his life. As far as his career was concerned, he knew he would get his Ph.D., and then a job. He was reasonably knowledgeable in chemistry and could teach and do some mediocre research, but he had no illusions about his ability to be innovative and achieve greatness in this field. He knew in his heart that he didn't have the bent of mind to conduct original research and publish high-impact manuscripts in prestigious journals. He wanted nothing more than a quiet life in Hyderabad, doing a routine job, and married to a pleasant and beautiful Andhra girl (just like his friend Ramu had done). He never forgave his father for throwing him into the cesspool of the scientific world. A world where you had to genuflect constantly to the top scientists in the field; a world where you were as good as your last paper; a world where you published or perished, and sometimes published *and* perished because no granting agency gave you money for your hare-brained ideas; a world where the research money was controlled by the old boys' network, and even God couldn't save you if you didn't belong to this mafia, no matter how good you were or how bright your ideas may be; a world where, in the name of peer review, the anonymous and malicious reviewers hid behind the compliant editors and blocked the manuscripts of their less powerful rivals; a world where even if your publications were proven to be based on fabricated or wrong data, you could talk your way out of trouble if you were powerful enough; a world where the "visible scientists" hogged all the limelight, gave meaningless keynote addresses at international conferences, and pontificated to their less fortunate brethren; a world where the graduate students and post-doctoral fellows, the unsung and unheard heroes of science, slogged day and night to churn out data that enabled the "visible scientists" to gallivant around the globe at the tax payers' expense.

In the meantime, Anant kept up his correspondences with Payal and Sara, and both women proved to be intransigent, refusing to provide their pictures or even telephone numbers. They preferred to communicate by e-mail alone. Since they both appeared to be interesting, he tolerated their behavior and thought they would eventually have to reveal their true identities, as he wasn't even sure if those were their real names. Payal was from Tamil Nadu, born and raised in Madras (now Chennai). She completed her M.A. in Journalism in Madras University, worked at *The Hindu* for few months, and then moved to the U.S. to pursue her doctoral studies. Right after she completed her Ph.D., she was offered a faculty position at a small university in Tennessee, and was tenured within a few years. Somewhere between her studies and job, she got married and divorced. She was reticent about her ex-husband and why the marriage ended. She never told Anant where she got married, or for how long she remained married to her husband.

Everything about her was a mystery, and Anant was sorely tempted to drop her. But her academic credentials really appealed to him, and he thought he should give her more time. It was also difficult to get a prompt e-mail response from her. He never kept any e-mail in his inbox unanswered if he could help it and didn't understand why she took forever to reply. When she wrote, she was apologetic, saying her mom and sister were visiting her from New Jersey, and that she was busy taking care of them. Finally, his patience running out, he asked her whether she was interested in pursuing their "relationship" further, and if so what he should do. To this she responded, "I definitely want to get married again to the right man, but at this point I am very confused about the whole thing." Anant said that they could end the confusion by meeting each other and volunteered to drive down to Tennessee. She agreed to this proposal and they set a date for his trip. She was decent enough to book him at a hotel and told him that she would pay for it as he was taking the trouble to drive for about seven hours. She met him at the hotel and took him to her place for dinner. He wasn't really impressed either with her looks or her clothes. She was dark, in her thirties, petite, short, flat-chested, and looked malnourished. She was plain, with dark spots around her eyes and absolutely no clothes sense. Her brown skirt was short, revealing her pencil-thin legs, and her white blouse had seen better days; at least she appeared to be clean. He wondered if that was the way she normally dressed or if she didn't want to appear to have taken trouble to dress up for his sake. She lived close to the university in a complex largely inhabited by students. She parked the car in the back and took him up to her apartment through the back door, as she was worried that some of her students might see her with a man. He wondered why a tenured professor such as herself should not be able to afford a decent house.

As though reading his mind, she said, "I got tenure last fall, and now I would like to buy a house. I have been busy looking for a house, but I am concerned about putting money down. If I get married, and if I need to move where he lives, I will have to sell the house. Too many ifs in my life, I am always confused."

Anant empathized with her predicament. "I know how it is not knowing where you might end up."

They had dinner. She was a pathetic cook; the food was barely edible. He somehow got through the meal, and after he finished she sat next to him and they talked for some time.

She said, "We have a good chemistry department in this university, and I know they get a lot of federal money for research. If you are interested, I can introduce you to some faculty members here."

He was polite and said that he would consider her offer.

She also said, "I can always find a job in your university. I know a faculty member in the journalism department there. We were colleagues at Ohio."

Anant wondered if she was hinting that she liked him or if it was just small talk. It was getting late, and he said that he should sleep as he planned to leave in the morning. She dropped him off at his hotel and asked him if he wanted to eat breakfast with her before he got on the road. He said that he was planning to leave very early as he had to catch up with work in his office. After he reached his home, he sent her an e-mail thanking her for her kind hospitality. He felt there was absolutely no chemistry between them, and therefore deleted her name from his "active file."

Sara was the most secretive of the four women. Her full name was Sara Bedford and she claimed that her family came to the U.S. from Mysore. She said that she was a Kannada-speaking Hindu Brahmin. She said she had an M.S. and worked in the computer industry. She declined to give any information about her family. In one of his e-mails he asked her about her strange last name.

She was upset about it and wrote, "There is nothing strange about it. Bedford is a common name in USA." He pointed out that it might be a common last name in the U.S., but he never heard of any Kannada-speaking Hindu Brahmin called Bedford. He didn't know why he included her name in his active file. He wondered if her mother was a Kannadiga married to an American. This might explain her last name. But in the absence of any clarification from Sara, he was left to his imagination. In the end he got fed up with her and sent her an e-mail: "It was a pleasure knowing you. But you are not forthcoming with details about yourself, and if I can't get this information, I can't go forward. Thank you." She never replied.

With no candidates left in his active file, this was the end of Anant's search. He considered advertising once more in the newspaper. But responses to his profile on the Indian matrimonial website were still trickling in, and he thought he should wait another month or two. The website appeared to be quite popular among the Indian community not only in North America, but all over the world, as he was receiving e-mails from women located in the U.S., Canada, South Africa, Malaysia, Singapore, the UK, and Australia. He didn't want to consider candidates who were not living in the United States, as he wasn't interested in communicating with women in all those faraway places. Also, he was concerned that some of the women who wrote to him were motivated more by their desire to come to America than by finding a compatible spouse. He got e-mails from twenty-year-old girls, and he wondered what on earth those girls could have in common with a man who was almost double their age.

One of the e-mails was from Meena, who lived in the U.S.. Anant did not realize at first that this was the same Meena he had met a few times and had a big crush on when he was living in Delhi, many years ago. When he saw the name Meena Rau on one of the responses, it did not ring a bell because he knew her as Meena Bhat. She wrote that she was a biotech scientist working for a pharmaceutical company in New Jersey. After exchanging a few e-mails with her, he realized that this was the same girl he had had the hots for long ago. She wrote that while she was completing her studies, her parents arranged her marriage to Ramana Rau who was settled in the U.S. After her wedding, she moved to America, and they had a son. When she told him that she got her Master's degree from Delhi University, he was absolutely sure that she was Meena Bhat. Although Anant was thrilled with this discovery, he did not say anything to her about it in his e-mails, fearing that she might remember how nerdy he was those days. A request for her picture was promptly granted; she sent him a picture that she took in one of those self-service machines. The picture confirmed that she was indeed Meena Bhat. Although it was difficult tell from the poor quality of the picture, it appeared that, after so many years, she still retained her good looks.

He remembered her vividly; she was well-dressed, pleasant, tall with a voluptuous figure, beautiful face with a small nose, luscious lips, big eyes, large forehead, and shining black hair down to her shoulders. She spoke English, Hindi, and Kannada. Her dad, an officer in the Indian Administration Service, was from Bangalore. In addition to her good looks, she was brilliant in her studies, participated in the university debating society, and acted in plays put on by a theater group in the city. For a fellow like Anant, who didn't do anything but read, she appeared unattainable. Anant had met Meena through Asha. When Anant came to Delhi for his graduate studies, he had met Asha through some family friends. In contrast to Meena, Asha was plain, short, petite, and not at all glamorous. But she was brilliant and always at the top of her class. She and Meena were classmates at Delhi University. Asha's parents were originally from Andhra Pradesh. Her father was a scientist at the National Physical Laboratories and her mother a school teacher. Anant's parents knew Asha's parents when her father was doing his Ph.D. at Osmania University. Anant went to their house in Delhi and they welcomed him into their family. He met Asha frequently for movies or to eat at restaurants. One day when Anant and Asha were out in the city, they ran into Meena. Asha introduced Anant to Meena, and they all chatted for a few minutes and went their separate ways. Anant was stunned by the drop-dead gorgeous looks of Meena. He asked Asha a lot of questions about Meena and learned a few things about her. He managed to get Meena's phone number and call her up, and he asked if she would meet him sometime for a cup of coffee. She was surprised at his telephone call, but she was pleasant. They met a few times in the university café and talked about this and that. But Anant couldn't bring himself to declare his feelings for her, as he presumed that she may not be interested in a nerd like himself.

While he was still debating about how he should proceed with Meena, his research advisor was becoming increasingly difficult to deal with. Even under the best circumstances, professor Saxena was arrogant, cantankerous, and unreliable. He was abusive and rude to his students and would yell and scream in the laboratory. He was also very particular that all the laboratory personnel—students, technicians, and post-doctoral fellows be present in the laboratory from early in the morning to late in the evening. When he was away attending meetings in San Francisco or London or Sydney, laboratory workers declared freedom and all the work came to a standstill for those few days. But the great man had his spies and was well aware of the situation in his laboratory during his frequent absences. Although he was a jerk, he was a successful scientist. His knowledge of chemistry in general, and his research area in particular, was encyclopedic. When students presented their work in departmental seminars, professor Saxena would question the students relentlessly, and if a student was found to be deficient, the professor was merciless and would publicly humiliate the hapless student. He expected nothing but the best, but he was never known to compliment a student when he or she did a good job. If he didn't say anything, that should be taken as praise. His publication list was prolific, and money for his research projects poured in from many granting agencies in India as well as the United States. In every aspect of his career, he was perfect, a great teacher, a fantastic speaker and an eminent scientist. His Achilles' heel was women; he had many affairs. He was supposedly happily married to the same woman for twenty years or so, and they had four children.

During the time Anant was working in the laboratory, the professor was involved with one of his students. The girl, Kethaky, was very pretty and tall with a striking figure. She was also quite intelligent and hard-working. The whole campus knew about this liaison, and people wondered what such a beautiful girl was doing with an old bandicoot who was not even passably good-looking. His face was always drawn and scowling, his skin was dry, and he was always scratching himself. His only redeeming feature was his height and bearing. He was about six-feet tall, well-built, muscular, and walked straight with long strides. It was rumored that professor Saxena seduced

Kethaky when she was in her first year. Apparently, when he wanted to, the professor could turn on the charm. The truth would never be known, but it didn't make sense for a girl as beautiful and intelligent as Kethaky to fall prey to such an obnoxious man. The burning question was whether she was subtly drawn into this relationship with the lure of fame and name. By the time Anant joined the laboratory, Kethaky was completing her fifth year and showed no signs of finishing her Ph.D. any time soon. She was oblivious to all rumors and innuendo surrounding her behavior, and went about her business in a placid manner. She was quite nice and unfailingly kind to Anant; she even used to advise him about his experiments.

Anant was given a difficult project and was expected to produce results rapidly. Although he worked hard, he was unable to make any progress. This infuriated the big man, and he scolded Anant in the presence of his colleagues. After a long tirade, the boss told one of the post-doctoral fellows to supervise Anant's work. In the beginning, Anant welcomed this and sought advice from the post-doctoral fellow, and things appeared to settle down for a few months. But when he started to get some interesting data, the post-doctoral fellow took all the credit and told the boss that Anant was lazy and hopeless. In reality, Anant only discussed the project with the fellow and did all the experiments himself. But the professor believed the fellow, and when the data was written up for a publication, Anant's name was not on it. This made him very sad and angry, and he wanted to quit the laboratory. Also, Anant was too sensitive and could not bear the domineering and ruthless manner of his adviser. But before making such a rash decision, he confided his problems to Dr. Valluri, a senior professor in the department.

Professor Valluri was always kind to all the students in the department, and consequently most of the students approached him for advice and help. Professor Valluri was the complete opposite of professor Saxena. Whereas Saxena was brash, arrogant, and full of himself, Valluri was humble, soft-spoken, and considerate. Valluri didn't care to build an empire like some other successful scientists; he was a serious scientist doing science for the sake of learning, and in spite of having graduate students, technicians, and post-doctoral fellows in his laboratory, he did his own experiments. He felt that if he didn't work with his hands, he would lose touch with the subject. That Valluri was also from Andhra Pradesh might have helped develop a bond between Anant and the unassuming teacher. Valluri listened to Anant carefully and said, "Before you decide to leave Saxena's laboratory, you need to have a plan. What are you going to do next? Can you find another laboratory? You must know that it will be impossible for you stay in this department if you quit Saxena's group. He is too powerful here, and no other faculty member would want to antagonize him by taking you into his group. You have two choices, go to a different university and start over or quit science and do something else. Since you have already spent some time doing your M.S. and a year here, I don't advise you to quit science altogether. Let me contact my friend at Indian Institute of Science, Bangalore, and ask him if he can take you into his laboratory. He is a good organic chemist, keeps a low profile, and treats his students humanely." Valluri was as good as his word, and within a few months Anant moved to Bangalore and started work on his Ph.D. He lost touch with both Asha and Meena.

Bangalore, the capital of Karnataka state, was such a contrast to Delhi. There were no dust storms, the city was full of greenery, and tall mature trees lined most of the roads. The people were courteous and kind, and when he spoke in Hindi they assumed that he was from North India and answered him in Hindi, if they were fluent enough, or else they spoke in English or Kannada. When he spoke in Telugu, they replied in Telugu. It was amazing to see that the populace was so adaptive and tolerant of other languages and cultures. His experience in North India was quite different from Delhi because the people there didn't care to accommodate people from other states, particularly the Southern states. They used to call him *"Madrasi"*—a common epithet for all South Indians. He felt bad for the North Indians because of their ignorance of the country's rich heritage and diversity. A lot of North Indians were not even aware that South India was comprised of four different states, each of them with a language and a culture of its own.

The picturesque campus of the Indian Institute of Science, spread over three-hundred acres away from the bustling city, felt like a park with its lush vegetation and quiet atmosphere. Those days, most of the city buses terminated their run at the eighteenth cross bus terminal, a ten-minute walk from the campus. Very few students had scooters or motorcycles, and those who needed to go into the city used the city buses. Most of the senior faculty members lived in faculty housing on the campus, and they walked to their respective departments. Some of the junior faculty members who lived off campus had either scooters or bicycles. Consequently, there was very little vehicular traffic on campus, and it was a pleasure to walk without being subjected to traffic and pollution.

Since Anant came from Delhi, the supervisor of the dormitories suggested that he enroll in "B" Mess, as food there was prepared in the North Indian style. That was when he came to realize that there were three mess halls—A, B, and C. The A mess was dominated by Tamil Brahmins, and they made sure that only vegetarian food was served. The B mess was divided into B vegetarian and B non-vegetarian. The B non-vegetarian was controlled by Bengalis from West Bengal. The C mess was ruled by Andhra people, and the food there was a bit spicy.

The Department of Organic Chemistry had about fifteen faculty members and fifty graduate students. When Anant reported to professor Ranga Rao, he was received by the man with affection and kindness. The professor, who appeared to be in his thirties, was dressed in light-colored pants and a white shirt; Anant never, in his four years in the department, saw the professor wear anything but light-colored clothing. He asked him if he had a comfortable journey from Delhi, and if he found the accommodation in the dormitory suitable to his needs. Anant was overwhelmed with the professor's thoughtfulness and told himself that he should work very hard to impress the man.

Ranga Rao had a sense of humor. He asked Anant, "What is research?"

Anant replied, "It is to discover how a particular system works and its underlying mechanism."

"Oh, that's great. You have the makings of a great scientist, but according my old professor, research is one part inspiration and ninety-nine parts perspiration."

At another time, when they were discussing new chemotherapeutic cancer drugs at a group meeting, the professor remarked wryly, "More people live on cancer than die of it."

Ranga Rao had spent a few years at Purdue University working with a Nobel Laureate and returned to India to take up a faculty position at the Indian Institute of Science. When he returned from the United States, he brought with him a blue car, as big as a boat, that he always parked under a tree. The car was his pride and joy and was always kept clean and shining. The car had a sign in the rear, "CAUTION LEFT HAND DRIVE," to warn the majority of Indian drivers, who had their steering wheels on the right-hand side of the car. Ranga Rao was a fun-loving person, and he enjoyed playing bridge and billiards in the staff club. He did his best work during his stint in America, and after his return to India, he didn't quite exert himself. But because of his association with the Nobel Laureate, he managed to get grant money for his research and publications in average journals. His laid-back attitude was quite common among professors at the Institute. Since there were very few undergraduate programs, the faculty members had a minimal teaching load. Most professors taught some graduate courses, and since they taught the same courses every year, they didn't have to devote much time to preparing for their classes. One teacher used the same notes that he had prepared some thirty years ago, and the students, who got the class notes from their seniors, knew exactly what the professor would say next. The effort the professors put into grading was equally pathetic. It appeared that most of the teachers didn't even bother to read the students' answers and gave the grades arbitrarily, depending on whether they liked the student. A student who was perceived as a trouble-maker because he or she asked too many questions or made smart comments in class invariably got low grades. Some students who referred to the latest journals and included up-to-date information in their answers were also given poor grades, as the instructor felt that the student was trying to show off. Some professors let their senior students or post-doctoral fellows teach some classes to the new Ph.D. students. Thus, there was plenty of time to do their research, and a small minority used the time wisely to publish in high-quality journals, while a significant number of professors tended to live on their past glory. Some of them were so indifferent to their research and students that they "visited" their laboratories for one or two hours each day and spent rest of the day taking care of their personal business. Their laboratories were run by senior students or post-doctoral fellows. The students somehow managed to complete their projects and write their theses, and in the end the advisor "corrected" the thesis and sent it off to a panel of examiners. If the student was lucky, the examiners were kind, their reviews were positive, and the candidate was awarded a Ph.D. There were some cases where the examiners were critical of a student's work and he or she had to repeat several experiments and rewrite the whole thesis. If things went smoothly, the advisor took the credit, and if they went badly the student got blamed for the sloppy work. Then there were professors who spoon-fed their students at every stage of their career. One particular professor, Annaji "Harem" Iyer, who always had more girl students in his group than any other laboratory in the department, was relentless in his efforts to make his students look good. He met with his students every morning and told them what to do in the lab. He would give them minute details and step-by-step instructions. This sort of spoon-feeding was counterproductive, and invariably, students who got their Ph.D. from Iyer's lab failed to become successful and independent scientists. When a student from his laboratory was scheduled to present his work in the departmental seminar, Iyer was more nervous than the student. Iyer would make the student rehearse the talk several times with the entire group and made sure of every little detail in the presentation. When a student was "writing" his or her thesis, Iyer would literally dictate the entire thesis, including the acknowledgements. It was strange that with so many girls under his tutelage, Iyer remained a bachelor. Some crude students commented that Iyer was spending all his energy on making sure that his car was always bright and shiny because he had no wife to spend time with.

No story of the unique faculty of "Harvard of India" was complete without a mention of the globe-trotting professors. These were few but very visible. They were powerful and rich because they got any amount of money they wanted (not needed) for their empire-building activities. One gentleman was so well-connected that he had access to the Prime Minister of India. These scientists got new facilities built with state of the art equipment and guarded their empires zealously. Needless to say, these scientists traveled all around the world, attending seminars and meetings while their students in the laboratory were being supervised by post-doctoral fellows or senior students. While some of them were fully aware of every student's projects and progress, others were not so well-informed because of their preoccupation with their travels and politicking.

Even though most of the faculty members were preoccupied with their private affairs or busy hobnobbing with their counterparts in the West, most of the students worked hard because they were aware that unless they got a Ph.D., their futures were dim. While the large majority of Ph.D. students were eager to complete their degree and go off in search of greener pastures, there were a few who, lured by the salubrious climate, the good food, and the easy lifestyle, stayed on campus for years, "working on their Ph.D.s." These super-senior students were in no hurry to complete their studies, as they were unwilling to face the rat race in the real world. In the end, the candidates were persuaded by the advisor and dean to finish their theses and vacate their dormitory rooms. The Institute's reputation was sustained in large part by the excellent student population. From the moment the students entered the campus, they knew that the next step in their career would be to work in America. Most of the students knew a lot about the United States; even some of the students who were ignorant about their own country knew the entire map of the U.S., each of its states, its political structure, and its history. Most of these students read *Time* and *Life* diligently and absorbed all the details about the country they would soon go to. The Indian Institute of Science, by virtue of its status as the premier center for research in India, attracted the best and brightest from all corners of the country. The selection process was long and arduous, and typically, one out of thousands of applicants were selected for admission into a Ph.D. program in any department. But once in a while, a few mediocre students, such as Anant, were admitted through the back door.

Ranga Rao first hired Anant as a project assistant, and once he was in the department, it was easy to coach him for the entrance examination. The interview process to select the candidates, although it appeared very rigorous to outsiders, could be manipulated to make a candidate look good. The committee knew beforehand about Ranga Rao's candidate and asked easy questions and gave him enough marks for admission into the Ph.D. program. For the trouble he took to help Anant, Ranga Rao was given a Bhatnagar Award. These awards were given in honor of Dr. Bhatnagar, who played a pivotal role in developing science and technology in India after independence in 1947. Awards were given annually in many basic as well as applied sciences. As a member of the Bhatnagar Award committee, Valluri played an important role in the selection of Ranga Rao. Not everybody who deserved the award got it, and not everybody who got the award deserved it. There were too many awards in India. There were awards to young scientists, awards to not-so-young scientists, awards to middle-aged scientists, and awards to the aging scientists. Most of the recipients of these awards were selected by the godfathers in each field and generally given to their cronies. Merit, unfortunately, had no place in the selection process. There were all kinds of rules and regulations for each award, nominating processes and committees to screen the number of eligible candidates each year for every award. But, in the end, it all boiled down to who you knew and not necessarily what you knew. There were some brilliant scientists in India who never received any award because they refused to kowtow to the mafia bosses of the science enterprise.

In her e-mails, Meena wrote that she had a son in high school. Even though she and her husband lived in the same house, they were, for all practical purposes, separated. She said that after her son got into college, she would get a divorce from her husband. This news perturbed Anant. Being a conservative and traditional guy, he wasn't comfortable dealing with a woman who was still legally married. But at the same he was curious as to how she looked now, after all those years. He didn't want to end this e-mail relationship just because of her marital status. Her e-mails were witty and full of information about herself, her son, and of course, her husband. Apparently, her husband worked for some big firms and held well-paid jobs. At some point in his career, he had decided to start his own company, and unfortunately the venture failed to take off. This drove him into deep depression, and he was forced to go on disability. What really upset Meena was the fact that he never tried to find another job after he got better. He continued to draw the disability checks and lived a carefree life. Moreover, all those medicines he had to take for his depression affected his libido.

Anant and Meena continued to exchange e-mails, and whenever possible, she called him at home. In the beginning, she e-mailed him from her work e-mail account, but Anant advised her to set up and use *hotmail*. He could not call her at home because her husband or son might be there when he called. Occasionally she sent him e-mails asking him to call her at a particular time when she knew that her husband and son would be out for a few hours. She also called him from pay phones using calling cards, as she didn't want to use her cell phone to make these calls; her husband paid all the bills and he would wonder about her frequent calls to the same number in a different area code. Anant felt good that she was putting so much effort into their relationship. During this period they both learned a lot about each other. When she asked the reason for his divorce, he was candid with her.

The only thing that had been missing in Anant's and Sheila's idyllic life was a baby. They both wanted a baby, any baby, a boy or a girl, it didn't matter. Sheila was thirty and was getting worried that something was the matter with her ovaries or tubes. They had been married for five years, and even though they never used any protection right from the very first time they made love, she didn't get pregnant. Anant was also concerned, but he didn't say anything to her because he knew it would only cause more anxiety. Her annual physicals, pap smears, and mammograms were perfect. During the first few years of their marriage, the lack of children didn't affect their relationship, as they were quite young and thought there was plenty of time for kids. But after five years, when Sheila still didn't get pregnant, she asked her gynecologist why she couldn't conceive. The gynecologist, after a thorough examination of Sheila's reproductive system, concluded that there was nothing wrong with her ovaries, oviduct, or uterus, and recommended that Anant get himself checked by a urologist. Anant had to give his sperm for testing. His seminal fluid was tested for its volume, viscosity, number of sperm per milliliter, sperm motility, and morphological examination of the sperm. All those tests indicated that his sperm production and function was normal. After this, the doctors recommended that Sheila go through an IVF procedure. Sheila went through many painful procedures to get pregnant. She was injected with hormones to induce ovulation, and then the oocytes were recovered and fertilized with Anant's sperm in cell culture dishes. The fertilized egg was allowed to develop and then transferred to her uterus. After trying this method for about three years, when Sheila didn't get pregnant, the doctors told them there was no hope. The news completely devastated Sheila, and she became very depressed.

While she was trying to get pregnant, she asked him, "Would you consider adopting a baby?"

He had no immediate answer. "I am not sure. Adopting is not like having our own child. Also, I am afraid of what we may be getting into. I have seen some cases where the adopted kids turned out to be mentally retarded or have other problems. I am not saying that all adopted kids will be problematic. But if we adopt and the kid becomes a problem, we will regret the decision."

"Sweetie, there is no guarantee that if we have a baby he or she won't develop some health problem."

"I know that. But if the child comes out of our own loins, it is an entirely different ball game. If the kid is ours, we will definitely love him or her no matter what."

"So you are not in favor of adoption?"

"I am not really comfortable with the idea."

Once she knew she would never be able to get pregnant, in addition to losing interest in sex, Sheila became ill-tempered and abusive. She would get mad over little things, yelling and screaming at Anant. She acted like everything that went wrong was Anant's fault, and she took out all her frustrations by punishing him. Although Anant was also feeling bad for not having at least one kid, he was more philosophical about it and continued to live his life as usual. In the beginning of the dramatic transformation of his wife from a loving, caring individual to a shrew, he tried his best to placate her and did not retaliate. But the fact that Sheila did not want to sleep with him anymore was difficult for him, and he was frustrated. His desire to be with her persisted, and he was aroused by her proximity in the same bed at night and had trouble sleeping. Therefore, he started sleeping in the spare bedroom. He still loved Sheila very deeply, but for him, sex was an important part of their marriage.

Although he had a pleasant personality and made friends quite easily, Anant was not comfortable around a lot of people, and he avoided big gatherings and loud parties. Some people misunderstood his nature and labeled him anti-social, a loner, and a party pooper. Even his parents used to say, "He doesn't like to be around people; he is always in his own dream world." But in reality he loved people as long as he was able to interact with them in small groups. When he was in school and college he had a few friends but only one close friend. While in college, Ramu and Anant were almost inseparable, going to college together on their bikes, eating lunch together in the cafeteria. In the evening, they met again and went for long walks. Being quite intelligent and well-informed, they talked about politics, world events, cricket, girls, and a lot of other topics. Anant's habit of having only one close friend at any particular period of his life continued even after he came to the United States. In the first few months of his stay in America, he was busy getting used to the system and standardizing his techniques in the laboratory. Once he was sure that things were going smoothly in the laboratory, he began to relax a little and hobnob with students and other post-doctoral fellows in the department, go to parties and bars. At about the same time, he developed a deep friendship with Heather. But he had to stop seeing Heather after he met Sheila. Their relationship blossomed, and Sheila became his confidante.

His need for a true friend was great, as he felt quite alone in this alien culture. However much he read about the U.S., its leaders, its cities, its people, all that knowledge was only theoretical and was of no use when it came to dealing with real people and real situations. Sheila helped him to negotiate this maze easily. He shared his joys, his small triumphs, his hopes, his frustrations, and everything else with Sheila. He was a lost soul when he couldn't talk to her during Sheila's bouts of depression, as they meant she was unwilling to communicate with him. He was getting increasingly lonely with no one to share his thoughts. Whereas in the beginning, he eagerly anticipated the clattering noise of the garage door at the end of the day, signaling her arrival, now he dreaded the evenings and did not look forward to her return from work. She would come home, without even acknowledging his presence, sit silently and read or watch TV. She spoke to him only when absolutely necessary, and then only in monosyllables. Sheila refused to go to a marriage counselor. Slowly but surely, the relationship deteriorated, and they decided to split up. This was very painful for both of them, but there was nothing they could do to bridge this growing chasm between them.

Meena understood Anant's feelings, as she was in a similar situation with her husband. Ramana loved her but was unable to please her in the bedroom. Apart from the lack of sex, what bothered her most was his unwillingness to find a job. When she confronted him, he told her not to worry because they had enough money to live on. Their beautiful house in an exclusive suburb and their luxury cars were paid off. Since he had held good-paying jobs in the past, he got a substantial amount from the disability payments. They only had to pay property taxes and buy food; money for the college tuition for her son was set aside quite some time back. Her husband never let her pay for anything out of her salary. Although Ramana was a kind and considerate man, living in the same house with him was difficult for Meena. She was brought up in a society that expected men to work until they retired. It upset her that Ramana, who was only in his fifties, spent most of his time sitting around or browsing the Internet. She decided to stick it out until her son finished high school.

Even though they e-mailed each other quite often, Anant and Meena enjoyed talking on the phone because it let them hear each other's voice.

In one of their conversations, Meena asked him, "Are you looking for a woman who can give you children?"

"I really don't know how to answer that question. Sheila and I were disappointed when we couldn't have any kids. But I am not sure if that's the sole reason for our divorce. I would have been happy if we had one or two kids. But I don't think that I will be devastated if I can't father a child or two."

"Anant, you are too vague. I want an answer to my question. Please say yes or no, do you want your next wife to bear you children or not?"

"Meena, you sound like an attorney! I would love to have kids. Does that answer your question?"

"In that case, you better look elsewhere because I can't get pregnant. After I had my son, there were some complications and I had to have my tubes tied."

"Look, aren't you jumping the gun a bit? We have a

long way to go before we can even consider this issue. As I told you, I won't be terribly disappointed if I can't father a child. Let's first meet and see if we are compatible."

"Okay, but I don't want to start this relationship with any false hopes."

Anant and Meena each knew exactly what the other was doing at any given time during the day. She was up by five, and after a cup of coffee and toast, she was at her office before eight. She was in charge of a division in her company and was busy with meetings, keeping track of the laboratory personnel, reviewing and analyzing data, and writing project reports. She went home by about five and jumped on her treadmill and worked out for about an hour. Then she watched the news, had dinner, and went to bed all alone.

Anant proposed to fly to Newark to meet Meena. But she didn't like the idea, because they could be seen together by some people she knew, having lived there for a long time. After some more discussion, they decided that she would visit him for a long weekend. Anant was excited at the prospect of seeing Meena. He was proud of his four-bedroom house located in a middle-class suburb, and he hoped that Meena would be favorably impressed with it. A couple of days before her arrival, he cleaned the house thoroughly, bought a lot of food, put new sheets in the guest bedroom, and placed fresh soft towels and Meena's favorite soap and shampoo in the bathroom. He got his car washed, purchased a dozen red roses from the neighborhood florist, and went to the airport to meet Meena. The day was mild, sunny, and bright, without a cloud in the sky. He arrived at the airport a little early, parked his car, and loitered around the gate area until her flight arrived. His heart was beating very fast when he saw her, and he was nervous. He gave her the roses and took her bags from her and escorted her to his car. As there were many people in the gate area, they had to walk single-file, and being a gentleman he let her go ahead of him and was amply rewarded by the sight of her firm, sexy hips; she was wearing high heels, and when she walked, those shapely hips wriggled and aroused him. She walked straight and was not bothered by the men who ogled at her curvaceous body. She was wearing beige pants, a white blouse, and a short denim jacket. It was a short walk to the parking lot, and after helping Meena into the passenger seat, Anant came to the driver's side. After closing the car door, he hugged her passionately and kissed her. She reciprocated his kisses by taking his lips into hers and gently biting on his lower lip. They would have proceeded to make love in the car but for the fact that it was around eleven in the morning and there were many people around. During the drive to his house, he constantly touched her thighs and looked at her lovingly. After they reached home and he got them both cold ginger ale, they both tried to carry on a conversation, but their minds were elsewhere. He set his drink on the side table and kissed her and made passionate love to her right there on the living room carpet. She reminded him of his first girlfriend.

When he worked at the University of North Carolina at Chapel Hill, Anant had met Heather. One day, he was walking to the university library and saw Heather; she was wearing a white T-shirt that accentuated her breasts. He had seen Heather around the campus but had no idea what she did or where she worked. He said hello to her, and after a few pleasantries, asked if she dated men. She smiled and said it depended on the man. Anant asked if she would go out with him. She said yes and gave him her home phone number.

Heather was a tall blonde with long hair, almost down to her waist, which she wore in a ponytail. She was slim with pleasant features. Her most striking feature was her bosom; when she walked, her breasts jiggled seductively, and most men couldn't keep their eyes off her. She worked in the purchasing department as an administrative assistant. Right after high school, she joined the department as a secretary, and with hard work rose up in the ranks. She enjoyed her job; although the pay was not great, the health benefits were good, the work was easy, and the hours not long, with a good amount of vacation and sick leave. Heather was religious, a member of a local Baptist church, and went to church every Wednesday evening and Sunday morning to listen to the preacher, Dr. Stevens. In spite of his education and knowledge, the pastor was a narrow-minded racist and a mouthpiece for the right-wing demagogues. He did not believe in the separation of church and state. During election time, mindful that his church would lose its tax-exempt status if he were to endorse any particular candidate, he would preach is such a way as to leave no doubt in the minds of his flock how he wanted them to vote. He lamented that the establishment of the welfare system was the direct result of abolition of slavery. He said many more outrageous and atrocious things, but nobody had the guts to castigate him as he was one of the most powerful pastors in the country, and he could bend the ears of influential leaders, including the President of the United States. Heather, like most Baptists, had a high regard for Dr. Stevens and believed whatever he said from the pulpit. She had spent her formative years listening to such biased opinions, and she never took the time to question their veracity. Like a lot of her friends, she voted Republican at every level—local, state and national.

After their first date, Anant and Heather met frequently. They went to movies, shopping malls, restaurants, and bars. Heather loved to dance, but Anant was clumsy; however, he eventually managed to learn enough to keep her company on the dance floor. Sometimes, in the neighborhood bar, when a man asked her to dance, she would look at Anant as though seeking his permission. But Anant was very possessive and never encouraged her to dance with other men. She loved to eat out and spent quite a bit of her money on restaurants. She never cooked at home if she could help it. Sometimes when the weather was lousy outside, she stayed in and ate an omelet or a sandwich. On the other hand, Anant was frugal and did not want to spend his money on restaurants. This led to some problems in the beginning, but eventually they both learned the art of compromise. They went out mostly for lunches, as it was cheaper to eat lunch at most restaurants.

On their first date, Anant picked her up in his brand-new car and took her to a Mexican restaurant. She was surprised that he drove such a nice car, saying, "Most foreign students here are not rich enough to afford brand new cars." He told her he was not a student, as he had a Ph.D. and worked as a post-doctoral fellow. She was not aware of the distinction between a student and a post-doctoral fellow and also had no idea how many years one had to go to school to earn a Ph.D. He was amused at her ignorance but was patient enough to explain that he had to work about eleven years after high school to get his Ph.D.

She said, "So now you make a lot of money after so many years at school."

He grinned. "I wish. Right now I am a post-doctoral fellow, and we don't make a lot of money. This is a sort of training program, and when I complete this in a few years, I hope to get a decent job with much better pay."

In the restaurant, she asked him a lot of questions about his country, his family, and his culture. When he ordered a beer with his chimichangas, she was surprised and said, "I thought y'all don't drink alcohol." The evening was full of such comments, and Anant had to patiently explain so many things about India, its people and culture, the various religions that people practiced in his country. He told her that it was the Muslims that didn't drink alcohol, and the Hindus that didn't eat beef.

She immediately said, "You are neither a Hindu nor a Muslim because you are eating a chimichanga with beef in it and drinking beer."

He laughed heartily, saying, "You are absolutely right! I don't believe in any religion."

"Didn't your parents teach you their religion?" She asked.

"Yes, I grew up in a religious Hindu family, went to

temples with my parents and learned how to worship the many Gods and Goddesses, knew about all the Hindu festivals. But once I left my parents' house, I developed my own philosophy and came to the conclusion that it was stupid to let religion dictate what one should eat or drink. I just abhor all these different religions. In the name of religion men are fighting unnecessary battles all over the world. In Ireland Catholics and Protestants fight, in Israel Jews and Muslims fight, in India Hindus and Muslims fight, and all this fighting can be avoided if we do not have all these different religions. Why can't man believe in one religion and one God? Things would be so much simpler and there wouldn't be any bloodshed."

For the first few months of his stay in Chapel Hill, Anant had managed without a car. He lived close to the campus and was able to walk to work or take the bus. There was a grocery shop about a mile or so from his apartment complex, and he would go there every week to buy milk, cereal, eggs, and other necessities. After his morning jog, he had a glass of orange juice, a bowl of cereal, toast, and two eggs sunny-side-up. His lunch was a bit late, around one, at the university cafeteria. The menu varied, depending on the day. The food was edible and cheap, and for about three dollars he could have a lot of food. Anant invariably had a dessert at lunchtime, apple cobbler or peach cobbler or pecan pie or carrot cake, depending on the day. After eating such a heavy lunch, he was never hungry for dinner. Most of the time he got home late, at about eleven or so, and had some milk and cookies or his favorite—butter pecan ice cream. He immersed himself in his work, wanting to set up all his techniques to lay groundwork for his research project. He worked very hard and impressed his boss, professor Martin. The professor, after seeing his progress, predicted a bright future for this new arrival in his laboratory. The professor was in his late fifties, tall and well-built with a ruddy face and a crew cut. He walked at a leisurely pace, never appeared to be in a hurry, and spoke slowly as though he had all the time in the world, the way the Southern people talked. He was generally dressed in khaki pants and a T-shirt, and taught his classes or went to meetings with the campus big-wigs in the same clothes. When the weather got a little chilly in the winter, he wore long-sleeved shirts. He was never seen wearing a tie or a jacket, except at scientific meetings where he had to chair a session. For all his knowledge and reputation in his field, he was an unassuming person and a real gentleman. With his extensive network of friends and contacts, if he wanted to, he could have built a large empire with many post-doctoral fellows, students, and technicians. But he chose to run a small operation with one or two post-doctoral fellows, a couple of graduate students, and a technician. He had written his first NIH grant in 1956, and the same grant was renewed eight times, each time for four years. This must have been one of the few instances where the granting agency was compelled to give money for a project due to its sheer intellectual quality and innovative nature. The trick, the great professor used to say, was, "Never ask for more money than you need, and always keep your budget reasonable." He sauntered into the laboratory at about ten in the morning, checked his mail, and worked in his small windowless office, which was sparsely furnished with a desk and a chair on one side and a couch on the other. His door was always open, except during lunchtime when he had his nap after eating his sandwich. Usually, he went home by about three.

Professor Martin lived on a large country estate about twenty miles away from the city, where he raised chickens and beef cows and grew tomatoes, cucumbers, okra, eggplant, and peppers. Some years, when he had good yield from his vegetable garden, professor Martin would share the produce with people in his laboratory. His wife was a successful realtor and made good money by selling residential and commercial properties. She also bought dilapidated houses fixed them up, and sold them for a profit. Such transactions made the couple quite rich, and they lived a comfortable life. When Anant first came to the United States, professor Martin received him at the airport and took him directly to his country estate and introduced him to his wife and the three children who were still living with them; one son was working in Washington, D.C., and the eldest daughter was married and lived only a few miles away. Two daughters were undergraduates at the university, and the youngest boy was in high school. Anant stayed in their house for a few days before finding a studio apartment. Professor Martin gave him a bed, a couch, a chair, and some pots and pans, and helped him move into the apartment. It was just a place for him to sleep. He didn't care to put up pictures or posters to adorn the white walls.

On Anant's first day in the department, professor Martin took him around and introduced him to various faculty members and the departmental administrative staff. They were all nice to him and welcomed him to the department. After the first meeting, he never met some of the faculty members again for a long time. But he had to meet with the office staff on a regular basis. When he needed chemicals or other laboratory supplies, he had to fill in a requisition form and give it to the lady in charge of managing their grant accounts. The girls in the office were friendly and always addressed him by his first name. He was brought up in a culture where such familiarity was seen only between close friends. In the beginning it bothered him that the office staff did not address him formally as "Dr. Prasad." As soon as he got his Ph.D., everyone in India had started calling him "Dr. Prasad." Even his father introduced Anant to his friends as "Dr. Prasad." Although professor Martin introduced Anant to everyone as "Dr. Prasad," most people in the department addressed him by his first name. But it was interesting that the people did not address another post-doc by his first name. His name was Don McDonald and all the office staff called him "Dr. McDonald." There was another post-doc from England named Claudia Hornsby, and nobody addressed her as "Dr. Hornsby." Claudia, Don and Anant joined the department at about the same time and they were of similar age; the difference was that Don was white. Anant thought, *Why is it that a white male is given more respect?*

Once he established himself in the laboratory, Anant's next priority was to purchase a car. Ever since he was little, cars had fascinated him, and he used to know the names and models of most of the cars that were manufactured in the world those days. It had always been his dream to own a Mercedes-Benz. But for now, with his meager salary he could only afford an inexpensive car. When he asked professor Martin for his opinion, he told him to buy a bare-bones model with absolutely no options, no air-conditioning, no power windows, no unnecessary gizmos. Professor Martin told Anant that he bought such a car for his daughter recently, and gave him the name of a dealer. He told Anant, "Don't buy a used car because you never know what you are getting. Buy a brand new car and try to get it for the least amount of money. Don't ever pay what they ask, always start low and go up only if you have to." Equipped with such sensible advice, Anant went to the automobile dealer and got himself a Japanese car that would last him for the next twenty years. This car was a far cry from the first car that he ever sat in, his father's Austin. One could not start that Austin with a simple turn of a key. A servant had to insert a handle into an ignition port in the front bumper and turn it while the driver pressed on the accelerator, and if you were lucky the car would start. Otherwise, two or three men had to push the car to help start the engine.

After Anant's outings with Heather, they invariably ended up in Heather's apartment. Anant never invited Heather to his place because it was not properly furnished. Heather never asked that they go to his place, maybe because she guessed the condition of his apartment or maybe because she was comfortable in her place, which she kept immaculately clean. Unlike Anant, she lived in a very small apartment complex comprised of eight units— four downstairs and four upstairs with just enough parking space for eight cars. Most people who lived in the complex were single. The complex was owned by a retired clergyman, and Heather could rent a unit in that exclusive complex because she was a Baptist and a white woman. The owner never rented his apartments to blacks or foreigners. Heather's apartment was nice, with a big living/dining room, a small kitchen, and a big bedroom with a walk-in closet. She had a comfortable couch on which they snuggled, kissing and fondling each other. Although he very much wanted to make love to her, he was scared because he had never come this close to a girl in all his adult life. He was embarrassed that at twenty-seven he was still a virgin. Even after several dates, when Anant didn't progress beyond kissing, Heather sensed something was not right. In her experience with the American men she had dated, no one was this patient, and they always wanted to get into her pants after a date or two. So she asked him if she didn't turn him on, and he had to tell her his situation. She was really surprised at hearing this and wondered why he remained a virgin despite his good looks and elegant behavior. In any case she was nice and supportive and helped him get rid of his virginity. She was astonished that he was not circumcised and told him about the practice of circumcising newborn boys in the United States. Apparently this was done because it was deemed unhygienic to have a foreskin. Anant said that in India only Muslim boys underwent circumcision, and Hindus never had it done.

Anant cared for Heather, although at times she exasperated him with her ignorance. When she asked him questions like, "Do you have trees in India?" it took all his patience to control himself. But he told himself that Heather grew up in a small town without the advantages he had while growing up. Her parents were separated. Her mom, Mrs. Thompson, after working several odd jobs, retired. Her father was lazy and only worked when he needed money for his drinking and gambling. He would be away from home for months at a time and suddenly appear, abuse his wife, make her pregnant and disappear; she had seven children—four girls and three boys. This abuse continued for several years, until she put a stop to it. One day he came home drunk and started to beat Mrs. Thompson because she wouldn't go to the bedroom with him. Hearing all this commotion, her two oldest daughters, who were teenagers at that time, got hold of their father and held him until their mom got her shotgun and aimed at him. "Never come back to this house. If you as much as touch me next time, I will shoot you."

After many years, when their father came back to town penniless and sick, Mrs. Thompson didn't even want to see him. By that time, since Heather and her siblings were all employed, they found the money to keep the old man in a nursing home till he passed away. Her mom didn't go to his funeral. She was a strong old lady, always doing her own work in her small house and was very proud of her kids as all of them became independent and held decent jobs. For her, a simple country woman with hardly any education and money, it was enough see her children lead a decent life, marry, and give her a lot of grandchildren. He remembered the first time he met her when Heather took him to her mother's house for a weekend visit. Before going, she told him, "No hanky-panky while we are at my mama's house. We can't sleep in the same bed; I will be sleeping in my mama's bed, that's what I always do whenever I visit her. You will sleep in the spare bedroom." Her mom's house was about three hours' drive from Chapel Hill. They left early in the morning on a Saturday and returned Sunday evening.

According to Heather, the visit was a success, as her mother was impressed with the foreign boy. It was difficult for Anant and Mrs. Thompson to understand each other, as each of them had an accent that the other couldn't decipher. Heather had to act as an interpreter most of the time. Mrs. Thompson lived in a small hamlet which had a gas station and a convenience store. There was also a café which served edible food and was the gathering place for folks to sit down for some coffee and gossip. If they needed groceries, they had to drive about ten miles to the nearest town. The village itself was spread out with large acres of farmland interspersed with houses of different sizes and shapes. Mrs. Thompson lived in an old farm house which she inherited from her parents. The house was always in need of repairs, and her children worked hard to keep it in a decent shape. At that time she was already in her late seventies, lived alone, and was drawing social security. She had to be frugal with her resources, and knowing this, Heather and her siblings routinely stocked the pantry with all kinds of food. Mrs. Thompson was a good cook and, according to Heather, went out of her way to prepare special meals for them when Anant visited her for the first time. She made meat loaf, fried okra, cornbread from scratch, and a peach cobbler that melted in the mouth. Mrs. Thompson never drank alcohol and didn't permit it in her house. Anant enjoyed the food; he particularly liked the way she prepared the okra. In India he was used to eating okra that were cut into small pieces and stir-fried; Mrs. Thompson mixed the chopped okra pieces with corn meal and then stir-fried the mixture after adding some salt and pepper. He thanked her for the exquisite dinner and complemented Mrs. Thompson on her cooking. After dinner that evening, they had visitors. Heather's relatives had heard about the visit of the foreign boy and were curious to meet him. Her two sisters and brother who lived in the same village first dropped in and checked him out; they were polite and talked about general things, asked him if he liked living in the U.S., how long he was going to stay in North Carolina and when he was returning to India. Then came Martha, Heather's niece who lived about thirty miles away. She visited her grandmother and her parents almost every weekend. First she would drop into her parent's house, catch up on all the gossip and then go to her granny's. That day, her mom must have told her about Anant's visit, and Martha couldn't wait to meet her aunt's boyfriend. Martha, a statuesque blonde, was a few years younger than Heather, being the daughter of her brother Fred. Martha took a liking to Anant and talked to him a lot, asking him all kinds of questions about India. Martha, like most girls in the rural United States, got married at a young age to a local boy. After completing high school in the village, Martha had moved to the nearest big town to work as a bank teller. There she met Doug, who worked for a local construction company, and married him. They had a three-year-old boy.

One Friday evening, Anant and Heather had dinner at her place, and after watching the news, they made love and fell asleep. They woke up only when the morning light came through the bedroom window. Anant rarely spent the night at Heather's apartment, always going back to his place to sleep. He knew about Heather's puritanical streak. She had this quaint notion that unmarried people shouldn't cohabit or make love. But she gave in, with a certain amount of reluctance, to his demands. He didn't take her frequent complaints that he was a sex maniac seriously. They were reluctant to leave the warmth of the bed and were cuddling and talking about their plans for the day. Suddenly the phone rang and Heather answered. Anant turned to the other side and tried to sleep some more. But he couldn't help hearing what Heather was saying. It appeared as though she was unhappy about something and in the end said yes to whatever the other person was asking. Anant didn't want to pry, but Heather was so livid that she had to tell him about the call. "It was Martha who called, asking me to lie to her husband. She wanted me tell him that she spent the night here in my apartment. Actually, she was with some guy. I don't know why she has to chase after other men when Doug is so nice and would do anything for her. I am fed up with her, always asking me to cover for her."

Anant didn't say anything as it was between Heather and her niece. But undeterred, Heather went on. "From the beginning, Martha had man trouble. It is like she has ants in her pants. Once she was dating this guy from Pakistan. Only I knew about it, and I kept it a secret. Then the dumb girl got pregnant and we had to find the money to get her an abortion. If her father had found out about her shenanigans, he would have been mad. He doesn't like his daughters or sisters dating foreigners or blacks. Privately, he still calls the blacks 'niggers' and the brown-skinned people, 'sandy niggers.'"

Anant wondered aloud, "How come he was nice to me

when we were at your mother's last month, if by his own definition I am a sandy nigger?"

"He knows not to show his dislike in public. But I know he said some things about my dating you to my mama. She doesn't really care what we do with our lives. She saw too much bigotry in her life time and now all she cares about is that her kids are all happy."

Her brother Fred was a typical white male from the rural South, poorly-educated and woefully uninformed, prejudiced, and intolerant of blacks, Jews or foreigners. Because he served in the Korean War, he got a state government job, which allowed him to lead a simple life in the country. He and his wife, Maryanne, with the help of five children (Martha was the third), raised beef cows and a vegetable garden in their back yard. Fred was generous to a fault and supplied beef and vegetables to all his family members who lived in the vicinity. When it came to his family, he was very protective and never hesitated to loan money (if he had it) in an emergency. He and Maryanne brought up their kids strictly, and all the kids, except Martha, turned out to be good citizens, God-fearing and Church-going. Not that Martha was not a good citizen in the sense that she had a decent job, paid her bills, kept her house neat as a pin, and loved her husband and son. It was just that she had this irresistible urge to experiment, and from time to time indulged herself with a willing man. While there was no dearth of men who were eager to sample her charms, she had to invent some excuse or the other to be away from her home for the night or weekend, depending upon the amount of time she and her paramour could spare. Heather and Martha grew up almost like sisters, and although Heather didn't approve of Martha's wayward ways, she genuinely loved her and hoped that with time she would calm down and come to her senses.

The Indians in Chapel Hill and surrounding towns had shindigs a few times a year, on some special Hindu festivals such as *Holi* or *Diwali*, and Anant was invited to the *Holi* function one Saturday. He asked Heather to join him, but she was going home that weekend. The local Indian association was quite active, running a Sunday School for the kids, meeting periodically to review the goings-on in India, arranging lectures by visiting Indian politicians or academics. *Holi* was celebrated in the early spring by the Indian community. Although the actual *Holi* day, depending on the Hindu calendar, could be on any day of the week, the celebration was always held on a Saturday so that people could stay up late and enjoy the festivities. When Anant was invited for the first time to the *Holi* function in Chapel Hill, he was filled with nostalgia, and some of the *Holi* events that he had enjoyed in India came to his mind.

Holi day was a national holiday in India, and the celebrations were not postponed to a weekend like in the U.S.. Nobody was so busy in India that they could not enjoy a festival on the actual day of the festival, as specified by the Hindu calendar. Even the thought of postponing it to a Saturday was blasphemous and would be met with indignity, demonstrations, public speeches, strikes, and in some cases even violence in the streets. In India, true democracy prevailed, and Indians were most vociferous when they perceived that their rights were being trampled upon by government rules and regulations. Therefore, the leaders of the country, very wisely, refrained from meddling with religious festivals and let the people celebrate festivals of all faiths—Hindu, Muslim, and Christian, and all important festivals were national holidays.

On *Holi* day, Anant used to go to the mess hall at about eight a.m., later than his usual time of seven, to eat the special holiday breakfast. This was a sumptuous meal with *alu parathas* and crisp French toast with tea or coffee. The *paratha* was crisp on the outside, and filled with spicy curry made of potatoes, onions, and green chilies. The French toast was a typical Indian adaptation, suitable for the Indian palate. Large slices of white bread were dipped in a mixture of eggs, milk, spices, and salt and fried on a skillet; the result was a heavenly dish, served with yogurt. On that day, most people drank tea laced with *bhang*, a mild narcotic. Only on *Holi* day did the authorities allow the use of *bhang* in tea. After a heavy breakfast and innumerable cups of tea, most students, equipped with colored liquids or colored powder, would do their rounds. First they would visit the Director's house to sprinkle him and his family with color; at this stop the students were respectful, used just a little color, and took the sweets that were offered. After that, they went around the campus to other professors' houses and, depending upon the age of the faculty member, were either courteous or rowdy. As the day progressed and the festivities became more and more rough, some of the students caught hold of some unsuspecting girls, who were going to and from the ladies' dormitory. They applied colored powder to their bodies, and some of the more unscrupulous boys fondled the girls' breasts and butts; luckily this did not happen all the time, and soon such elements were warned by the authorities to behave themselves or else face strict disciplinary action. In spite of this nonsense, the day was filled with fun and everyone enjoyed themselves.

Compared to all that, the *Holi* celebrations in Chapel Hill were insipid and tame. But since it was the best they could do, everyone still came to the function and enjoyed the camaraderie. The food, catered by a local Indian restaurant, was not particularly tasty, and the conversation was dull. People felt compelled to attend because their friends worked hard to plan the program. The positive aspect of the function was that it was an opportunity to interact with people one didn't meet on a regular basis. Anant was bored to death at this particular event. Since he had come to town only a few years back, he didn't know many people, and compared to him, most people at that gathering were much older; he couldn't relate to many of them. It was quite warm inside, and he came out of the hall to breathe some fresh air. They had just finished eating the appetizers—samosas, pakodas, chicken tikkas. None of the items were spicy enough for him, and it appeared that they were prepared by a timid cook with the American palate in mind. Actually he went to that party because Dr. Murthy, one of the senior professors in the university, invited him. Dr. Murthy had a good reputation as an excellent teacher and researcher, and he was an active member of the Indian community. He was a vocalist in the local carnatic music group, well-versed in Sanskrit and was known to officiate in religious ceremonies when the local pundit was busy elsewhere. As Anant loitered in the foyer, contemplating whether he should go home and curl up with a book, Dr. Murthy spotted him and asked, "How are things, young man, are you enjoying the party?"

Anant politely replied, "Yes, sir."

Dr. Murthy said, "You must meet some people, come with me," and dragged him back into the hall. There, he introduced him to many luminaries of the community— professors in the university, engineers working in the local industries, and doctors working for hospitals or private practices. Seeing that Dr. Murthy had taken Anant under his wing, they were all nice to him, inquiring about him, his work and his family. When they found out that he was single, some of the ladies took more interest in him and asked some probing questions about himself, his surname, his education, his job, his hometown in India, and his father's occupation. By nature he was shy and never talked about himself or his family. But he could not brush those nice ladies off and was compelled to talk about his antecedents.

His father, Durvasula Venkata Bala Subramanyam, was a professor in mechanical engineering at Osmania University at Hyderabad, and everybody called him professor Bala; his mother, Lalitha, was a gynecologist and had her own clinic near their house in Banjara Hills. His parents were deeply religious and spent most of their free time praying, chanting *slokas*, visiting all the major temples in India—Kanchi, Madurai, Rameswaram, Badarinath, and a number of others. Anant grew up in this highly-charged religious atmosphere, and at times he felt that he couldn't even breathe properly; when he was little, life was always about God, religion, *poojas*, *homams*, and *yagnas*. During those early years, he did not fully appreciate the religious fervor of his parents but went along without questioning their way of life. After he completed his high school, his parents wanted to send him to America for undergraduate education. This decision was not endorsed by his grandparents on either side. They felt that their grandson should be in Hyderabad, close to all the relatives, so that he would grow up with proper Indian values. They were old-fashioned and were worried about the "corrupt" Western influence on their grandson. Anant was the oldest grandson, and it was his responsibility to carry on the family name and traditions. His paternal grandfather owned thousands of acres of fertile land in the Godavari Delta, producing a variety of crops worth millions of rupees. Anant's mother's family was also from that part of Andhra, and his parents' marriage was arranged by the elders.

In the face such strong opposition from his parents as well as Lalitha's, professor Bala decided to send Anant to a college in Hyderabad. His original plan to enroll his son in an engineering school did not work out, as Anant's grades were not good enough to be admitted even to a mediocre engineering school. Therefore, he was enrolled into college to pursue a bachelor's degree in science. Anant was a smart kid but never really applied himself to studies, just managed to get through each grade without failing. This was a source of constant worry to his parents, and they goaded him to study hard. He would listen to them respectfully and pretend to study. But the moment he was alone, he went back to his favorite pastime—reading novels. Before he became well-versed in English, he read whatever Telugu books he could get hold of, and when his English improved he started to read a lot of English novels. That was his passion, and he was always reading some book or other, anything but his textbooks. Just before the exams, he crammed for a week or so, wrote his answers quickly, and got out of the examination hall. The fact that he never failed any exam was not enough for his parents, who achieved academic distinction in their lives. Although they both got married when they were very young, his father twenty and his mother sixteen, they both studied hard and went to good colleges. When they got married, his father was in his final year of B. E. in Hyderabad, and his mother had completed high school.

After their marriage, professor Bala's father bought a house in Hyderabad, furnished it, and sent a cook and servants from the village so that the young couple need not worry about cooking and cleaning. He expected his daughter-in-law to stay at home, supervise the household staff, take care of his son, and produce children. But Lalitha had different ideas. She was very strong-willed and was determined to become a doctor. In those days, there were very few women in medical schools in India. But first she had to convince Bala. They were married for about a month and living by themselves in the big city. Actually, they didn't have much privacy in the house, as either his or her mother would pop in now and then to make sure they were doing okay. Bala's younger brother, who was studying at the university, was also living in the same house. In addition, the cook and the servants were always there in the house doing something or other. Only when the newlyweds retired to their bedroom at night did they have some time for themselves; but that time was very precious for them as they were just discovering each other. One night, after some extremely satisfying sex, Lalitha broached the topic of her education. She knew that Bala was satiated and therefore in a good mood to listen to her. When she told him about her dreams about becoming a doctor, he got very perturbed and said, "What about me?

Who will take care of me if you are away in the medical college? Do you know how much hard work it is to become a doctor? You have to study day and night."

She said, "I will always be here to take care of you, my dear. You have to let me do this. Please don't say no."

Then he talked about how their parents would be upset if she went to college as everybody was eager for them produce an heir ASAP.

She said, "We can work on producing kids. What's the big hurry? We are both very young anyway."

After a lot of back and forth, when Bala would still not relent, she used the final weapon she had; she started to sob inconsolably, with tears falling from her beautiful eyes. This was something that Bala was not prepared to handle. He hated to see her cry. He took her into his arms and consoled her and told her she could go to medical school. Once she had Bala on her side, tackling her parents and in-laws was a piece of cake. Although they all fretted and fumed and said a lot of things, she and Bala stood their ground firmly. So she enrolled herself in a pre-med program for two years and then got admitted into the Osmania Medical College. Meanwhile, Bala joined the Master's program in mechanical engineering in Osmania University.

Immediately after completing his M.E., Bala was offered a faculty position in the same department. This suited Bala well, as he did not want to disturb Lalitha's studies. While he carried out his teaching duties, he pursued his doctoral studies in his spare time and got his Ph.D. in a few years. Although they both worked very hard, they found time to go to movies, eat at their favorite restaurants, and have some fun and frolic in the bedroom. But she took precautions not to get pregnant until she completed her final year of medical school. When they announced her pregnancy to their parents, there were tears of joy, celebrations, poojas, trips to Tirupathi temple, and a lot of other religious hoopla. Both of their mothers had almost given up on seeing a grandkid, as it had been almost six years since Bala and Lalitha got married. In Andhra, where women were as fertile as the farmlands of Godavari Delta, it was unusual for a woman not to conceive for such a long period, and everyone thought that Lalitha was barren. The mothers pleaded with Lalitha to visit some of the temples in the South to pray for a child. But Lalitha, always busy with her studies, told them to pray on her behalf. So the mothers took off to visit various temples, consult astrologers, and perform poojas. Now that their dreams had finally come true, there was nothing to curb their enthusiasm. They went crazy shopping for their grandchild, but not knowing the gender of the baby somewhat hampered them. During those nine months, Lalitha was not allowed to exert herself, although she kept telling her elders that it was okay to do some work and take walks. She passed her finals with distinction, was presented a gold medal by the vice chancellor of the university, thus joining the ranks of a small number of female physicians in the state. She postponed doing her internship until after the birth of her baby.

3

A few weeks after the *Holi* party, Anant got a phone call from Dr. Murthy's wife, inviting Anant to their house for dinner on a Saturday. As Heather was visiting her mom that weekend, Anant had no plans on that particular day, and he accepted the invitation. He took some flowers for the lady of the house and a bottle of wine for Dr. Murthy. There were other people at the party, and Dr. Murthy made the necessary introductions. Anant had met some of them at the *Holi* party and was glad that he had a good memory for names. The party was small and intimate, the kind of get-together that Anant liked, where one can get to know the others and carry on a decent conversation instead saying hi and bye like at a big gathering. While they were all having drinks and appetizers, a young woman walked in, saying, "I am so sorry I am late, I just couldn't get away from work." Mrs. Murthy, the ever-gracious hostess, said, "My dear, don't worry, we are just starting and you are on time," and turned towards all of them to introduce the woman. "Everyone, this is Sheila." Anant could not take his eyes off Sheila. She was gorgeous in a black sari with red roses embroidered on the borders as well as on the *pallu*. Her black blouse, with red roses on the sleeves, revealed a good part of her slim waist. She was petite, not particularly tall, even with her heels adding a couple of inches to her height. She was dusky, with wavy black hair reaching down to her shoulders. She had big expressive eyes with long lashes, full lips, and a nice smile revealing straight white teeth. The only blemish, if one considered it as such, was slightly big nose for such a well-sculpted face. She had generous hips, a slim waist and, although it was difficult to determine due to the *pallu* cover, a nice bust. From the moment she walked into the room, Anant couldn't stop staring at her.

Anant was still in a trance when she walked gracefully towards him and said, "Hi, how are you doing, I am Sheila Puri."

Anant was tongue-tied and mumbled something incoherent at first, but slowly regained his composure and blurted out, "You look terrific! You are very attractive!"

Sheila's American accent indicated that either she was born in the United States or her parents moved here when she was little.

"Thank you, you are cute too! What is your name?"

"Oh! I am sorry, my name is Anant."

"What is your last name?"

"Durvasula."

"So, you are Anant Durvasula?"

"Well, I don't write my name like that; I am from Andhra Pradesh, and the surname always precedes the given name. So, my full name is Durvasula Ananta Naryana Rama Prasad."

"So your friends call you Anant?"

"My Indian friends call me Prasad and the Americans call me Anant. Only after I came here I started using Anant because of the American obsession with first and last names."

"By and large people here are less formal, and they want to use first names whenever possible."

"I understand that. But in India, when I tell people that my name is Prasad they accept it without any question, and they don't ask what is my first name and all that. In India we know most of our friends by one name only. My friends from North India, I know them only by their last name as that is the way they write their names, like Malhotra, Mehta, Duggal. We know that these are surnames but never even think of asking their first names. On the other hand, in Andhra it is the reverse, most of us know each other only by our given names as that is the only name people get to know. For example, my grandfather's name is D.N. Swamy, and everyone calls him Swamy. Only very few people know his full name."

"But now that you are here in America, don't you want to conform to the norms here?"

"You are right, I should. Only problem is that I have already published a few papers when I was in India, and now to change the order of my surname and given name will be a headache as I will have two different names in my *curriculum vitae*. In the papers that I previously published, my name was given as D.A.N.R. Prasad. Now if I change the sequence of my name, it will be A.N.R.P. Durvasula. Do you see how confusing it will be?"

"That is true, but why do you have such a long name?"

"Naming ceremonies in my family are a very elaborate process, involving not just the parents but the grandparents as well. Because everybody's opinion had to be taken into consideration, my name became long. But this is not unusual in Andhra. I have a friend whose name is V.B.V.S. Nagendra Rao. I can give you many more examples, but I don't want to bore you to death."

"Okay, one last question. What do your parents call you?"

"They call me Puttu. Everyone one of us has a pet name. I don't even know how my pet name evolved, may be when I was little someone might have called me Puttu, meaning small, and it stuck. My parents and all my relatives call me Puttu. Actually, most of my aunts, uncles, and cousins don't even know my real name. Even I don't know the official names of most of my cousins because we all refer to each other by our pet names."

"In my family, no one has a pet name, everybody calls me Sheila."

Just then Mr. Murthy walked towards them and joked, "So you both are now calling each other by pet names?"

Sheila quickly replied, "No, sir, we were discussing the complicated naming customs in Andhra Pradesh."

Dr. Murthy looked at her. "What is so complicated about it? When we were little, the grandparents decided the name, and the parents obeyed them and gave the name to their kids. So the names were strictly based on family tradition and the Gods they worshipped. Nowadays I am seeing Indian kids with simple names that can be easily pronounced by the Americans. Maybe these days, the parents in India are aware that their kids might go to

America to study, and therefore give them simple names, such as Maya, Natasha, Lisa, and not tongue-twisters like Subbalakshmi or Balasubramanyam."

This discussion was interrupted by the announcement that dinner was served. They all trooped into the large kitchen where a lot of items were placed on a center island—nans, alu gobi curry, eggplant curry, spinach and potatoes, mixed vegetable rice, plain rice, sambar, and yogurt. Anant helped himself to some of the delicious food and found a place to sit in the living room, as all the chairs in the dining room were occupied. Mrs. Murthy went around making sure the guests were comfortable and well-fed. She told Anant that the food was from a local Indian restaurant, and Anant complimented her on the choice of items and said that the food was great. After dessert and coffee, Anant had to leave as he had an experiment running in the laboratory; he thanked his hosts and said good night to other guests. At about the same time, as Sheila was also leaving, he politely to walked with her to her car down the street.

She asked Anant, "Are you going home?"

"No, I need to go to my laboratory to terminate a reaction."

"Are you going to work all night?"

"No, just a few minutes. I have to switch off a machine and make sure all the data was properly recorded. After that I am going to my apartment to relax with a drink and a book."

"That sounds like a good idea."

"What are your plans for the rest of the evening?"

"Not much, do laundry and watch TV, and sleep."

He made sure she was in her car. "Great, good night then, see you around."

In the next few days, Anant thought about Sheila and wondered if she would be willing to go on a date with him. In spite of his good looks, he didn't have any luck with girls when he was in India. This was due to the fact that he grew up in a society where girls and boys were segregated most of the time. Even in some of the coed colleges, the girls hardly mingled with boys, and it was a big deal if a boy and a girl exchanged a few words. In the circles he grew up in, it was almost impossible to meet a girl his age one-on-one. Consequently, he had very little experience in how to approach a girl in order to start a relationship.

While doing his Ph.D., Anant had fallen madly in love with Shalini, a beautiful Iyengar girl from Bangalore. He and a thousand other boys were smitten by this haughty beauty. There were probably at least two-thousand male students on campus and maybe a hundred girls. With such a paucity of females, the males were starved, and even an ugly girl had a good chance of catching a reasonably good-looking guy. It was such fun to see the guys waiting for the girls to arrive in the mess hall for their meals. As soon as a girl entered the mess hall, all eyes would follow her movements, and everyone would stop eating or drinking. Most of the girls moved around the campus in small groups of two or three, maybe to keep the boys at bay. An eager male would be less disposed to approach a girl if she was with other girls. But Shalini always went around alone. She walked very fast, so fast that some of the boys nicknamed her "express train." She was quite tall for an Indian girl, and, as was the case with most Iyengar women, extremely fair-skinned. She had a slim figure, a pleasant face with high cheekbones, and a long, slender nose. It was difficult to understand why and how Anant fell head over heels for this girl who was always aloof and taciturn. It was an irrefutable fact that he fell in love with her, and that it was a one-sided affair. His friends knew that he was crazy about her, and they all felt great pity for his unreciprocated love, as they knew that Anant had absolutely no chance of winning the love of the sultry Shalini. The only person who was unaware of his fate was, of course, the poor besotted fool. He tried asking her out to movies, ice cream, dinners, and each time she would curtly refuse, saying that she was busy or had to go somewhere. In desperation, one day he approached her in the mess hall at dinner time, and somehow managed to sit with her and poured his heart out to her. She listened to him courteously, ate her meal silently, waited for him to finish his, and asked him to walk with her. He was overjoyed at this piece of good luck. Even though they were the same age, Shalini was much more mature than Anant. They walked on the quiet road going towards the swimming pool and sat on a bench near the pool.

Then for the first time, she spoke clearly to Anant. "You say that you are in love with me. What do you love in me? Me the person, or is it my body and the pretty face? But do you know what love is? You hardly know me, you don't know my likes and dislikes, my hobbies, my moods, what kind of food I like, what movies I like to watch, the kind of music I listen to. Do you know that my father died when we were little and my mother had to bring up six kids all by herself? Even with some help from my uncles, it was difficult, but we coped. Somehow we all managed to study hard and all of us got into good colleges. I don't have time for love now. Maybe one day I might meet a man and love him. But that day is far off. Right now my focus is to complete my Ph.D. I know you are a nice guy. But please leave me alone."

With that she got up and walked back to the ladies' dormitory. She never spoke to him again until a year or so later, when she gave him an invitation to her wedding. He was as surprised as everybody else at the news. Here was a girl who said that she was serious about her career in one breath, and in the next she goes off and gets herself engaged to a rich guy from America. Anant was shocked and furious that she misled him and a number of other hopeful boys, and jealous of the guy from America who grabbed his girl (he still thought of her as his girl). But in reality he had nothing to offer her except maybe his good looks. In her eyes, he was a struggling student who had a long way to go before he could support a wife in style. In contrast, the fellow from America was well-settled and was in a position to offer her financial security.

Some of those jilted boys, because it was mostly the male of the species who suffered from unrequited love, took to drink; some went into deep depression and refused do anything, not even eat a proper meal. One could easily identify the poor soul from the way he picked at his food in the mess hall; his friends dragged him there in the hope that interaction with others might bring him out of his shell. Observing the lack of productivity in the laboratory, his research adviser tried in vain to coax the student back into the laboratory. Sometimes it took months for a lovesick fellow to get back into shape, and when it happened, all his well-wishers celebrated. In one particular case, when a brilliant student was discarded like a worn-out glove (to borrow a phrase from Wodehouse) by a sexy siren, it almost led to a tragedy. The love affair between Somnath and Savita was the talk of the town. The beautiful Savita was from Coorg, a region in the Karnataka state known for its natural splendor, coffee plantations, and beautiful damsels. Savita's father, a brigadier general in the Indian Army, was stationed at Bangalore. Savita was very fair, reasonably tall, with a sensuous figure and gait. Her appearance was closer to a Bollywood star than to that of a Ph.D. student. She was probably the only girl in the campus to have her hair styled by a professional at an expensive salon. She had manicures and pedicures at regular intervals and dressed as though she was going to a grand gala evening, and not to a test-tube-filled laboratory that smelled of chemicals. To say the least, she was overdressed for a chemistry laboratory. Somnath was her senior by about three years in the department, and was well on his way to finishing his project and off to the United States. Because of his extraordinary knowledge and hard work, he was the darling of the faculty, and everyone predicted a bright future for this budding young scientist. Somnath and Savita became inseparable, and everyone thought that they were engaged to be married. Nobody understood why such a beautiful girl fell for a nerd like Somnath. Everything about him was average, his height, his looks, his behavior, with the exception of his scientific knowledge. The affair came to an abrupt end when Savita suddenly disappeared from the campus for about a month. That swift vanishing act coincided with the onset of Somnath's depression. After a month or so Savita reappeared on the scene. She was the same sexy Savita, dressed to kill and elegant, but without the sparkle in her eyes and her characteristic bright smile. It was said that she went away to get an abortion. Somnath and Savita were never seen together after her return to the campus, and for all practical purposes their once-sizzling relationship fizzled out. Neither Savita nor Somnath would talk to anyone about what happened and why they were not together anymore. It was generally known that, a week or two after Savita's absence from the campus, her father, the brigadier general, visited the campus in his gleaming olive green official car. The car was parked in front of the department building and the driver was sent to fetch Savita's advisor. The advisor and the brigadier general spoke to each other for about thirty minutes or so. According to reliable sources, Savita's father informed the adviser about the reason for her absence. Upon her return to work, she was studious and worked hard under the close supervision of her ever-vigilant advisor. On the other hand, Somnath was completely devastated, and his research came to a complete standstill. It was believed that he took to drink. Despite repeated pleading from his advisor and other professors, he never set foot in his laboratory for almost six months. His clumsy attempt to commit suicide by swallowing potassium cyanide was thwarted by an alert senior student in the laboratory who yanked the bottle out of Somnath's hands. After saving his life, the good Samaritan told Somnath, "If you let a silly girl like that ruin your life, what good are you? We all know you have the potential to become a good scientist. You must forget that girl and move on with your life. Girls are like buses, you miss one, you will catch the next one." The story had a happy ending just like a Bollywood movie. Somnath got his Ph.D., married a girl arranged by his parents, and went off to America with his new bride.

Although most of the anecdotes were about the discarded males, there was one compelling tale of a beautiful damsel ditched by her lover. Usha, a petite and busty Iyengar girl, and Hemant, a dashingly handsome fellow, had been seeing each other for about a year when without any warning Hemant told Usha that it was over. She was dumbfounded and cried, "What do you mean, it is over? I thought we were going to get married soon. How can you do this to me? I gave my virginity and my youth to you, and now you are dumping me."

He was unmoved by her tears. "Didn't you have fun too? Why do you complain about being used? You used me too."

There were many more such stories of failed romances, and there were also stories of couples coming together and getting married and flying off together to America to start a new life.

Luckily, Anant neither got depressed nor abused alcohol or tobacco. He became a workaholic, determined to succeed and show the world that he could overcome. He made up his mind to work day and night and complete his Ph.D. in less than four years. He never let the world know how sad he was at "losing" Shalini. But in his private moments, he succumbed to his blue mood and took to singing the tragic songs of Talat Mahmood. He memorized all the sad songs sung by the great singer and sang them in the bathroom, on the way to the laboratory, and even in the laboratory while conducting his experiments. (*Sub kuch lutake hosheme aya*—What is point in coming to my senses after I lost everything; *Ansu samajke kyoo mujhe ankse tumne giradiya*—you brushed me off your eyes thinking that I am just a tear drop). His colleagues and friends tolerated his idiosyncrasy, telling themselves that this was much better than alcohol or cyanide.

His lack of experience with women was a handicap when Anant moved to the United States, and Anant had a difficult time adjusting to the culture where men and women interacted in such a free manner. Also, his approach to American women was different from the way he approached Indian women and, to a certain extent, influenced by what he saw on TV and movies. He thought that it was okay to ask an American girl out soon after he met her. But his cultural bias kept him from treating Indian women this way, even those born and raised in the U.S. who were American in their outlook. Moreover, he observed the way Indian parents "protected" their daughters from becoming too Americanized, keeping them from consuming alcohol and dating. But the same parents had no problem when their sons indulged themselves with American girls, went to bars to drink and dance and maybe even had sex. Although he found her very attractive, he wasn't sure how to approach Sheila. She was constantly on his mind for the next few days, and after weighing the pros and cons, he made up his mind to call her, thinking that the worst that could happen was she would reject him. He looked in vain for her number in the phone book. He thought Mrs. Murthy might have Sheila's number and called their house but got no answer.

Heather took Anant to a farewell party for her best friend, who was moving to Atlanta. Anant had never met the girl and told Heather that he might not be comfortable in that gathering. She overruled him and almost dragged him to the bar where they all met. After settling down at a table and ordering drinks, Heather took Anant to the dance floor and began to dance to the loud music. Anant did his best to keep up with Heather but was clearly uncomfortable on the dance floor. He wished Heather would let him go back to the table. Suddenly he heard a voice over the cacophony. "Hi, I see you are having fun." He looked around to find Sheila dancing away with a good-looking fellow, and by the time he said hello, she was not to be seen, as there were many people on the dance floor. After a couple of dances, Heather and Anant went back to their table. Debbie, the girl who was leaving, was happily getting drunk in honor of her last day in North Carolina. The next day, she was supposed to drive off to Atlanta to life in the fast-lane. She was getting increasingly maudlin, reminiscing about her life in Chapel Hill, talking about her ex-husband, how he was always drunk and spent all their money on gambling. Anant was embarrassed and he wished Debbie would sober up and they could all get out of the noisy and smoky bar. He looked at Heather, hoping she might move things along, but even Heather was drinking a bit more than usual. Anant had had just one beer and didn't feel like drinking anymore in that crowded atmosphere. When he went out for a few minutes to breathe some fresh air, he ran into Sheila.

They said hi to each other again, and she asked him, "Where is your girlfriend?"

He lied. "Heather is not my girlfriend, she is just a friend who happens to be a girl."

"Oh, really, the way she was clinging to you, I thought that you two were very close."

"That is the way we dance, as I am afraid I will lose my balance if I don't hold on to her very tight. I am terrible on the dance floor."

"You are crazy! Why dance if you don't like it?"

"I hate to displease people, and it doesn't hurt to pretend that I am enjoying it."

"Are you always like this, doing things you don't like just because you want to please somebody?"

"No, not always. But there is no harm in being polite. Anyway, I was meaning to call you but couldn't find your number in the phone book."

"That's because my number is unlisted."

"Will you give me your number?"

"Sure, I will give it you. But why did you want to call me?"

"I thought I will ask you out for dinner."

"Why are you so sure I will accept your invitation? After all, I might be happily married." She said with a twinkle in her eyes.

"Well, I knew that I was taking a chance. Fact is, I know nothing about you except that you are very attractive and I couldn't think of anything else but you for the past few days. I even tried calling Mrs. Murthy to get your number. If it turned out you are married, I would have cursed my luck and tried to forget you, may be go to Himalayas and become a *sanyasi*."

"For God's sake, don't be so melodramatic. To the dismay of my parents, I am still single. I am free this evening. If you are also free, let's go to Taj."

"I thought you are with your friends. Aren't you going back into the bar?"

"Oh, no, I am done there. This is our monthly thing, all my colleagues get together to have a good time. Some of them are still there inside and I wanted to leave."

Anant wanted to go with Sheila, but he was worried about Heather's reaction. He knew Heather expected him to join them for Debbie's farewell dinner. But the very thought of listening to Debbie's diatribes at dinner did not appeal to him. "Sheila, can I see you at the restaurant in a few minutes?"

"Do you know where Taj is?"

"Yeah, I went there a couple of times, I know how to get there. I will see you there."

He went into the bar and was accosted by Heather. "Where have you been? I have been looking all over for you. We are ready for dinner. Shall we go?"

"No, Heather, I don't feel well. I have nausea and headache, that is why I went out for some fresh air. But it didn't help. Why don't you all go and have a good time. I think I will go home and sleep it off. Goodbye, Debbie, have fun in Atlanta." Since he didn't want to give Heather a chance to coax him to go with them, he walked out of the bar quickly and drove off.

On the way to Taj, he thought about how mad Heather would be at him for ditching them. He wondered if she really believed him. But he had cultivated the habit of telling a lie as though he believed what he was saying, and most people fell for it, as he came across so sincere and honest. He did feel guilty about the episode but told himself that he should be selfish once in a while and that he didn't have to put up with Debbie's behavior at dinner. His clothes smelled of smoke from the bar, and he thought of going to his apartment to change and then go from there to Taj. He rapidly calculated the time this would take and concluded that there might be just enough time to do that. So he drove fast to his place, which was only a few minutes away, had a quick shower, changed into a blue shirt and khaki pants, and drove to Taj. He was glad to see that he arrived before Sheila and that he hadn't kept her waiting. He got a nice secluded table by a window and waited for her. In a few minutes, she walked in, and Anant got up and escorted her to the table and helped her to her chair. They looked at each other and smiled, as they couldn't help but notice that they had both taken the trouble to change clothes. She looked stunning in a pale green silk blouse, beige pants, a short white jacket, and open-toed sandals with wide white straps. The bright red polish on her toenails accentuated her shapely feet. This was such a contrast to the way she looked at the bar. Anant complemented her on her outfit and said, "You must have driven very fast to accomplish so much in such a short time."

"You look great too, the blue really suits you."

"Thank you. I like blue, pink and green. What is your favorite color?"

"It all depends on my mood, I don't have any specific favorite color. If the whole ensemble looks good and suits me, I will wear almost any color."

Anant wanted to find out more about Sheila. "I am a post-doctoral fellow in the chemistry department at the university. Where do you work?"

"I completed my M.D. and now doing my residency in Internal Medicine."

"How many more years do you have to do this?"

"I will complete my first year this coming June, and then I will have two more years of training."

"After that, will you be able to practice medicine anywhere in the country?"

"Yes, but first I have get a state license to practice. But I will worry about that when I am closer to completing my residency. Anyway, at about the same time I will also have to sit for my board exams for certification by the American Board of Internal Medicine. But enough about me. So you already have your Ph.D. Where did you get your degree?"

"From IISc, Bangalore."

"What is IISc?"

"It is an abbreviation for Indian Institute of Science, just like we use IIT for Indian Institute of Technology."

"Oh, I know about IIT. My cousin did his B.Tech at IIT/Delhi. It is so tough to get into IIT/Delhi. He had to go to special classes in the evenings for almost four years before he finished high school. All that preparation helped him do well in the entrance examination, and he managed to get into IIT. Now he is a big shot in Silicon Valley. But how come I never heard of IISc? You must think I'm dumb."

"No, not at all. It is true that IISc is not as well known as IIT. But IISc is the premier research institute in India, and it was established long before India became independent, whereas IITs were set up after independence."

"So you must be a good scientist."

"Not really, I am just an accidental scientist."

"I never heard that expression. What exactly do you mean by that?"

"By that, I mean that I never really planned on becoming a scientist. My life was a series of accidents, not in its literal sense, but what I mean is that when I did my B.S. I never even thought of doing a Master's in Chemistry. It just happened."

"How can it just happen, unless you enrolled for the program?"

"Of course, I did enroll, but not because I wanted to, because my father pushed me into it."

"I know Indian parents can be very pushy. Indian parents push their kids into studies they are not interested in. If the father is a doctor, he wants his son or daughter to be a doctor, and if he is an engineer, the kid should study engineering. The mothers are not as demanding as the fathers, but they also want their children to achieve great things. You'll be hard pressed to find an Indian parent wanting their child to become an artist or a singer. Sometimes the parents push the kids so hard that they drive them to drugs, or worse, to suicide. It is only when it is too late that the stubborn parents come to their senses. I am lucky, my parents are different. They left the three of us alone to do whatever we wanted. At first I wanted to be a journalist, and in fact I took some courses during my undergraduate days, but soon found out that it is tough with my skin color to succeed in that field. I then chose a safe profession where I can excel if I work hard. If you were pushed into doing your Master's, why didn't you just stop there? Did you suddenly develop an interest in science?"

"Oh, nothing of that kind. With a Master's degree from a mediocre university, it is difficult to get a decent job. That is why I was forced to do a Ph.D. Once I completed my Ph.D., I was again left with no choice but to come to the United States. It is one of those rites of passage, almost all of us go abroad after completing Ph.D. None of my professors advised me stay in India and work there. Everybody I spoke to said, 'Go West, young man.'"

"I have seen so many well-qualified Indian engineers, doctors, and scientists coming to the U.S. and settling down here for good. I wondered, why does a country as poor as India train so many professionals only to lose them to the west?"

"Well, you do have good point there. But we must remember that the founding fathers of the country sincerely believed and hoped that a well-educated group of people would be an asset to the country. But unfortunately, most of those educated fellows were unable to find suitable jobs in India, and they were forced to migrate to greener pastures. There is a misconception that people like me come here because of a better life. It is true that in America we have a better quality of life, clean air, less pollution, better roads and communication. When I said that qualified professionals can't find jobs in India, I mean suitable jobs. If I really wanted to settle for any job, I might have found a teaching job in a small college. But at those colleges one can't do anything but teach, as facilities for conducting research are almost nonexistent. After all, having studied at IISc, one would like to continue to do some research, however mediocre it might be. In my case, another reason for coming to USA is India's obsession with 'foreign returned' candidates. Most of the top scientists in India have spent some time in the western countries and, from what little I have seen, faculty positions at the top Indian universities are given only to those with post-doctoral experience abroad."

Sheila tucked her hair behind her ears and turned the pages of the menu. "OK, I understand your situation, but what about all those engineers from IITs? Why can't the Indian government try to keep them in the country by creating more opportunities?"

"It has to do with finding money to invest in manufacturing, research, and development. Indian engineers are second to none, but if the money for private investment is limited and the government-run factories invariably run under loss and are poorly managed, how can we have new jobs?"

"When countries like Taiwan, Singapore, and South Korea can do it, why can't India?"

Anant took a sip of his water. "Those countries are beholden to the multinational corporations and do their bidding. India's leaders are certainly aware that inviting the big Western corporations to open their ventures in India will create more good jobs and help stem the brain-drain. But unfortunately, along with money will come the foreign influence. It will only be a matter of time before the large amount of money at the disposal of the multinationals to makes its way into the hands of the political parties and influence elections. This will be followed by the influence of the West on India's foreign policy, and pretty soon the

Indian Prime Minister will be nothing but a puppet in the hands of the leaders of USA and UK."

"You talk as though you don't really care for the Western system and its values."

"Oh, no. You misunderstand me. I have nothing against the Western societies. It is their nature to pillage and exploit the poorer countries. As long as one is aware of the rules of the game and play it by their rules, we will be OK."

"Do you regret coming to the U.S.?"

"Not anymore, now that I met you!"

The waiter came, and they ordered drinks and appetizers. Anant asked for an Indian beer and Sheila wanted white wine. They started with vegetable cutlets, and for their main course they ordered tandoori chicken, fish curry, *parathas, palak paneer,* and lamb *biryani.* Over the sumptuous dinner, they talked about their families and their hopes for the future.

Sheila's parents had moved to the U.S. from Delhi right after they completed medical school. Due to the shortage of physicians in the late 1950's, it was easy for Indian doctors to immigrate to the U.S.. They were given VIP treatment when they arrived, got their green cards almost immediately, and were on their way to well-paid jobs. Her parents worked for some time and then got advanced training, her father in cardiology and her mom in allergy medicine. Now, after some thirty-five years in this country, they were well-established, their children well-educated, and on their way to becoming self-sufficient. Sheila was the middle child; her older sister studied molecular biology and worked for a pharmaceutical company in California, and her younger brother was a college senior in Charlottesville, VA. Since her parents lived in Silver Springs, Maryland, her brother could drive up there in a few hours whenever he had a few days off from school. As he was the youngest, he was a bit spoiled and was more attached to his mom than his sisters were. While their parents were very successful financially as well as professionally, they brought up their kids to be fiscally responsible, never to spend a penny more than they should. When they were little, the whole family used to fly to India in economy class, and it was invariably quite stressful. By the time they reached their grandparents' home in Delhi in the middle of the night, they were all dead tired, and for the next three days all they did was sleep and eat. When Sheila was old enough to know about first-class travel, she asked her dad why they couldn't travel by first class. He said that the money saved by traveling in economy class would come in handy for the innumerable gifts they had to purchase for their relatives back in Delhi.

Sheila sipped her wine. "Most of the guys from India are either married or engaged by the time they reach your age. How come you are still single?"

He joked, "No one wanted to marry me. To the parents of the prospective brides, a Ph.D. is not very appealing compared to doctors or engineers."

While Anant was doing his Ph.D., his parents tried to marry him off to an Andhra Brahmin girl from a traditional family. Since he was the scion of a big landlord, there was no dearth of parents trying to offer their girls in marriage to Anant. At that time, Anant was in Bangalore trying to decide on his Ph.D. research project. His advisor offered him several alternatives, and Anant was conducting some initial experiments to determine the feasibility of some of those problems. This process was crucial, and he didn't want any distractions at this stage of his career. So he appealed to his parents to leave him alone for a few years. Although they didn't like the idea, they reluctantly postponed the bride-screening process.

Anant wasn't too fond of the traditional way the marriages were arranged in his family, as he knew only too well what his uncle, professor Bala's younger brother, had had to go through. His poor spineless uncle Ganesh, while doing his Ph.D. in physics at Osmania University, fell in love with a gorgeous Reddy girl, who was also pursuing her doctoral degree in the same department. When Ganesh's father heard about his son's escapade, he immediately summoned Bala to the village and gave him a piece of his mind. "You are the elder brother and you shouldn't have allowed Ganesh to go around with a Reddy girl. Have you ever heard of such nonsense? How can a Brahmin boy marry a Reddy girl? The reputation of our family is at stake unless we do something immediately. Bring the boy home and we will get him married to a Brahmin girl." When Bala tried to tell his father that he couldn't control what Ganesh did, his father wouldn't listen to him anymore, telling him only to get on with the job.

Bala had the unpleasant task of convincing Ganesh to forget the Reddy girl. Ganesh was made to visit many peoples' houses to "see" the prospective brides. Tiffin and coffee were invariably offered at every household and served as icebreakers. After the guests ate and drank their coffee, the bride was then presented for "viewing." The boy and girl had absolutely no say in the initial part of the process. This first "meeting" was arranged by the families in consultation with various intermediaries. Ideally both families should belong to a similar socio-economic class, the bride's family should be in a position to give a substantial dowry to the groom's family, and last but not least, the horoscopes of the prospective couple should be made available for matching by an astrologer. On the day of the groom's visit, the bride would be dressed up carefully by a coterie of aunts and other relatives and "presented" to the groom's party. The groom would then be permitted to look at the bride and, in some cases, they were allowed to talk to each other, although not in private. After several weeks of this torture and drugged by all that caffeine, Ganesh became quite indifferent and let the elders choose a girl they thought might be suitable. Unfortunately for Ganesh, the girl he was forced to marry was almost illiterate, hadn't finished high school, and didn't speak a word of English. On top of that, she was a lousy cook and a terrible housekeeper. Somehow the couple managed to produce three kids, but poor Ganesh suffered for the rest of his short life with that most unsuitable woman. He was an intellectual and a scholar and probably would have been happy married to a like-minded girl. But he was too timid to go against the wishes of his dictatorial father, and consequently took to drink and suffered a massive stroke and died at the young age of forty.

Although he knew that he would be fighting a tough battle, Anant was determined that he would never go through the ordeal of an arranged marriage. After a few years, when he was on the verge of completing his Ph.D., he did not inform his parents that he was applying for post-doctoral fellowships in the United States. After everything was settled, he went to Hyderabad and told them that he had to leave within two weeks to accept a fellowship in North Carolina. His parents were upset at this news and tried to force him to stay back at least a month so that they could arrange his marriage. But Anant convinced them that he couldn't delay his departure because the professor in North Carolina was in a hurry to fill the position. He promised them that he would be back in six months, a promise that he did not intend to keep.

They just ate their appetizers when the waiter brought their entrées. Anant asked the waiter for more beer and wine.

Anant asked Sheila, "You are so beautiful and sexy. How come you are still single?"

Sheila replied, "Oh, there was someone, but he was crazy and I broke up with him. That was few years ago, and after that I never dated anybody else. My parents tried to fix me up with some suitable boys, but I didn't want to go through the whole rigmarole."

During her third year in medical school, Sheila had met Kishore Khanna. Kishore was a first-year resident; they bumped into each other in the cafeteria, and he introduced himself and thus began a relationship that lasted a year or so. He was good-looking, charming, articulate, and knowledgeable. He had completed medical school in Delhi, and after passing the examinations for foreign medical graduates, joined a residency in Internal Medicine. He spoke English with a strong Hindi accent, and sometimes it was difficult to understand him. They saw each other quite often and got along well. Although they held hands and kissed, it was quite a while before they went all the way.

Sheila didn't have much experience, as she never dated anybody until she was a junior at the University of Maryland at College Park. Scott was a senior, and they met at a dorm party. Everybody was drinking beer and dancing and having fun. Sheila was with a bunch of Indian girls when Scott approached her and started talking and she found out that his parents also lived in Silver Springs. After a few weeks, they met again in the cafeteria, and Scott asked her out. They dated for a couple of months and slept together a few times. He was her first man, and she thought that sex would be great, like what she read in the romantic novels. But Sheila was disappointed with the experience, as Scott was an inconsiderate lover. He graduated and went off to graduate school at Penn State. After that, she never met anyone interesting, and no one asked her out either. She got so busy with her studies and applications to various medical schools that she didn't have time to date anyone. She got into medical school at Charleston, South Carolina, and then life became more hectic. In the meanwhile, her parents tried to find a groom for her, but she never encouraged them, as she didn't care for arranged marriages. After a while they gave up, telling themselves that it was all in God's hands.

Kishore and Sheila were compatible in many ways. They were from similar family backgrounds, both spoke Hindi, and shared a passionate interest in medicine and patient care. Although she was in her third year of medical school and he was her senior by several years, he was considerate and patient with her and treated her as an equal. Their relationship grew out of their passion for their profession and blossomed into intimacy. She also liked the fact that he didn't pressure her to have sex like Scott had. Not that she didn't want to have fun with the right man, but she was not promiscuous like some of her friends.

After they made love for the first time, Kishore asked, "Aren't you a virgin?"

She could have lied and said that her hymen was ruptured due to the use of tampons, but didn't want to begin their relationship with a lie. "No, I am not a virgin."

She could tell that he was upset about it.

She asked him, "Were you a virgin before you met me?"

"No, there was a woman in Delhi. We were very close, but she got married to another guy and I came here."

"So if you are not a virgin, why did you expect me to be one?"

"It's different with men. In our culture, the man should be experienced."

"Does it bother you that I am not a virgin?"

"Yes, to some extent. When I think of some other guy touching you and making love to you, I get very annoyed. You know that I want to marry you, and I always thought you were never with another man."

Then he asked her with how many men she had been with and how many times with each man. He wanted to know each and every detail about her past sex life. He was obsessed with her virginity and went on pestering her to tell him everything. She didn't mind sharing her past sexual experience with him, as there wasn't that much to tell. When she told him that she had sex with only one guy before and that she never got any pleasure from it, he didn't seem to believe her. In every other aspect he was a great guy: a decent, compassionate doctor, a good friend, and a mentor. But the virginity issue was making him nuts, and she felt it was best if they parted ways.

Anant and Sheila finished dinner and decided not to have dessert because they were full. Anant was happy to see that, unlike some women, Sheila had a good appetite and didn't constantly worry about her weight. As it was a Friday evening, they were both relaxed and didn't notice the time. They were the last customers in the restaurant, and the staff was closing down for the night. Anant paid the bill, and they walked out of the restaurant. Neither of them wanted the evening to end.

Anant said, "I want to invite you to my place for a drink, but you may not like my shabby place. For me it's just a place to sleep. If I knew that I would be meeting a gorgeous girl such as you, I would have rented a posh apartment."

"Anant, don't worry about your apartment. Mine may not be any better, but I do have a good view of the river and the downtown. You can come to my place for a drink."

He said yes and followed her car. He had a tough time keeping up with her as she drove like a maniac. He was happy to arrive at her apartment complex in one piece. She made fun of his driving. "You drive like an old man! You are so slow, I had to slow down so many times to make sure you were still behind me." He thought, *If this is slow, I hate to see her normal driving*. But he didn't say anything.

She took him into the foyer of the multi-storied complex. "These apartments are owned and maintained by the hospital and rented to the residents at a subsidized cost. The units here are one, two or three bedrooms, and a resident is entitled to a two- or three-bedroom unit if he or she is married with kids."

They went up in the elevator to the fifth floor to her one-bedroom apartment. Her place was in great disarray, with books, magazines and journals lying all over the living room. It was sparsely furnished with a comfortable looking couch, a matching chair, a coffee table, and lamps on either side of the couch. A TV was in the corner facing the couch, and right next to the TV was a sliding door leading to a balcony.

Sheila removed a pile of journals from the couch and

the chair. "I am sorry this place is such a mess, I never get time to clean. I have some white wine, will you have some?"

He followed her into the kitchen to help her. The kitchen was also very messy, dishes lying everywhere, cups and glasses left on the counters, begging to be washed. He didn't say anything, but she was apologetic. "I didn't expect any company today, I normally do all the washing and cleaning on Saturdays." She got two clean wine glasses from the cabinet and a bottle of chardonnay from the fridge. She explained, "I never drink when I am alone; I need company to drink wine. Somebody gave me that bottle of wine for last Christmas and I just stuck it in the refrigerator."

He opened the bottle and poured the wine into their glasses, and she suggested that they go to the balcony to see the view. From the balcony they could see the river, and beyond the river was the downtown. The reflection of the bright lights in the river was spectacular. They just stood there, sipping wine and admiring the view. She stood so close to him, he could smell her subtle perfume. He was glad that she had good taste, unlike some women who smelled like they poured a whole bottle of perfume all over their body. The wine, the view, the perfume, and her sensuous body just inches away from him were enchanting. He threw caution to the winds, put his hand around her waist, drew her to him, and kissed her softly. She responded by embracing him and kissing him passionately.

"Let's go inside," Sheila took him to her bedroom, where they made love all night. After each time, they slept for an hour or two, then woke up and again lost themselves to the rapture of their two bodies coming together. Finally, holding each other, they slept until about ten in the morning. He wasn't sure who woke up first, but both of them opened their eyes slowly and looked at each other. He drew her closer to him and kissed her and fondled her gently. "It was great, honey."

"I enjoyed it too, you were very energetic."

They were both hungry and decided to go out for breakfast. Anant said that he would go to his place, have a shower, and join her at the restaurant.

She asked, "Why don't you have a shower here? I'll give you a clean towel."

"But I have to brush my teeth and shave, and wear a fresh shirt."

"Sweetie, I will give you a toothbrush, and you don't have to shave, you look sexy with a day-old beard."

"Oh yeah, if I let it grow for a couple of more days, I will look like Yasir Arafat."

She laughed. "You are funny."

"OK, let's get moving, I am starving."

"Let's brush first and then shower."

"You mean together?" he asked mischievously.

"You are very greedy! Yes, we can shower together, but don't start anything now."

"Agreed. I will behave myself, I will just admire your beautiful body and rub your back."

After breakfast, they went to their respective apartments to catch up on their weekend chores.

Anant called her in the evening, and she asked him to come to her place. He got a bottle of Merlot and a six-pack of beer and went to her place. The apartment was sparkling clean. All the books and journals were neatly placed on the coffee table, and the kitchen was scrubbed, and the cups and other utensils put away. He was impressed. "You must have worked quite hard all day, this place looks wonderful."

She looked at him. "After a sleepless night, this was hard, but I had to do it." He took her into his arms and kissed her passionately and she kissed him back and led him to the bedroom. Afterwards, they ordered a pizza to be delivered.

"I like being with you, you are so wonderful", Anant said, stroking her hair.

"What is so wonderful about me? I am just an ordinary girl."

"But I like you very much. You are fun to be with."

"I like you too."

"We should see more of each other."

"That's fine with me. We can meet as often as my schedule allows. My calls tend to be hectic and on those days, I don't do anything but work. I guess I am too intense. I know some of my colleagues are so nonchalant about their calls, they go golfing or watch movies."

"I am sure we can work something out."

The next day, he was busy doing work in his laboratory and writing a manuscript. Heather called him that evening, "What happened to you? I called you several times yesterday and today, and you were never there. How are you feeling?"

He completely forgot that he complained about nausea and a headache on Friday evening. "I am fine. I was in the laboratory today, working on a manuscript. How was your weekend?"

"It was fine. I thought we might go for lunch somewhere, but I couldn't get in touch with you."

"I am sorry, I should have called you. But I was quite busy and didn't think of going out."

Heather asked him if he would like to come to her apartment. He declined, saying that he had to work on his paper. Then he rang Sheila and asked if she was interested in his company.

She said, "I was thinking of you all day. I tried calling you several times. Where the hell were you? Are you going around with that girlfriend of yours?"

"What girlfriend?"

"That girl you were dancing with in the bar on Friday."

"No, I didn't see her this weekend. I was at my laboratory working."

She was mollified. "OK, do you want to come to my place now? I will cook something for dinner."

"Fine, I will be there in a few minutes."

The moment he walked in, they both embraced each other and made love.

Afterwards, she said, "I missed you very much all day. Why didn't you call me?"

"I was in the laboratory. Besides, I thought you needed to catch up on your sleep."

"I am all caught up on my sleep. I slept like a baby on Saturday night. What about you?"

"I too slept well, but I missed you."

She cooked delicious food. She made eggplant and squash curry with onions and garlic and other spices, rice, and a spicy sambar with potatoes and small pearl onions. She cooked everything very quickly, moving about in her small kitchen efficiently. They had their dinner, and he helped her with the dishes and after the kitchen was cleaned up, they went back into the living room and cuddled on the couch with their wine.

Sheila said, "I am on call tomorrow night. I must get some sleep tonight."

"Is that a hint for me to go?"

"Don't be silly, I didn't mean it like that. I have to be in the hospital by eight in the morning, alert and ready to handle the patients."

"I guess I am lucky, I don't have to worry about timings. I go to my laboratory whenever I feel like it and I work when I am in the mood. Sometimes, I go swimming in the middle of the day. My boss doesn't care where we are and when we do our work as long as it gets done."

"If I get that kind of freedom, I will never do anything. I need to be under pressure to accomplish anything. If I don't have to work I can watch TV or sleep all day."

They spent some more time together, and at about ten, Anant got up very reluctantly. "I better go. Sleep tight. I will call you day after tomorrow."

She kissed him, and clinging to him, did not let him go. "To hell with my sleep. Let's go inside."

Anant and Sheila met frequently, and their relationship became very close in the next few months. He spent most of his free time at her place and even slept many nights there. Although she enjoyed their love-making, Sheila didn't have the patience for long-drawn marathon sessions. Anant went on and on, so much that she complained that she was sore and begged him to finish it off. In the beginning, when he did it for a very long time, she said, "How come you take so much time to come? Usually it is over in a few minutes." From this he surmised that her previous lovers were very speedy and inconsiderate, and felt that he should give her the satisfaction she might have missed with them. In spite of those minor issues, they enjoyed being with each other and couldn't bear to be apart.

Sheila had a few days off and was planning to visit her parents in Maryland.

She asked Anant, "Sweetie, I want you to come with me. Can you take a few days off?"

"I can take some time off. But are you sure that you want me to go with you? I am afraid that I may be in the way."

"Don't be silly. I want you to come with me because I hate to be away from you. If you come with me we can drive up together and go sightseeing in Washington."

The drive to Maryland would take about six hours, and he hoped that the weather would be nice. They reached her home by evening, and Anant was received courteously by her parents. Dr. Puri, dressed in an expensive suit, was short, chubby, dark-skinned, and almost bald; to cover his bald head, he combed his hair from one side to the other, and the effect was grotesque. Mrs. Puri appeared to be slightly taller than her husband, and although there were a few wrinkles on her face, her features were sharp, suggesting that she must have been beautiful when young. They were both pleasant and made Anant feel at home. When Mrs. Puri offered tea, Dr. Puri suggested that it was almost cocktail time and asked Anant what he would prefer to drink. Caught between tea and a real drink, he would always prefer alcohol but hesitated and looked at Sheila.

She understood his predicament. "Daddy, you always

complain that you never find a drinking buddy since most of your friends are teetotalers, and at home we women just drink a little wine now and then. You will like Anant, he never refuses a drink."

Anant was embarrassed. "Sheila, your parents may think that I am an alcoholic!"

"Don't worry, Anant," said Mrs. Puri. "We know how Sheila exaggerates everything. We take what she says about you with a pinch of salt."

Dr. Puri looked at Anant. "Shall we have some whiskey?"

While the men had whiskey, the two women went into the kitchen, presumably to get dinner ready. Dr. Puri enquired about Anant's family in India and asked him whether his parents ever visited the United States.

Anant's father never cared to go out of India. Professor Bala was one of those individuals who was happy in his environment—his teaching, his students, his department, and his family. He couldn't think of leaving all that to go off on a tour of America. Although professor Bala could have gone abroad for a sabbatical, he wasn't interested in it. Some of his colleagues went abroad almost every year for a couple of months during summer holidays. Professor Bala was aware that his colleagues published in prestigious journals as a result of their collaboration with their Western counterparts. In addition, they saved some money during their stint abroad. Typically, a professor from India visiting the U.S. for one year lived frugally and saved at least ten thousand dollars, which when converted into Indian currency multiplied by about forty (depending upon the exchange rate at that time). In other words, a person could save about four-hundred thousand rupees in about a year, which was equivalent to the net annual salary of a professor in most universities in India. Moreover, they also got their full pay for the whole year at their parent institution. Some of the more enterprising professors would invite themselves to lectures at various universities where they had some contacts. Each lecture would fetch anywhere between two and three hundred dollars, and this would add up to quite a bit if they managed to give a few talks. Professor Bala never understood this lure of money, maybe because he was rich. Also, the fame and glory associated with amassing a large number of publications in prestigious journals, the rat race for Bhatnagar awards, and chasing grant money never appealed to him. He was content with teaching his classes and the reputation he had in the department as a good teacher. Although Anant suggested that his parents visit America so that he could take them around the country and show them some of the tourist spots, they demurred, saying that they had too much work that they couldn't delegate.

Dr. Puri complained, "I built all this—this life, a good name in the community, this nice house—but my parents have never seen all this." Then he took Anant on a tour of his house. Dr. Puri's house was built on a large lot of at least thirty acres. The land was surrounded by a white picket fence, presumably to keep deer away. All the rooms in the three-story house were very large; Anant thought that one of the bathrooms in this house was as big as his entire apartment. A basement, which opened up into the back yard, was equipped with a small kitchen and a fully-stocked bar. Also in the basement were two bedrooms with attached bathrooms. The living room, den, kitchen, dining room, and master bedroom were on the first floor. On the second floor, there were four large bedrooms and two bathrooms. After the grand tour, Dr. Puri and Anant went into the kitchen to join the ladies. They had a simple dinner consisting of chapathis, rice, mixed vegetable curry, dal and yogurt.

After dinner, Dr. and Mrs. Puri retired, and Sheila and Anant went upstairs to their separate bedrooms. Sheila showed him into his bedroom. "I am right next door, and we share the bathroom." The bathroom was between the two rooms, and both of them had access to it. This proved to be convenient, as Sheila would sneak into his bedroom through the bathroom after her parents had retired for the night. They had a great time for the whole week. Sheila was not bothered with her night calls and her patients, and Anant was free from his laboratory work and writing manuscripts. Every night, they made love quietly, as they were worried that any noise would wake up her parents who slept downstairs. Sheila had to curb her proclivity for loud screaming during her orgasms, and Anant had to restrain himself from getting too vigorous so the bedsprings wouldn't creak. Although they lacked the complete privacy of her apartment, the love-making was different but exciting.

After dropping Anant off at the Smithsonian or the Library of Congress, Sheila and Mrs. Puri would go shopping and pick him up in the evening. Dr. Puri would be back from his office by about six and ready for his cocktails with Anant. Dr. Puri liked Anant and talked to him about his early days in America and his work at various hospitals.

He told Anant, "During my first few years in this country I worked like a donkey. I had a regular job that was keeping me quite busy, but whenever I had some free time I used to moonlight at a different hospital to make some extra money. My wife never liked that I was always working and would tell me to take it easy. But those days I was very ambitious and wanted everything very fast, a big house, a luxury car, and vacations at exotic locations. I wanted to make my first million dollars in a very short time. When six of us started this private practice of cardiology some twenty years ago, all of us worked long hours and built up the practice. Today, our group has about fifteen cardiologists, and we are probably the best in this area. After all those years of hard work, now I am slowing down. I told my people last year that I will no longer do night calls. I will be in my office from eight to five, and after that nobody should bother me."

When Anant and Sheila left for North Carolina, Mrs. Puri cried a lot, telling Sheila, "Come back soon, my dear, I miss all you of very much. Your sister comes home only once every year, and you are always busy with your work, and that brother of yours never even calls me now that he has a girlfriend."

Sheila was embarrassed at her mother's behavior. "Please, Mom, don't cry like that. I will be back very soon." Dr. and Mrs. Puri told Anant he was always welcome in their house.

Anant couldn't help but think of how his parents had behaved when he went home from Bangalore. Although it was only an overnight journey by train from Bangalore to Hyderabad, he went home only twice a year. In those days, telephone calls between cities were expensive. So he wrote home almost every month, sometimes to his father or mother, but mostly to his sister Swathi. Anant and Swathi, although five years apart, were close and corresponded regularly. When he joined the Indian Institute of Science, she was doing her pre-med at a college in Hyderabad. It was at Swathi's insistence that he periodically went to Hyderabad. When Anant went home, he spent most of his time with Swathi. She did most of the talking and brought him up to date about everything at home and in his grandfather's village. His parents hardly communicated with him, as they were always busy with their work or religious activities. They acknowledged his presence by saying, "So you have come from Bangalore, how are things there?" He didn't say anything, as he knew that they didn't care about his answer. Anant and Swathi went out to eat and saw Bollywood and Telugu movies, and came home laughing at the plots and the characters. He enjoyed spending time with his sister, and when it was time to leave she would cling to him, telling him to return soon. When he was leaving, his father would give him some money and say, "Work hard." His mother would hug him perfunctorily and tell him to eat properly. There were no tears and no melodrama.

Sheila asked Anant one evening, "Are you still seeing that girl?"

"Which girl?" he teased her, knowing full well that she was referring to Heather.

"You know, the one in the bar you were dancing with."

"Yes, sometimes when I have my lunch at the university cafeteria I do bump into her."

"Sweetie, that's not what I meant. Are you going out with her? After we started seeing each other regularly, I didn't go out with any other man."

He pretended to be hurt by her lack of confidence in him. "Oh, Sheila, how can you even think that I would go out with any girl after I met you?" He got up and walked out into the balcony.

Sheila was upset that she hurt his feelings and came out and hugged and kissed him while he was still acting like he was sad. "I am sorry, sweetie, I didn't mean to be nasty. It's just that I hate to share you with another woman. You know I love you."

"I love you too, Sheila. Heather is just a friend, and I don't go out with her anymore. In fact, the day after we had dinner at Taj, I stopped going out with Heather. I want to be with you all the time. In fact, I have been thinking of asking you to marry me but wasn't sure when to propose to you."

Sheila had definitely entertained the idea of marrying Anant, but she didn't want to put pressure on him. She was happy to hear that he felt the same way. She asked him mischievously, "Do you have to consult a pundit for an auspicious time to propose to me?"

"No, nothing of the sort. I wasn't sure of your reaction. I mean, will you marry me?"

She kissed him. "You are really hopeless. How can you not see that I liked you from the very first day we met?"

"Great, when shall we get married?"

"Where is the ring?"

"What ring?"

"You know, when a guy proposes to a girl, it is customary to give her a ring. Don't you know that?"

"Yeah, I have seen it in the movies, the fellow goes down on one knee in a public place and proposes to the woman. I will do no such thing. If you agree to marry me, I will take you to a jewelry shop and buy you a ring of your choice."

"You kill the romance of the whole thing! I didn't know that you were so miserly that you didn't want to spend money until you are sure that I will accept your proposal."

"Well, I am not rich enough to throw my money away. What if you were only interested in having fun with me? Also if I buy a ring beforehand, I am not sure if you will like it or even if it will fit you properly."

"Stop it, sweetie, I was only teasing you. But seriously, we have to consult our parents about setting the date for our wedding. Don't worry about the ring now. We can get it later. And I promise that you need not kneel in a restaurant or some other public place to propose to me. I never thought that it was romantic to show one's love in public. What we have between us is private and should remain that way."

When Anant told professor Martin about his engagement to Sheila, he congratulated him and arranged a party at his house to celebrate the occasion. All of the laboratory members and the Martin family had a good time. Mrs. Martin was very gracious and asked Sheila about her family and siblings. When Sheila told her that her parents lived in Maryland, Mrs. Martin said, "My folks live in Massachusetts, and I grew up there. Now my mother is getting quite old and feeble, and we are thinking of bringing her here so that we can look after her."

Professor Martin served dark beer that he brewed himself. When Anant complimented him on the great-tasting beer, he said, "I learned how to make beer from my father. We buy all the ingredients and make a few gallons at a time. The advantage of making our own beer at home is that we can avoid adding all those preservatives, and also it works out quite cheap. A six-pack at the store may cost around three to five dollars, depending on the brand, and when we make it at home, the cost per bottle is a lot less."

After they got home, Sheila told him, "Martin is very fond of you and thinks you are a superb scientist with a bright future. Coming from such an eminent scientist, it is a compliment. I am really proud of you."

The three days that Meena spent in Kansas City with Anant were hectic. They drove around the city, did some sightseeing and window shopping, ate out, took long walks in the evening, and made passionate love. One evening they returned home after eating some really great barbecued ribs at a place that was supposed to serve the best ribs west of the Mississippi. He was glad that Meena, unlike a lot of Indian people, didn't have any objection to eating beef.

Sheila was one of those individuals who disliked beef. Once, when he asked her if the reason for avoiding beef was religious, she said, "No, although I am religious and try to pray every day, I don't care about the holy cow and all that. But my parents never ate beef, and I know their reasons were religious." Anant loved juicy hamburgers and barbecued ribs, and whenever he got a chance he ate them with gusto. Some of the best ribs were served at hole-in-the-wall-type joints, mainly run by black people, and Sheila refused to go to those places. When Anant was seeing Heather, they went to these out-of-the-way places, but after his marriage to Sheila, it was difficult to find someone to accompany him to eat ribs or hamburgers. He went to those restaurants by himself during the weekends when Sheila was on call.

Back at Anant's house, Anant and Meena opened a nice bottle of Merlot and sat down in the dimly-lit living room, chatting, cuddling, kissing and fondling each other. Between sips and kisses, they talked. During the final year of her Master's program in Delhi, Meena met a handsome chap through the amateur theater group that she was a part of. She worked with him in one play, and they spent a lot of time together rehearsing and studying their parts. One thing led to another, and pretty soon they became intimate. Unfortunately for Meena, the fun turned into a nightmare when she got pregnant. She didn't want to inform her boyfriend about her situation because she was quite aware that he was a penniless student without any access to the kind of money she needed for an abortion. Telling her parents about her pregnancy was absolutely out of the question, as she felt that they might disown her. While they gave her a lot of freedom, they expected their daughter to remain a virgin until she got married. She was desperate to get rid of her pregnancy. She spoke to a close friend, who introduced Meena to a rich guy. He was willing to help on one condition; Meena should agree to have sex with him and four of his "friends." Meena was totally distraught at this indecent proposal. Being intimate with one or two boyfriends was quite different from having sex with total strangers. She spent sleepless nights considering her options. She had no intention of going through with her pregnancy. That would be totally devastating to her family prestige, and also for her future prospects. Who would be ready to marry a tarnished woman, however beautiful and accomplished? She had only one avenue open to her; just get rid of it immediately before her belly became big. She arranged to meet the men in a hotel room, and they used her one after another. While one of the guys was with her in the room, the other fellows were in the adjoining room making lewd comments and generally being obnoxious. She endured the nightmare, physically and mentally tortured. She expected her "protector" to leave her alone after the abortion, and she was sadly mistaken. The fellow called her up whenever he felt horny. On the one hand, she was happy that her pregnancy was terminated and that she emerged from the ordeal in one piece; but on the other, the man's persistent demands were not acceptable to her. It was a stressful period of her life, as she had to keep the fellow happy and at the same time study for her finals. Just when she thought that she was helpless, Ramana Rau appeared on the scene. Although he was about ten years her senior, she accepted his proposal of marriage with an alacrity that surprised her family and friends.

Anant was shocked to hear Meena's story. He was sad that she had to go through that sordid affair with those despicable guys. He was angry that Meena had put herself in such a desperate position. He was extremely jealous that she gave herself away to some fellow just because he was handsome, while he, Anant, was crazy about her. Anant was all the more distressed that this squalid episode took place at about the same time he was living in Delhi. He wondered if Meena would have reacted positively if he approached her assertively and told her about his feelings for her. It was true that at first he was attracted by her physical attributes, and he had absolutely no idea of her persona. Although everything happened many years ago, Anant couldn't get over the thought that somehow his failure to make his feelings known to Meena could have led to her difficulties.

By the time she completed telling her story, they were quite tipsy having opened a second bottle of wine.

Meena asked, "Do you still want me, after knowing my sordid past?"

Anant was not quite sure how to answer her question. In arranging this weekend, they made no promises to each other about the future. It was simply a meeting of two friends with no strings attached.

He said, "Past is history and future is mystery. Why don't we enjoy the present?" He took her into his arms and gently kissed her and made love to her.

She said, "You are very nice to me, Anant. I am glad that you didn't judge me for what I had to do. Thanks for your support. I now wish that I was nicer to you and encouraged you to get close to me in Delhi when we met those few times."

Anant was flabbergasted. He had never realized that she remembered him after all those years. "How come you never told me that you remember me?"

Meena looked at him tenderly. "You must think that I am really dumb not to remember you; you were such a nice guy, always a gentleman. The problem with you was that you didn't know that you were such a good catch. I was attracted to you when we first met, but I never encouraged you because my friend, Asha, was interested in you. Of course, we both knew you lived in a dream world and were completely unaware of anything that went around you. Asha was crazy about you, and she wanted to marry you. Knowing her feelings for you, I just couldn't jump in and take you away from her. Oh, how I wish that I could turn the clock back. If only we were together during that time, all those dreadful things wouldn't have happened to me."

"Meena, I knew who you were when you first wrote to me, but I thought you may not recollect our meeting in Delhi such a long time back. But I never thought that Asha had such strong feelings for me. I always treated her as a good friend, used to respect her a lot as she was so knowledgeable. When I left Delhi, I wasn't in a great mood, as I felt I wasted my time there with that fool of an advisor and the lousy research project. I never said goodbye to anybody."

He couldn't believe that Meena found him attractive and that she might have responded to his advances if he had been more persistent in his approach. He never thought that Asha had such deep feelings for him. He never gave her any idea that she was anything more than a friend to him. If she was so much in love with him, why didn't she come out with it and tell him? He couldn't understand these women, why they had to make everything so complicated. If only he knew of Asha's feelings, he would have once and for all dispelled that silly notion from her mind and moved on. But then again, did he have the guts to approach Meena, who appeared beyond his reach? He thought, *"Life was a bloody mess, we both wasted our lives. At least Meena had a son from that loveless marriage of hers. I got nothing."*

The next day, Anant took her to the airport and went with her up to the gate and they talked some more and held each other very tightly and kissed. When the final boarding call was made for her flight, Meena said, "You are very good to me. I love you, I will be back soon."

He smiled. "Have a good flight, call me when you can." After he came home, he felt sad that again he was alone in his house with only his music and books to keep him company. He wondered if the average Indian guy had gone through so much emotional trauma. Most of his contemporaries had gotten married at an early age and were now settled happily with children. His friend Ramu, after completing his B.S., got a job at a bank, got married and moved up the ladder to a managerial position. Life was so simple for Ramu. No heartache, no disappointment, and no divorce.

Anant thought that he should have returned to India after a few years of post-doctoral experience in the U.S. At that time, he was still quite young, and he might have been able to land a decent teaching job in a university, or a position in a pharmaceutical company. By now, after almost sixteen years, he would have been nicely situated, with a wife and a kid or two. In his quest for independence, he ruined his life. Why hadn't he listened to his parents' repeated advice to return and settle down in Hyderabad?

They were so mad when he told them about his intention to marry Sheila. His first instinct was to call his parents to inform them of his engagement to Sheila. But when he considered the amount of money he had to spend on the telephone call, at the rate of about two dollars per minute, he decided to write a letter first and then call them after about ten days. He wrote to his father in English as his ability to write in his mother tongue had vanished long ago. In high school era, Anant had been fluent in Telugu and could read, write and speak the language very well. Once he entered college and then his graduate studies, he didn't get the opportunity to use Telugu much, as English was the only language used in and out of the classroom.

My Dear Father:

I hope you all are doing well there. I am fine here and working hard on my research projects. My boss is pleased with my progress and we are going to send another manuscript for publication in the *Journal of American Chemical Society*. We hope that it will be accepted without many problems. We had to revise the last one a few times before the editor was satisfied, and we lost precious time in the process. I am hoping that the work I am doing here will pave the way for a faculty position at a decent university in this country, as I feel (and my boss supports me) that I should teach for some time here before making plans for the future. Compared to Hyderabad weather, it is quite cold here but I got used to this climate now after almost three years. My car is running well and, whenever I get some time during the weekends, I am exploring nearby areas. I have some good news to convey to you. I am in love with a girl. Her name is Sheila Puri, and she is a doctor doing her residency here at the medical center. Her parents are from Delhi and they speak Hindi at home. Sheila and I decided to get married. I will send you her picture as soon as I get one. I hope you will all be happy to find out that I have finally found a nice girl. I will call you in about ten days and then we can discuss the dates for the wedding.

With best regards,
Yours affectionately, Puttu

When Anant called Hyderabad, there was an uproar at the other end. His father was apoplectic. "How can you write such a letter to us? Do you think you are old enough to arrange your own marriage? Did you consider the consequences of such an action? How can you marry a North Indian? Is she a Brahmin?" He went on and on, ranting and raving, and when he was done his mother came on line and gave him a piece of her mind.

"After all the sacrifices we made to raise you, this is how you repay us? With this indignity? What a shame you bring us! How can we even raise our heads and walk in the street? You are our eldest son, and we depend on you to do the last rites when we die. Now you are going off to marry some creature from the North."

During this monologue, Anant kept quiet, drinking his cold beer and watching a movie on the TV with the volume turned low. He let them have their say and finally asked, "I need your help in fixing a date for the marriage.

Sheila's parents want to perform the wedding in Maryland. Are you going to come?"

This was received with more disapproval from his parents. They were vehemently opposed to the wedding because they were not consulted about it in the first place. They ordered him to return to India immediately, which of course he ignored. Then they threatened to disown him, saying that he would not get a single paisa from them when they died.

They resented the fact that Anant did not involve them in the selection of his bride. He explained to them patiently that there was never any such selection process and that once he met Sheila there was no question of his meeting other women. They fell in love with each other and decided to get married. His parents never understood this phenomenon of love before marriage. They were brought up in a society where a couple gets married first and then love grows out of the relationship. Most importantly, they felt cheated that their eldest son, who was the torch-bearer of the family name, should resort to this type of marriage without the involvement of his elders. They were more worried about the reaction of their friends and relatives than their own son's happiness. It bothered them that tongues would wag and spiteful people would say, "Bala's son is marrying a North Indian girl, as though there are no eligible brides in the entire state of Andhra Pradesh." This kind of talk would be a blow to their prestige, and they were very sad that Anant would not listen to them.

Anant wasn't surprised by their reaction and told Sheila about his conversation with his folks. She was upset with the news and said, "What's wrong with me? I am young, not bad- looking, well-educated, and my family is well-established. What more do they want? I don't want to start our marriage with problems with our elders. Why don't you go to Hyderabad and try to convince them? If you want, I will come with you." Anant told her that it would be a futile undertaking, as his parents were pig-headed. Sensing that Anant was deeply hurt by his parents' reaction, Sheila kept quiet.

He gave his parents a few weeks to cool off and then called them again. But the passage of time didn't seem to help their demeanor. They were still angry at his "betrayal" and refused to discuss his marriage to Sheila. He thought that his fiancée's education would impress them and they would eventually relent. They were vehemently opposed to the wedding because Sheila was not a Brahmin. They had strong feelings about caste, and they believed that inter-caste marriage was a recipe for disaster. The fact that Anant was no longer a Brahmin, in the strictest sense, didn't seem to matter. He told them that he didn't live his life as a Brahmin should; he ate all kinds of meat, including beef. He didn't do pooja every day morning, nor wear the sacred thread. He didn't go to temples, and most importantly he didn't even believe in God. He asked them, "Why are you so hung up on this issue, when I don't even care about it?" This question was only met with vituperative language from the other end. After trying a few more times, he gave up and told Sheila, "Forget about my parents. They are not going to agree to our marriage. Please tell your parents to fix the date." Sheila was in tears because she guessed how bad Anant must be feeling in his heart. He never understood his parents. They keep on saying that all they want was that he should be happy and that they knew what was best for him. If his happiness was all they cared about, why couldn't they see his point of view?

Anant went ahead and got married to Sheila. Her parents were happy about their daughter's engagement, and they were planning a big wedding in Maryland. Their marriage ceremony took place in March, and Dr. and Mrs. Puri planned the entire event meticulously; the ceremony was carried out according to Hindu tradition, with pundits chanting in Sanskrit and the air filled with the fragrance of flowers, sandalwood, and incense. The marriage ceremony was conducted in the morning at their house and was followed by a reception at the country club. The reception in the evening was a grand gala affair with a DJ, music—mostly old and new Hindi film songs—food catered by an exclusive Indian restaurant, and the most important of all, an open bar with every conceivable beverage to please the most discerning palate. The guests, a mixture of Indians and Americans, were friends and colleagues of Dr. and Mrs. Puri. Most of the men wore suits. The Indian women, who always looked forward to these special occasions to show off their saris and jewelry, wore their glittering diamonds and gold ornaments. Sari, the most versatile garment ever invented, covered the bulging bellies of the middle aged women and revealed the flat stomachs, slim waists, and navels of those damsels blessed with a slender figure. A sari could be worn in many different ways, depending upon how the *pallu* was arranged. Also, the *pallu* could be used to cover the complete upper body or it could be strategically placed so as to subtly expose the cleavage of a well-endowed woman. Most American women were dressed conservatively, either in nice dresses or pantsuits, but few of them wore saris. All in all, it was a great heterogeneous gathering, and everyone had fun.

The DJ was boisterous and kept the party on the right track. The party started at about six in the evening, and the guests circulated, greeting each other, chatting, eating appetizers, and sipping drinks. After the appetizers, the guests were asked to take their places at the dinner tables in the grand ballroom, and after all the people were seated, the DJ announced the names of Dr. and Mrs. Puri. Right on cue, they entered the ballroom to the accompaniment of music and a lot of clapping. Finally, the bride and groom made their grand entrance, and everybody got up from their seats and cheered them along. Dr. Puri spoke very briefly, welcoming the guests to the celebration of his daughter's wedding. He told them all to have a good time, and then he let the DJ take over. To work up an appetite for the delicious dinner that would be served, the DJ invited the bride and the groom to the dance floor. A Hindi song played: *"Pehala Nasha, Pehala Khuva, Naya Pyar Hai, Naya Intazar,"* —something about the intoxication brought about by the first love, the deep desire of the lovers, and the anxious wait to consummate their love. Luckily for Anant, this was not a fast song; the experience he had had holding Heather on the dance floors of various bars came in handy, and he comported himself quite creditably. Once the first song was over, other couples joined them on the floor, and the party was in full swing.

They went to Niagara Falls for a short honeymoon. They stayed at a hotel only a block from the falls, and spent most of the time walking around the park, enjoying the beautiful scenery and the magnificent falls. Everything was clean, and the park area was well-maintained. It was amazing to see the large number of Indians visiting the falls. It appeared as though the whole area was taken over by Indians speaking Hindi, Gujarati, Bengali, Telugu, Tamil and other Indian languages. In most cases an older couple was accompanied by a younger couple, suggesting that the old folks might be the parents of one of the younger couple. It was *de rigueur* that all visiting parents from India be brought to this wonder of the world. One couldn't help but wonder if all those Indians visiting Niagara Falls had seen the other wonder of the world— the Taj Mahal. Having seen both, Anant couldn't help but compare the two, one a natural wonder and the other man-made. When he went to the Taj Mahal, the visitors were required to take off their shoes and go barefoot or in socks into the mausoleum. When he came out after seeing the interior, his snow-white socks were filthy. Being fastidious, he took the socks off and wore his canvas shoes without socks and walked out. He wondered why such national treasures weren't properly taken care of and kept clean in India. With thousands of tourists visiting the Taj Mahal every year, one would think that the authorities would pay attention to such a simple thing as cleanliness.

When they returned to North Carolina after their wedding, Sheila and Anant moved into a two-bedroom apartment in Sheila's apartment complex. Being married, she was now eligible to rent a two-bedroom unit. This meant that Anant had to drive to work, but he didn't mind the commute. It was convenient for Sheila to continue to live in that complex, so she could walk to the hospital. Since Sheila made sure that the new apartment faced the river, they still had the spectacular view of the downtown lights. She had roughly another year and a few months to complete her residency. They both liked living in North Carolina and had every intention to settle down in that state. Once she completed her residency, Sheila shouldn't have any problem finding a job anywhere in the state.

Sheila told Anant, "Now that we are married, I will sponsor you for a green card and then you can apply for any job you want. It may take a few months for you to get the actual card, but your status will change to a permanent resident as soon as we apply for it. So in the meantime you can start applying for jobs." Anant agreed to the proposal and got the necessary forms from the Immigration and Naturalization Service (INS), and they sat together and filled all those forms and submitted them to the INS office.

Anant spoke to professor Martin about his job search and was glad that the boss was supportive.

Martin said, "It will take a good year for you to find a suitable job. You have been in this lab for more than three years and have been very productive. I am sure you will find a good job. Where do you want to look?"

"Sheila and I like this state, and we both want to settle down wherever I can get a job. As you know, she can pretty much find a job anywhere. So it all depends on my job."

So he applied for teaching jobs in universities and colleges all over the state, as well as some jobs in the pharmaceutical industry. To be on the safer side, he also applied for teaching jobs in South Carolina, Georgia, Virginia, and Maryland. When he was applying for those jobs, he never thought that he would have difficulty in securing a suitable job. After all, he had published a total of forty papers in good journals, and had expertise in many research techniques. But by late fall and early winter, when he didn't even get one interview call, he began to worry and shared his thoughts with Sheila. "I have put in so many applications that I lost count. It is getting late now and if they don't call me in the next few weeks, I will never find a job by next fall. They start interviewing in winter for all the vacant teaching positions. The job offers are usually made in spring."

"Don't worry, sweetie. You are doing your best. Even if you can't find something by next fall, I am sure you can continue to work in Martin's lab for another year or two. By next July, I can start working as an attending physician and we will be in a good shape."

"I agree. But I don't want to remain a post-doc for the rest of my life. I am surprised that nobody is calling me for an interview. There is this fellow Don McDonald in our department who has published only six papers and he got at least three interviews so far. That fellow is always boasting about how much salary he will demand and how much lab space he needs to do his work. And he is hopeless and utterly incompetent."

"But, sweetie, please understand, he is a white guy. My father always told us that we have to be a lot better and work harder than the white people to succeed in this country."

"I know that. But look at my record. I got a degree from one of the most prestigious schools in India and have published forty papers. I have another five papers that I have to write."

"Be patient, sweetie. It will work out."

When another month went by without any good news, Anant went to Martin. "Dr. Martin, I am worried about my job. So far I haven't gotten any interview calls. As you know, I sent out a lot of applications."

"I take it you are applying only in a few states in the East Coast, is that correct?"

"Yes, sir. Sheila wants to stay close to her folks."

"Let me tell you something, Anant. Right now the industry jobs are very competitive, and candidates from Ivy League schools are being picked for those jobs. As far as teaching positions are concerned, the situation is not too bad. There are still some schools that are having difficulty finding good candidates. You just have to look hard and spread your search. I think at this stage if you stick to a few states, you might not find a job that you like. I suggest that you apply to as many schools as you can all over the country. I don't think it is too late if you do it in the next few days. I will keep on sending recommendation letters on your behalf. Don't worry. I will do my best to help you."

After a few days, Martin called Anant into his office for a talk. "Williams at Kansas asked me to recommend a candidate for a faculty position in his department. Would you like to move to Kansas? Talk to Sheila and see what she thinks, but will you let me know soon so we can call Williams and get things moving?"

When Anant told her about the job, at first Sheila balked. "Why do you want to move to the Midwest? It is either too cold or too hot. Can't you stay here for another year or two and keep on trying to find a job in this area?"

"I know that it will be convenient for us to stay on

the East Coast, but this is a good opportunity for me. You know that if I apply by myself without Martin's backing, my application would end up in the trash bin. I have a few handicaps and unless he goes to bat for me, I can't make it in this country. First, my degree is not from an American university, second, I speak English with an Indian accent, and third and most important I am a brown-skinned foreigner. If I listen to Martin now and take that job, after a few years we might be able to move back east. You should not have any difficulty finding a job there in Kansas. Please, let's go to Kansas."

Faced with such irrefutable logic, Sheila couldn't object anymore, as she knew how important this was for Anant's career. Martin spoke to Williams, and Anant was offered the position. They went through the charade of an interview, but that was just a formality.

Anant and Sheila moved to Kansas in the summer, right after she completed her residency. Since they didn't have too much stuff, it was an easy move. They hired a U-Haul truck and put all their belongings into it, hitched one car behind the truck, and Anant drove the truck while Sheila followed him in her car. They lived in an apartment for a few months before buying a house. After they got settled, Sheila started to look for jobs. She had a choice of two reasonably big medical centers—one in Kansas and the other in Missouri, and a fairly large Veterans Administration hospital (generally called VA), and plenty of private practices. She applied for a job at the VA hospital as well as at some of the multi-specialty private groups in town. Within a few weeks, she was asked to interview for a job at VA, and was offered a job. In the meantime, one private group called her for an interview, and they also offered her a position. So, armed with two job offers, she was pondering which one to accept.

She asked Anant's opinion. "Sweetie, what do you think I should do?"

"Tell me a little about each job, and then we can decide."

"The VA job is pretty much eight to five and no night calls. It is a mixture of out-patient and in-patient practice. I will get a fixed salary of one-hundred-thousand dollars per year. But it is not challenging. We will mostly see psychiatric and alcoholic patients, and I am not sure that I like that. When I did a rotation in the psychiatric floor, I didn't like it at all. Most of those people are noncompliant, smelly, and many of them are alcoholics. I want to deal with normal people with illnesses, not crazy people. The multi-specialty group has about a hundred physicians working under one umbrella. They call themselves the Midwest Health Organization (MHO). There are fifteen internal medicine doctors in the MHO, and they have five offices in different parts of the city. They have offered me a job at their Lenexa branch. At this branch, there are three physicians now, and if I join it will be four. The patient population is by and large well-educated and decent. This job pays one-hundred-thirty thousand dollars per year. But I will have night and weekend calls."

"How many calls per month?"

"It is usually one night call every week, and one weekend call every six weeks. Each call I will be covering some eight physicians. Weekend call starts Saturday morning and ends Monday morning."

"When you are on call, what do you do?"

"I have to answer patients' phone calls and listen to their problems and sometimes call in prescriptions. Since I will be covering eight physicians, there are bound to be many phone calls. Then if a patient goes to the emergency room, and the ER physician determines that the patient has to be admitted under our service, I will be paged."

"Does it mean that when you are on a weekend call, you will be very busy?"

"It all depends on the particular day. But since I will be covering eight physicians, and assuming that each of them has at least three thousand patients, the total will be twenty-four thousand. It is quite possible that at least a few out of such a large number will get sick on a weekend, and may need to be admitted into the hospital. So, to answer your question, yes, I will be very busy on a weekend call."

"So, what do you want to do?"

"I want your opinion first."

"Well, if I were you, I would take the VA job, as it seems more reasonable."

"But, sweetie, it will be so boring. I will get tired of all those loony characters."

"But if you are going to be so busy in the private practice, what's the point? We can't have any time together, and what will you do when we have children?"

"I know it will be very busy in the first three or four years. Once I am well-established, I can cut back my hours and work only for four days per week. I may work long hours if I join the private group but I will make thirty thousand more per year and there will be bonuses if I can see more patients every quarter. They told me that on the average most physicians make about twenty thousand in bonuses every year. I prefer to make more money."

"You know I don't really care that much about money. As long as we have enough to live on, why should we struggle so much? You have asked my opinion, and I have given it. It is up to you now."

"Are you mad at me?"

"No, I think you are making a mistake by taking such a high-pressure job. I know I don't make a lot of money. But even if you make only sixty-thousand dollars per year, we will have a total of about one-hundred-thousand dollars and that is quite enough to live a good life."

"Sweetie, if we have more money, we can afford more luxuries."

"I know. But I hate to see you kill yourself working so hard. I don't care for luxuries. We can live happily with less money. I married you because I found you attractive and sexy. I fell in love with you the moment I saw you walk into Dr. Murthy's house."

In spite of his advice, Sheila joined the private group.

During the weekends, they went house-hunting with the help of a realtor. One of Anant's colleagues in the department recommended an Indian realtor. This fellow, Mr. Kutty, was an interesting character. He was an engineer from Kerala and had worked in the U.S. for many years. Somehow he ended up in Kansas and decided to quit his engineering and start selling houses. He was reasonably competent, although not very punctual. With his help they saw many houses, some as old as fifty years and some very new. Due to Sheila's busy schedule, it was Anant who first saw most of the houses and made a short list of the ones he liked. Then they went back to those houses when Sheila could find some time. After almost three months of searching, they found a house that was reasonable and made an offer. They made the offer on a Thursday, and Mr. Kutty told them that he would send their offer to the selling agent. Sheila and Anant weren't completely satisfied with the house but thought that they could purchase the house for the time being and move into a better one after a few years. They decided to make an offer because the house was in a nice neighborhood and close to the university. On Saturday morning, while they were having breakfast, Anant was reading the local newspaper and small advertisement caught his eye and he immediately showed it to Sheila. The advertisement was for a four-bedroom house at a much lower price than they offered for a three-bedroom house. This was a bit surprising, but on closer examination they saw that the house was for sale by owner. Since that fellow had eliminated the middle-men, he could afford to sell his house for less. Anant called the number and they made an appointment to see the house that same day. It was a nasty day, gray and gloomy, and it rained intermittently. They got out of the apartment quickly, finished their grocery shopping, had lunch at a Chinese place, and went to the house on time.

The house was close to the university campus, and on a nice day Anant could even walk to his office in about fifteen minutes. The house was located in a quiet cul de sac, away from the street traffic and right opposite an elementary school. There was a baseball field adjacent to the school. Since all the land opposite the house was owned by the school, no one could build anything on it. The owner, Tom Shafer, received them and requested that they remove their shoes before entering the house. It was a reasonable request in view of the rain; he didn't want them dragging the mud in and spoiling the white carpet. In spite of the cloudy day, the living room had a lot of light as there were tall and wide windows all around the big room. The living room had a cathedral ceiling and the windows extended from floor to ceiling. The living and dining rooms were contiguous, and the den and the kitchen were adjacent to the dining area. The den had a sliding door leading into a nice-sized deck, and they could see a reasonably large back yard.

Tom explained, "In this subdivision, we discourage people from putting up fences so as to maintain a park-like atmosphere. Although my back yard is not very big, it appears big, as the back yards of my neighbors are not cordoned off by ugly-looking fences. In the spring, me and my girlfriend sit here and watch the red robins and the yellow finches fly up and down. Also, you can see that forsythia bush there in Amy's yard, now it's green, but in spring it's bright yellow for almost a week and that is a very beautiful sight. We have daffodils planted all around the back yard and they also bloom in the early spring. You will enjoy this house and the neighborhood."

Anant asked Tom, "Why are you selling this house?"

Tom looked at him sadly. "I have to move to Seattle to take up a new job there. My job here came to an end; my company is downsizing."

Four bedrooms and two full bathrooms were upstairs. The stairs were carpeted, and were not at all steep like in some of the houses they saw. Another attractive feature of the stairway was the wide and tall window on the first landing, letting in daylight to brighten up the staircase. Subsequently, they found that on full-moon nights, the bright moonlight illuminated the staircase. The master suite was large, with a bedroom leading into a walk-in closet and a huge shower and tub. There were two vanities side by side.

They returned to their apartment and discussed the house. Sheila said, "I love the house, we must get it. But how do we get out of the offer that we made on the other house?"

"We made the offer, but the owner hasn't yet made a counter-offer. So if we withdraw our offer before he makes his counter-offer, we should be okay. If the fellow is hard-nosed, we might lose our earnest money."

"It's only five-hundred dollars. I don't care if we lose it. Let's call Mr. Kutty and tell him about Tom's house."

"I don't think he will be happy, he is going to lose quite a bit of money if we don't buy the house through him."

"I know that. But he can't force us to buy a house that we don't like. Also, he never showed us any houses in Tom's neighborhood. While we were returning to the apartment, do you remember seeing another house for sale? And that was listed by an agent. I understand that Mr. Kutty can't show us Tom's house as it was for sale by owner, but what prevented him from showing us the other house?"

"I agree with you that Mr. Kutty didn't do his homework even though we kept on asking him to show houses close to the campus. I really don't feel bad about ditching him. This is what we should do. We will call Mr. Kutty and tell him that the deal is off. Then we will call Tom and make an offer on his house."

After a lot of resistance, Mr. Kutty agreed to withdraw their offer. They bought Tom's house and moved in after a month.

The walk-in closet was built for men's clothes, and Sheila was upset that her dresses wouldn't fit. Since Anant didn't have that many clothes to fill the entire closet, he suggested that Sheila could keep her pantsuits and blouses in it, and her dresses in another closet in the adjoining bedroom. The most attractive feature of the house was the big windows all around the living room. On a nice sunny day, the room was ablaze with sunlight, and they could lie on the couch and read or listen to music. They were careful not to purchase too much furniture quickly; they bought only those items that were absolutely essential.

Sheila didn't like to do housekeeping chores. She didn't care to vacuum the floors or clean the bathrooms and toilets. She would wait until the last cup was used up before she did anything about the dishes. Anant hated to see a dirty kitchen, and would wash the dishes as soon as they appeared in the sink or put them in the dishwasher. Pretty soon it became Anant's responsibility to take care of dishes, laundry, and cleaning the house. After he did those chores for about a year or so, he realized that this work in the house was leaving very little free time for him to indulge in his favorite pastime—reading books. He then found a lady to come once a week to clean and iron clothes. Sheila wasn't happy with the way the maid pressed her pants. She complained bitterly about the lack of a proper crease on her pants, and because Anant wanted to have peace and quiet in the house, he pressed her pants. Even then, she wasn't satisfied and said that the iron he used was not good enough and made him buy a terribly expensive model. He tried to explain her that the old iron was good, and whether a particular pant could retain the crease depended on the type of fabric.

Their neighbors were interesting, to say the least. To the right of their house were Bill and Jane, on the left were Jim and Pam, and facing their back yard were Dennis and Amy. Actually they could walk to Amy's house through their back yard, as the two back yards were adjacent, with only a few trees and shrubs between them. On a nice day, when Anant and Sheila sat on their deck, they could see Dennis and Amy having coffee in their patio, and sometimes Amy would walk across her back yard into Anant's and chat with them. Dennis and Amy were a friendly couple. Amy was an investment broker who still worked hard in her sixties and appeared to make a lot of money. She was always well-dressed in designer garments and went on exotic vacations. As for Dennis, he told Sheila and Anant he was doing some business with biotech companies, but they could not pin him down and get any concrete information about his work. But given a chance, he talked incessantly about his business dealings with the high and mighty in the biotech field. In the beginning, Anant and Sheila thought that Dennis and Amy were married, but eventually they found out that they were only living together. They had been together for more than fifteen years, a much longer than some marriages. In spite of their friendly nature, the couple constantly bickered about everything in the presence of other people, and this bothered Anant and Sheila. Also, when Amy tried to make a point, Dennis would constantly interrupt her, either to contradict her or to correct her. At other times, Amy was the one who behaved obnoxiously. After they put up with it for a few months, Anant and Sheila slowly dissociated themselves from and the couple; when Amy and Dennis invited them over, Sheila would say that they had a prior engagement. Anant had a soft spot for Amy and would tell Sheila, "She should kick that fellow out of her house. He is always putting her down."

Sheila would retort, "Amy is no better. She is just as horrible as Dennis. I think they are made for each other."

Bill was a retired engineer, and his wife was a housewife. Their kids were grown and had left the house long ago. They traveled when the weather permitted. Sometimes, Bill came over to ask Sheila's advice about his health. Sheila was patient with him, although she felt that Bill shouldn't bother her at home with his problems. But Anant suspected that he came not only to talk about his health but also to admire Sheila's beauty, particularly her perky breasts. After he left, she would complain, "Look at that old bandicoot. He is very close to eighty, and he wants to look at my bosom. I don't like it when people constantly stare at my chest. It's disgusting." But the next time he came, she would smile and talk to him nicely.

Jim and Pam were in their seventies. Jim was a retired professor who had worked at the university for several decades. Jim and Pam were crazy about their yard, and whenever the weather permitted, they would be outside pruning, raking or mowing their lawn. In the fall, Jim would work long hours to pick up literally every leaf that fell on his side of the yard. In the weekend, when Sheila was resting after a rough Friday-night call, Jim would start his old noisy leaf-blower. This would make Sheila mad, and she cursed "that yard fanatic." In the beginning of their stay in that neighborhood, Anant mowed his lawn almost every week. But every once in a while he wouldn't be able cut the grass, either because it rained or because he was too busy with work in his lab. When he saw Anant outside, Jim would smilingly ask, "You are going to cut your grass today, eh?"

Anant didn't like being told that his lawn needed cutting, but he didn't want to be unpleasant to his neighbor. He would be nice and say, "Yeah, I think I will do it this weekend." But after a few such encounters, he thought that it was best to have a lawn service cut the grass.

Another thing that irritated Anant and Sheila was Jim and Pam's assumption that they were Muslims. During the Ramadan time, Pam would comment, "It must be hard for you to fast all day." Anant wondered what she was talking about, and then it dawned on him that she thought he was a Muslim. Or it could be that she was trying to find out whether he was a Muslim. Anant was not at all religious and never liked to discuss religion. Sometimes when people asked him about his religious affiliation, he would say, "I was born into a Hindu family, but I am not religious." On the other hand, Sheila believed in God and religion; she had a pooja corner in the house with a big idol of Lord Ganesha, and smaller idols of other Hindu gods and goddesses. In any case, Anant and Sheila found it bothersome that Pam would probe into their personal details.

Apart from these minor irritants, Jim and Pam were decent and caring. Whenever Sheila and Anant went out of town, they kept an eye on the house, and during Christmastime they always brought some baked goodies or a bottle of wine. Jim and Pam sent Sheila and Anant greeting cards on Valentine's day, Easter, and Christmas. At the beginning of every spring, Jim left a bouquet of spring flowers at their doorstep.

Sometimes, Anant thought that Sheila would have been happier if she married a physician. She would often come home in the evening and rattle off some medical jargon, trying to explain an uncommon diagnosis she had made.

After talking for about five minutes, she would stop and ask, "Are you following anything at all?"

"Yes, some of it. But I can't follow every little detail."

"I am trying to educate you, but you don't pay attention to what I say. I don't think you listen."

Anant felt bad for Sheila because she was so eager to discuss a particular case and there was no one she could talk to when she came home. He knew that at work it was very difficult for her to have a leisurely discussion with her colleagues, as everyone was pressed for time. In her group there was constant pressure to see a large number of patients every day.

Some days, she would come home and complain, "Today Tom Mills saw sixty patients. How can he possibly see so many? It makes me very angry. It's like a conveyor belt. He goes into an examination room and comes out in less than two minutes and he goes into the next room. For me it takes at least twenty minutes to listen to a patient's complaint and then diagnose the problem. I can't see more than twenty-five per day, and usually I run behind by at least one or two hours. That fellow goes home by five after seeing so many patients. I hate it when they make a mockery of medicine. For him, it's always the bottom line, not patients' health. A lot of his patients are coming to me because they must have heard that I take the time to treat them like people, not just a number."

Sheila was always changing her hair-stylist. She would go to one person a few times and complain. "She is lousy, she didn't do a good job. Look at my hair, it is all over the place and I have to use so many clips to keep it in place. Also the girl was constantly on the phone, talking to her daughter, her husband, and God knows who else. I am sure she was distracted and didn't do a good job. Next time I have to find someone else." She would let her hair grow for a few months and suddenly decide that she needed a haircut. Again the scramble to find a suitable hair-stylist began in earnest. She would call some of the Indian ladies, get some phone numbers, and call one of them to make an appointment. After the haircut, she would come home and ask Anant's opinion. "What do you think? Do you think she did a good job?"

"Oh, yeah, you look terrific and sexy."

"You are saying that to keep me calm and quiet."

"No, really, I am honest. I find it sexy. This haircut suits you very well. I think you must stick to this person and go to her every month or so."

She wasn't convinced with Anant's assurance and would look at herself in the mirror from all angles and say, "No, I am not sure. I think it looks funny."

She would be convinced only after she got many compliments on her new hairstyle from her colleagues in her office. The next month, she would go to the same person and come back angry. "She is really bad. She gossips too much. I learned everything about all the Indian women in the town. Who is in town, who is out, who is buying a new house, who is moving out. What do I care about all those people? Why can't she keep quiet and do her job?" After this she would find another hairstylist, and the saga continued.

Anant found a barbershop on forty-second street and stuck to it for all those years. When he first went into the shop, all the male barbers were busy with other customers, and only a fat female barber was available. She asked him to sit in her chair, and at first, Anant was apprehensive about getting his hair cut by a female, as he was used to only male barbers all his life. But he didn't want to be rude and thought, "It's only one haircut. If she is no good, next time I will go to someone else." But to his pleasant surprise, she did a very good job, and he always went back to her. He always had the same person cut his hair in North Carolina and in Bangalore. In Bangalore, the barber was located in a big room in one of the dormitory blocks. By virtue of his several decades of service to the members of the Institute, some students called him an honorary professor, and everyone referred to him as "professor" Krishnappa. He was a genial fellow and would regale the students with his witty anecdotes. Most of the younger faculty members, who had their haircut by Krishnappa, were also his customers when they were students at the Institute. He knew everybody on campus, and the new students were in awe of his contacts. Everyone came to his shop to get their haircut and waited their turn patiently on the bench outside. Krishnappa made an exception in the case of the Director, the Registrar, and the Chief

Medical Officer of the institute and went to their houses on campus to cut their hair. Krishnappa would comment on a newly appointed faculty member, "I knew him when he was a student here; he came to me every month for a haircut. Then he went to America and now see, he is a big man. But he didn't forget poor Krishnappa. The moment he returned from America, he came for his haircut and said that the barbers in America are lazy and don't cut the hair as well as the barbers in India."

People relax in many different ways. Some people read books, some listen to music, some drink alcohol, and some simply sleep. Sheila needed something visual to help her relax. Sheila loved to watch TV, and it didn't matter what she watched; as long as the picture moved, she was happy. Many times she didn't even care to know what she was watching, and more often than not, she simply fell asleep on the couch with the TV on. She loved to watch the commercials, and never liked Anant's habit of muting the volume when a commercial came on. He loved commercial-free TV and watched PBS or movies from the video store. When Sheila didn't like a movie, she would be restless and move a lot on the couch, and talk a lot, and this used to irritate Anant. He never understood her peculiar habit of channel surfing. When she did that, she didn't even allow ten seconds to see what was playing on a particular channel. She simply used the remote and went on changing channels very quickly. In the beginning, they would sit together to watch some program on PBS, and if it wasn't interesting, she would resort to her favorite pastime of channel surfing. Most of the time, Anant controlled his irritation, but every once in a while he snapped. "Why the hell do you go on changing channels without even watching? Keep it on one channel and watch the program. I am tired of this."

Sheila would drive him nuts by not coming to bed until midnight. Sometimes when he had a glass of wine, he fell asleep, but on the days he did not drink, he would be awake and waited for her to come to bed. After she came to bed, she would want to talk to him and tell him about the show she watched. All this disturbed his rest, and when he got up at five in the morning, he was not a happy camper. He never figured out how Sheila could function with so little sleep. He needed to sleep at least eight hours each night. No matter what time he went to bed, Anant would wake up with the birds, the moment the morning light arrived. He was so regimental in his habits that at Bangalore that his friends called him Colonel Prasad. He was in the mess hall for breakfast at seven sharp, and he always sat at the same table. Jayant, the senior waiter, would bring him crisp buttered toast, orange marmalade, two eggs sunny-side-up, and tea. Jayant, a kindly middle-aged gentleman, always had a smile on his face and was well-liked by the students. In spite of his heavy work-load of taking care of so many tables, he kept an eye on Anant's table, making sure that his favorite student was taken care of. Jayant knew that Anant liked his toast crisp, and brought two more pieces the moment he saw that Anant ate his first two pieces, and he would make sure that the tea in the pot was hot. By the time Anant finished eating, and was on his second cup of tea, a couple of his friends would arrive and sit at his table, and they all chatted for a few minutes before going to their respective departments. Some of his friends who wondered why the mess staff was so nice to Anant didn't realize that Anant's unfailing courtesy and kindness towards the staff was simply being reciprocated. Also, when the students collected money and gave it to the staff at major holidays, Anant was one of the few students who gave consistently large sums of money.

Anant jogged in the neighborhood, following the same route every day. He got out of his street and followed the curved road to the small bridge into the university campus. Once he was on campus, he could jog happily on the sidewalks without worrying about traffic. After going around the perimeter of the campus, he left campus by the rear gate and then got onto the road leading back to his house. Sheila didn't like to jog but preferred to walk. So, on those days she came home early enough in the evening or during weekends when she was not call, they both walked together, and took the same path that he always took everyday. One day when they got out of the rear gate, suddenly a fierce-looking black dog appeared and tried to pounce on them. They stopped right where they were, and didn't move, as they didn't want to make the dog nervous. Meanwhile the owner of the dog, an old lady, was calling out, "Sparky, come back here," but Sparky couldn't care less, as he found Anant's shin more interesting. The dog went on barking and circling around him. Anant was very scared. He thought, *Oh my God, now this dog will bite me and I will have to get rabies shots*. He was afraid and yelled at the owner, "Why don't you keep your dog on a leash like everybody else? If you can't control it, why do you have a dog?" The old lady kept on calling the dog to go back into the house, without any success. In the end, a neighbor, hearing all the commotion, came and got hold of the dog and saved them. After going home, Anant called the dog-control officer at the police department and complained. After that, they never saw that dog on the street again. But he wondered why so many Americans had dogs and cats. While most of them were careful to see that their pets didn't bother other people, some were careless and left their dogs to roam about, jump on people, and lick them. When the innocent person looked at the owner for help, the owner would say, "Ben won't bother you, he is such a friendly dog. He likes people."

Anant wanted to say, *The dog may like people, but I don't like dogs.*

For their fifth wedding anniversary, Anant and Sheila went to Sarasota, Florida. When Anant was dating Heather, they had driven to Orlando to see Disney World and gone on some of the scary rides, and had a good time. But he never went to the Gulf side of Florida. Sheila was familiar with that area, as she had been there several times for vacations with her family. They spent a week at her father's condominium by the beautiful Sarasota Bay. Every morning, they got up late, ate a light breakfast, and walked for about an hour on a walking trail by the bay front. The weather was quite decent for March, the temperatures in the seventies and sunny. After lunch at one of the innumerable restaurants downtown, they went to the beaches, to Siesta Key or Lido Key or drove to Venice, which was about twenty miles south of Sarasota. They walked on the fine sandy beaches, hand in hand, sometimes letting the cold seawater touch their feet, and talked about their future life together. Some afternoons after their walk on the Lido Key beach, they went shopping at St. Armand's Circle, buying things they didn't really need. Sheila had an incessant urge to stock up on clothes, and she would walk into a shop and see a nice blouse and say, "This will go well with my green jacket." At the end of the day they would have a few parcels to carry back to their place. Each evening, after dinner at exotic restaurants— French, Mexican, or Colombian—they returned to their condominium and opened a bottle of wine and relaxed in each other's company. They enjoyed the time they spent at the sunny Gulf Shore town, and they decided that they should return to Sarasota to whenever possible.

The Indian community in Kansas City was small, not more than a few hundred people. While most of them were physicians, engineers, or professors, there were a few Gujaratis who owned motels and gas stations. From time to time there were weddings, graduations of children from high school or college, and these occasions were generally celebrated in the banquet hall of a hotel owned by two Patels. It was as though the banquet hall was reserved only for Indian shindigs. Generally, the food was mediocre and barely edible, and the guests had to endure boring speeches. At these gatherings, people formed small groups, mainly based on the language they spoke. Gujarati people got together and spoke Gujarati and Tamil people sat at a different table and talked in Tamil and so on. Anant and Sheila didn't really fit into any linguistic group, as they spoke mostly English with each other. Sometimes Sheila went over to Hindi-speaking group and exchanged a bit of gossip. Although Anant spoke Hindi quite fluently, his Hindi wasn't without an accent, so he avoided speaking in Hindi. He sometimes joined the Andhra or Kannada people. The Andhra people thought that he was from Bangalore, and the Kannada folks assumed that he was from Andhra. In any event, he was welcomed by both the groups and felt happy to be with them. Anant always gave a check for one-hundred dollars if it was a wedding, and fifty for graduation. A few times, they weren't invited for a party, and when Sheila heard about it, she would get mad. But Anant would say, "Look at the bright side. We have saved some money, and we don't have to eat that lousy food. Now that we don't have to go to that boring party, let's go somewhere and have fun. You always see the same people and try to smile and talk some useless things. Also, you don't have to worry about back-rubbing Bhaskar and video-wielding Vinod." He was referring to the menaces that some of the younger women in the community complained about to their husbands. Back-rubbing Bhaskar was in his late fifties and always looked as though he needed a shave and shower. He and his anemic wife were physicians. They made a lot of money, but they always dressed so poorly that they could be mistaken for homeless people. Whenever Bhaskar met Sheila, he rubbed her back while talking to her, and this irritated her very much. She complained to Anant about it. He said he would warn Bhaskar to keep his hands off his wife's back, but Sheila didn't like the idea because it would lead to unnecessary complications in such a small community. Neither Sheila nor Anant saw Bhaskar rubbing the backs of other women. The case of Vinod was also a cause for concern, as he videotaped all the people at every party. It appeared that he focused particularly on women and their cleavages. One of the irate women complained to her husband, who accosted Vinod and threatened him with dire consequences if he so much as focused his video camera on his wife. This warning put a damper on Vinod's enthusiasm, but he didn't completely stop his videotaping activities.

Every Saturday, it was Anant's duty to do grocery shopping, as Sheila was either on call or at her yoga class. Sometimes when she accompanied him to the grocery store, some of her patients approached her and bothered her with their medical problems, or asked about their test results. Even though she didn't like it, she was patient and told them to make an appointment and see her in the office. All this took some time, and Anant would get impatient because he wanted to finish the shopping and go home to catch up on other things. Sheila didn't like that he was always in a hurry to finish shopping, and she would say that because of his hurry they forgot some item on their list. She generally made the grocery list and, of course, no one could read it except the pharmacist. Finally, after many such altercations, they both decided that it was better if Anant went to the store alone. So he went to the store every Saturday and got the stuff for the next week. The store was always busy at that time, and there were too many people in the aisles. Sometimes, some of the old ladies would push their shopping carts around the aisles at breakneck speed, almost hitting each other. Some of them would maneuver their carts in such a way that the person opposite them had no choice but to yield. If he or she didn't yield, the old lady would say in a menacing tone, "Excuse me," accompanied by a dirty look. Those intimidating tactics got worse on a long weekend or before an important holiday. After all that rush, some of the same ladies would spend a lot of time at the check-out counter, making sure that all their stuff was safely placed in the cart, and finally, when the clerk gave them the bill, they would take out their checkbooks to write a check in their spidery handwriting. It drove Anant crazy to see the antics of these old people. He thought, "*Why the hell do they shop on a weekend, when they are retired and have the whole goddamn week free? They not only get in the way of innocent, hard-working people like me, and now they take forever to write that check. Why can't they use cash like most of us?*" After this sort of thing happened a few more times, he started to go to the store at eight in the morning, and got out quickly before the avalanche of the golden oldies began.

Anant never learned to cook. So it was Sheila's job to cook for them. On those weekends when she was not on call, Sheila would unleash her culinary skills and cook all kinds of items—some were edible, and others ended up in the trash. When a dish turned out nice and tasty, she rejoiced, and when it didn't, Sheila would get upset. "I can't even make such a simple item. The trouble is you never let me do anything in the kitchen. On the weekends all you want is bedroom activity." The fact was, Anant didn't want her to spend so much time in the kitchen when they could do other things like watch movies, go for walks, or just cuddle on the sofa listening to music. For him, food was something one ate to keep the body and soul together. Not that he didn't relish tasty dishes like lamb biryani, spicy fish curry or barbecued ribs. He wanted Sheila to stick to what she knew best and not go off experimenting with all kinds of exotic stuff. In the beginning of their marriage,

Sheila cooked elaborate meals—dal, two vegetables, white rice, and parathas. They ate what they could for dinner, and the left-over food ended up in their lunchboxes. In the beginning of her career, Sheila was not very busy and came home by five or six in the evening, which gave her ample time to get dinner ready by about eight. But as her practice picked up and she got more and more busy, she returned home at eight and then started cooking. Anant would be hungry and eat all kinds of junk food until dinner was ready, sometimes as late as ten. Sheila got mad at him when he could not eat what she cooked because he was already full. After this went on for a few weeks, she realized that she had to modify her cooking habits. Sheila was not in a position to cut back her hours at the office, as her practice was still picking up, and they both had to accept the fact that she would not be home before eight.

Eventually, a four-letter word saved their marriage—S-O-U-P. They both hit upon the brilliant idea of preparing a large quantity of soup in a big stock pot and keeping it in the refrigerator for the entire week. Sheila bought a book that had excellent recipes for many different soups. Once she became proficient at making soups, they started preparing soup for dinner and mixed vegetable rice for lunch boxes. Saturday morning, Anant went to the store and got all the ingredients for both the items, and Sunday after breakfast, they both worked hard in the kitchen for about four hours and finished the cooking for the entire week. Anant was in charge of chopping all the vegetables for the soup and for vegetable rice. In the beginning, they used a food processor, but Sheila wasn't happy with the way the machine delivered unevenly cut veggies, and therefore started chopping them herself, and let Anant wash the dishes. Slowly, after watching her, he learned the right way of chopping celery, fennel, asparagus, bell peppers, squash, carrots, onions, and potatoes. The onions had to be chopped in two different sizes, big pieces for soup and small ones for rice. For soup, the cubes from two or three big baking potatoes were first boiled in a saucepan and kept aside, and for rice the cubes were kept in a separate dish until further use. They got a pound each of whole green peas, green split peas, cow peas, black-eyed beans, pigeon peas, navy beans, small white beans, red kidney beans, pink beans, and small white beans, and mixed them all up a big container. Each time, a cup of this mixture would be boiled separately and added to the cooked soup. The rice contained a lot of vegetables—chopped spinach, mixed vegetables, lima beans, and snow peas. They prepared salmon or flounder curry and added small pieces of the fish to their rice in the lunch boxes. Although they slogged for half a day every Sunday, it was well-worth it as, during the week-day evenings, Sheila had some time to relax and read or watch TV, and the household was again peaceful, without dinnertime tension. They worked well together, he her loyal helper and she the Great Chef. If it was warm outside, they opened all the windows to expel the cooking odors out of the house. Since they had plenty of privacy, Anant wore only his jockey briefs and Sheila wore her bikini, and they kissed and fondled in between their cooking, and most often, stopped everything and made love in the sunny living room. They enjoyed those mid-morning sessions, with sunlight on their naked sweating bodies, kissing each other's salty lips and skin. On every Saturday, if Sheila wasn't on call, they would go out for lunch and then do some shopping and return home by evening, and then go for their walk. After getting back, they made love and afterwards opened a bottle of Merlot or Cabernet and watched a movie or TV.

At the university, there were some graduate students from India in various science departments. Among the few Indian professors in the campus, Anant was probably the most friendly and accessible, so the Indian students used to come to his office to talk about their problems and seek his advice. He was courteous and affectionate because he was once in their shoes, in a new country and culture. Once in a while, he invited some of the Indian students to their house for an evening, and Sheila cooked some Indian food. They all loved Sheila, and looked up to her because she was a doctor, and they addressed her as "Dr. Sheila". It was fun to spend time with the youngsters who came all the way from India to pursue their education. They were brilliant, hard-working, and ambitious. They knew that a degree from an average American university was worth more than one from a good university in India. The boys were more aggressive than the girls; they got their driver's licenses, a used car quickly, and some of them started dating American girls. On the other hand, most of the Indian girls were not that outgoing and refused to date American boys. Once, when Anant asked one of the girls why she didn't date, she replied, "None of us want to date the boys here. Our parents would be furious if they found out about it." Sheila told them that dating doesn't necessarily mean that they have to sleep with the boys. She explained that dating an American boy would expose them to a different culture and expand their horizons. But the girls were scared, probably thinking that in addition to expanding their horizons they might end up expanding something else. One of the girls, Nalini, was particularly outstanding, as she came to this country after completing her M.D. at Bombay, to do her Ph.D. in Biology. Sheila liked her a lot, maybe because she could talk to her about medical issues. Nalini visited their house frequently and stayed for dinner, and they would all talk about various issues. Sometimes when Sheila was on call, Nalini would come and spend time with Anant, and he fed her whatever he ate, mostly left-over food from the previous day. She talked to him about her family, her brother in New York City, her parents in Bombay. Anant and Sheila sensed that she was homesick and were extra nice to her. Nalini was attractive, although she was short and chubby. When she visited them, she dressed up nicely and applied lipstick and make-up. She used to sit close to Anant and sometimes rub her thighs against his and bend low so that her cleavage was visible. After a while, Anant got uncomfortable with this, and told Sheila about Nalini's odd behavior. Sheila laughed. "Sweetie, she has a crush on you. You have to ignore it, and pretty soon she will get over it."

But Nalini's attitude only got worse, and she started telling him about personal stuff, like her irregular periods. Finally, it became too much, and he told Sheila, "You have to handle Nalini. When she comes to the house next time, I will be in my study doing some work. Don't let her come near me. She is doing her best to seduce me."

Sheila teased him. "If something should happen to me, you know you have another doctor who is equally crazy about you." He managed to avoid Nalini, and eventually she got her Ph.D. and moved to California.

Anant met Kevin at the auditorium when he went to attend a lecture by a Nobel Laureate. Since it was expected to draw a large crowd, the lecture was arranged in the auditorium. Although Anant arrived ten minutes before the program started, the hall was packed and there were few empty seats. He sat next to Kevin, and at the end of the lecture, Kevin introduced himself to Anant, and they started to talk in the hallway. Kevin was a professor in the Biology department working on prostate cancer. He was trying to develop a screening test for prostate cancer, as the current methods for detection were woefully inadequate. Anant was impressed with Kevin's research and arranged to meet him for lunch on another day so that they could talk more. After that lunch, they met frequently to discuss not only science but other topics as well, and pretty soon Kevin was a frequent visitor at Anant's house. Kevin had a variety of interests in addition to his teaching and research. He kept bees, extracting gallons of honey every fall. He owned every conceivable tool and loved to work on cars. In order to make use of his tools, he bought thoroughly hopeless cars, rebuilt their engines, and made the cars drivable. In addition, he was a great cook and an avid reader. Anant and Sheila admired him, and wondered why, with so many talents and interests, Kevin remained single. They privately thought that Kevin might be gay. When their friendship became stronger, Anant did ask Kevin whether he was gay, and Kevin said he was not gay. But Anant never heard Kevin talk about any girlfriend, past or present, and it concerned him that his friend was living like a monk.

One Friday evening Kevin, was visiting Anant and

Sheila. The three of them were having drinks. Sheila was trying to cook some new dish with Kevin's help. They were discussing the divorce of an Indian faculty member and how he avoided paying alimony to his ex-wife. Kevin told them that Dr. Patel had sent his wife and daughter to India on a vacation, and while they were there, he had filed for a divorce and told his wife that he would send her a lump sum if she didn't contest the divorce. The wife, unaware that she was legally entitled to half of the estate, plus child-support, had agreed to take the paltry sum of money.

Anant was shocked. "What a slime bag, I will never even think of doing such a thing."

Kevin remarked, "Anant, you are not an Indian, you will never do what Patel did."

"What do you mean I am not Indian? You know I am from India."

"The only thing Indian about is you is that you are from India. In every other aspect you are an American."

Sheila said, "That's not quite true, Kevin. Although Anant has lived in this country for many years, in some aspects he hasn't assimilated. For example, his taste in music, it is still predominantly very Indian. He does listen to some country music from time to time, but I know he prefers Hindi songs. Also he has some quaint habits which were probably practiced by his folks in India. For example, after a haircut he never touches anything in the house, he goes straight to the shower. And he never starts anything important on a Tuesday, as it is not supposed to be an auspicious day. While stepping out of the house, if anyone sneezes, he will wait for a couple of minutes before leaving. I can tell you more things to convince you that he is completely Indian."

Kevin looked at Anant curiously and asked, "I understand that you are a neat-freak and don't want hair all over the place in your house after a haircut, and that's why you have a shower right away. But what's with this Tuesday and sneezing business?"

Anant explained, "These are old customs in India, practiced in the South as well as the North. I don't know how they originated, but in our family we were never permitted to begin an important project on a Tuesday. Also, none of us started a journey on a Tuesday. Actually, in Hyderabad and Bangalore most of the barbershops are closed on Tuesdays. As for sneezing, I never understood why our elders told us that it is not auspicious to go out of the house right after someone sneezes. I guess every culture has its superstitions. Like here in America, people don't like to walk under a ladder or a black cat crossing their path."

"This is quite interesting, Anant. But all this is personal stuff. I still think that in your attitude, your views, the way you look at issues, you are very American. The Indians I met are by and large cheap and narrow-minded, and you are not like that. This Patel guy I was telling you about is very well-funded, but he is so miserly he never spends his grant money to purchase enough laboratory supplies. His students always borrow chemicals and supplies from other laboratories. The fellow has no shame, and they never replace any of the items they take."

Anant mildly interjected, "You know, Kevin, not all Indians are cheap and narrow-minded. We must keep in mind that the Indians in this country, at least the first generation, are still quite insecure despite their accomplishments. In the beginning of their careers here, they have this tendency to convert every dollar they spend into Indian rupees, and this makes them hesitate to spend much money. Once they become more prosperous, some of them become less tight-fisted and do enjoy life. They may come across as narrow-minded because of their behavior. Most Indian boys, whether they are born here, or born in India and raised here, go back to India to find a bride. This may be because the Indian parents insist that their sons marry "unspoiled" girls, or it could be the boys are intimidated by the local girls. This lack of assimilation into the American culture is what makes the Indians feel perpetually alien in this country. Maybe things will change when the third generation of Indians comes of age."

In addition to his heavy teaching load, Anant had to find time to write grant proposals to get money for his research projects. He was given start-up funds for purchasing equipment, chemicals, and other laboratory supplies. The money he was given was significantly less than that allotted to the white faculty members hired at the same time. Anant was not aware of this discrepancy at the beginning, but when he saw that those guys purchased expensive equipment and hired experienced technicians, he knew that they got more money to help them build their labs. He had neither the extra money nor the ability to hire good technical help. Consequently, he had to work very hard during the first few years and watch every penny he spent. He was frugal by nature and shopped around for the best deal for chemicals and other laboratory supplies. Also, he made friends with the sales representatives of the scientific companies and got some good discounts. Moreover, he was lucky in his choice of graduate students. Two candidates from India joined his laboratory, and those two were invaluable. They worked long hours, were fast and efficient, and helped him put together manuscripts and grant proposals. But in spite of such hard work, Anant found it difficult to publish in top-notch journals, and as a result could not get grant money. He had only two more years to get a grant before his case for tenure would be reviewed by the Promotions and Tenure Committee of the department. Although Williams, the chairman of the department, was supportive of his candidacy for tenure, he was not the only one who decided, and there were a few old faculty members who didn't go along with Williams. If he got a major grant within the next two years, Anant was sure to get tenure, notwithstanding the objections of the old guard. But first he had to publish at least one or two papers in first-class journals, and this proved to be tough. The reviewers were, to say the least, brutal and critical of his work, his hypothesis, his data, and even his English. This really infuriated Anant, who knew that his work was original and deserved to be published in a prestigious journal. It was ironic that, during his stint at the Martin laboratory, similar ideas were praised by the reviewers when manuscripts were submitted with professor Martin as the senior author. When they went to national or international meetings, professor Martin took pains to introduce Anant to all the bigwigs in the field. He always gave credit to Anant for his ideas, and almost everyone in that field was aware that this new area of research was Anant's own brain-child. But when he met some of those same people at a different meeting and said hello to them, he was completely ignored by the big shots. This was when Anant went to some meetings by himself, as sometimes professor Martin had other commitments and could not go a meeting. These senior scientists never even bothered to stop by at his presentation when he was by himself. But when he saw those senior people joking and carrying on with other white junior colleagues, it dawned on him that the predominantly white scientific community did not really care to hobnob with him, as they did not perceive him as their equal. Not even one of them had a kind word or a pat on his back for the new ideas he brought to this small area of research. He knew that his ideas were neither earth-shattering nor Nobel-Prize material. But they were refreshingly novel and opened up a new dimension in the study of anti-cancer compounds. While at first he was hurt by the indifference of his peers, he did not let himself wallow in self-pity but told himself that he would work hard to win their respect. By nature, he was not one to seek compliments, but when people didn't treat him properly, he felt bad. Because in his mind, he did not see a white person as either superior or inferior to himself, only his equal. Before he came to the United States, he was never discriminated against in India, maybe because of his family's wealth and position or maybe because he was born into a Brahmin family. Wherever he went in India, Anant was received with respect and dignity. In fact, he never thought of this issue of discrimination before he experienced it first-hand in the U.S.. When in India, he was not unaware of discrimination against "lower" caste people and Muslims. Because some of his good friends were either Muslims or from the "lower" castes, and since he always treated them as equals, the issue never made an impact on him. Of course he was aware of the slums where poor Muslims lived in Hyderabad and Bangalore. But he also knew that well-educated people, both from the Muslim community and from the "lower" castes, lived in decent areas and were treated no differently from other educated people. But in the U.S., in spite of Anant's education and good manners, most people, even the educated ones who should know better, did not treat him as their equal, and this sometimes bothered him.

Anant had this strange feeling that, for reasons best known only to themselves, the reviewers were trying to block his publications, and the reasons they gave for their rejection were flimsy with no solid scientific foundation. When he tried to bring this to the editor's attention, he was given the usual story—the editor was only following the reviewers' recommendation, and he couldn't go against their advice. Finally, in desperation, Anant appealed to Martin, an old-hand in these matters who not only knew exactly how to out-maneuver, but also had enough clout to make the editor listen to him. Martin called the editor and persuaded him to reconsider Anant's papers. Martin didn't tell Anant how he pulled it off, but Anant could guess that there was some *quid pro quo*. Martin was on many review committees of granting agencies, and the editor, like other scientists, was dependent on money from these organizations for the work in his laboratory. The fact that Martin called him to request a favor was a signal to the editor that when his grant came up for renewal, Martin would support his application. Because Martin had the power to block his grants, the editor reconsidered Anant's work. Finally, Anant had two papers published back-to-back in one of the most prestigious journals, which paved the way for his first major grant. When the Promotions and Tenure Committee met to consider his case, there was unanimous approval for his promotion to associate professor with tenure. Those old professors who wanted to block his promotion kept their mouths shut, as they knew that the committee would overrule them and they would look foolish if they objected to the promotion of such a good candidate.

Meena and Anant continued to communicate by e-mail and telephone, and their friendship was growing stronger. Meena came to Kansas for another long weekend, and they both enjoyed the visit. This time, they slept in the same bed and shared the bathroom in the master suite. They were comfortable around each other and had showers together, and she was not shy at being nude in his presence. The first time she had visited him, she was shy and never emerged from her room unless fully dressed. Even when they made love, she came to him in a robe, got out of it quickly, and joined him in the bed. This time she was free, parading in front of him without any clothes. Although Anant had made love to her several times by then, seeing her beautiful and sensuous brown body during the daytime was erotic. In addition to some fun and games, they discussed their future plans. Anant asked her, "When are we going to get married?"

Meena replied, "As soon as I get a divorce. Next year my son will go to college, and then I should be free to marry you."

"I want you to move to Kansas once you file for a divorce. It may take a few months to finalize the divorce, and there is no point in your staying in New Jersey. Once the papers are ready, we can get married. Until then we will live in sin!"

She laughed. "That sounds great, but I am not sure I can find a job here in these boonies. There is nothing here but the university. I think I have a better idea. Why don't you move to New Jersey? I know our medicinal chemistry division is looking for people, and I can send your resume to that division chief. I don't know him that well, but we have met a few times. Usually, when an employee recommends a candidate they will give it a serious consideration. I am sure they will be happy to hire an experienced organic chemist such as yourself. Once you move there, we can see each other every day, and when my divorce becomes final, we can get married."

"I like the idea. The only thing is I have tenure here and if I move to an industrial position, I may not have the job security that I have now."

"That is true. The jobs in the industry are not secure, but you will probably get at least three times the pay that you are getting now as a professor. Also, if you lose one job in a particular company there will be jobs in other organizations. People keep on switching jobs all the time. Please give it a serious thought."

Anant promised to think about her proposal. Her short visit came to an end much too quickly, and he was again lonely.

After professor Williams retired, professor Sam Fong took over as the chairman of the department. The new chairman was eager to change the research focus of the department. Although he filled three faculty slots with people in his research area, he wasn't satisfied with that. Therefore, he made it as uncomfortable as he possibly could to drive out the faculty members hired by the previous chairman. It appeared that professor Williams anticipated such a move from his successor, and he made sure that the faculty members he had hired were given tenure before he retired. But Fong had some old tricks up his sleeve. He gave the "Williams people" more teaching duties and took away their laboratory space if their research funds were not renewed, and due to lack of laboratory space they could not take graduate students, which reduced the manpower in their laboratories. All those dirty tricks affected the morale of the faculty members, and some of them found jobs in other schools and moved out, while others went into industry jobs. Of the "Williams people," only Anant and Petra Sokoloff were left, and they lived in constant fear of chairman Fong's dirty tricks (they called him Mao, privately). He was really tired of the new chairman and would have gone elsewhere if only he found another job. But the job market was tight and he was now almost forty, an age at which most people stayed put wherever they were. When he applied for faculty positions at smaller schools, he got regret letters saying that they received as many as sixty applications for one position and that his credentials, although impeccable, did not match their requirements. He found that some of the smaller schools were hiring candidates who got their Ph.D.s from Ivy League schools. It appeared that many brilliant candidates from prestigious universities preferred to teach at smaller universities and colleges where they could focus on teaching. Although research activities were encouraged, they did not expect their faculty to bring in large sums of grant money from extramural agencies. In effect, he was stuck in Kansas City, and unless he got a lot of grant money, his ability to move to another university was severely hampered. His godfather was long gone, and there was no one else to help him.

A few months after his promotion to associate professor, Anant got a call from North Carolina to inform him of the sudden death of professor Martin. Anant came to his office after teaching a class and was making himself a cup of instant coffee. The phone rang, and he picked it up and heard the familiar voice of Janet, the senior technician in professor Martin's laboratory. Even though he had left that laboratory many years ago, Anant kept in touch with professor Martin and Janet. When he called the laboratory for a protocol or some other information, it was Janet who usually answered the phone. He sensed that something was wrong because Janet sounded hoarse as though she was crying. She said, "The boss passed away this morning. It was a massive heart attack." Anant couldn't believe her because when he had met Martin a few months back at the American Chemical Society meeting, he had looked healthy and happy. It seemed that Martin was working in his vegetable garden with his youngest son, and suddenly keeled over and collapsed. The son ran into the house and called 911, and by the time they took him to the hospital, it was too late.

Anant flew to North Carolina for Martin's memorial service. As soon as he landed in Raleigh, he went to Martin's house. Mrs. Martin was taking the death of her husband very hard but received Anant graciously, and asked him about Sheila and his work in Kansas. He was very emotional and wanted to tell her so many things that he admired about professor Martin, but he could not bring himself to talk because at any time he might burst into tears. The house was full of relatives, neighbors, and friends, and Anant left as soon as he could. The funeral was a private affair, and only close family members were present. The next day, the memorial service was held at the university, and all dignitaries of the university attended the ceremony. Many of professor Martin's colleagues spoke about the man, his contributions to science, his humanity, and the extraordinary role he played in shaping the careers of so many students and post-doctoral fellows. Sitting with him were many of the professor's former graduate students and post-doctoral fellows, now at good positions in academia, industry, and government. Some of them Anant knew only by name, as he referred to their publications while working at the Martin laboratory, and some of them he had met at various scientific meetings. After the speeches, the choir sang "Amazing Grace" and "Battle Hymn of the Republic." The speeches and the songs moved Anant, and he was embarrassed at the tears in his eyes, but there were others who were also equally emotional. The moment was sad, and Anant felt terrible losing a man who was so nice to him in his personal as well as professional life.

Anant's grant application to the National Institute of Health was not renewed. It was funded for the first time for four years and had been renewed for another three years. When he submitted his proposal for the third time, the agency rejected it, saying that the ideas were not novel and exciting enough for it to be funded. It was a blow to Anant's research activities because without money he couldn't purchase chemicals, laboratory supplies, and equipment for his work. Now that Fong was the chairman, Anant's situation was more precarious, irrespective of his tenure. Fong couldn't fire Anant, but he had the power to make it difficult for Anant to continue to work in the department. Anant had some money left over from the previous year's budget, and his lab could pull on for another year or two. But after that, the future looked bleak. His teaching load might get heavy once his grant money ran out, and that would be the end of his research. Also, his failure to get another grant would kill the chances of his promotion to a full professorship. Right now, the two students in his laboratory had almost completed their experiments, and were ready to write their dissertation. Hopefully, in another six months or so, they should graduate and move on. Anant was trying to work in a new area that might be interesting to a granting agency, and he encouraged his students to work on the project in their spare time. But the new project was risky and might not yield useful data for a grant proposal.

Thus, after serious consideration, Anant told Meena that he was willing to relocate to New Jersey. Meena was excited about the prospect of his moving close to her and asked him to e-mail his *curriculum vitae* to her. After she received it, she made extensive changes in his *curriculum vitae*, telling him that people in industry had a different perspective compared to the academia. She circulated his *curriculum vitae* in all the divisions of her company where there was a need for organic chemists.

Meena visited Anant again for another weekend, and they enjoyed each other's company.

She joked, "I hope you get a job in New Jersey soon. Or else I have to spend most of my salary on airfares to be with you."

Anant said, "You know that I can visit you, but you don't like the idea. And when I wanted to pay for your ticket, you refused."

"I know, my dear. But I hate to take money from you. As it is, you lost a lot of money in that divorce of yours."

"Do you have any idea when they will make a decision about hiring me?"

"I spoke to Dave Abbott, who is the chief of the medicinal chemistry division. He is impressed with your credentials, and will contact you in a few weeks. Don't worry, my dear."

It was the third time Meena visited him, and Anant felt happy that she took the time to fly all the way to be with him. With each visit their relationship grew stronger, and Anant felt lucky that he found Meena. This time, Meena said that she would cook for him, as she didn't want to eat out all the time. She was a superb cook and prepared all kinds of items such as *idli*, *dosa*, *upma* and other Indian dishes. In addition to her culinary skills, she was prompt about dishes in the sink and general cleanliness in the kitchen area. The three days she was in Kansas City, they enjoyed each other, eating good food, taking long walks, and making love whenever they felt like it. Sex with Meena was great, the best he ever had with any woman. She was innovative in bed, always trying something new, and never complained about his ability to go on making love to her for a long time. In fact, she complimented him on his virility and enjoyed it. She liked being on top, and only after she was satisfied in that position, she allowed him to try other positions.

Dave called Anant to fix a date for the interview. After a few weeks, Anant traveled to Newark. He flew in on a Wednesday evening and checked into a hotel near the pharmaceutical company. Dave and his colleagues took him to dinner, and they discussed various things about the company, their products, and the future plans for developing new drugs. Anant was amazed at the wide array of the company's products and their vision for the future. The next day, his talk was attended by most of the technical people from many divisions. After his lecture, there were a bunch of individual meetings with Dave and other senior Ph.D.s in the division, and lunch at the company cafeteria. After lunch, Dave took Anant around the campus and showed him various divisions of the company. At the end of the day, he was dropped off at his hotel to take it easy until the next morning when a realtor would give him a tour of the neighborhoods.

In accordance with their previous arrangement, Meena came to his hotel room in the evening, and they spent a glorious night together. She told her husband and son that she was spending the night with a bunch of her girlfriends. They hugged and kissed each other and made passionate love, urgently and without any preliminaries. They both were eager and starved, as they hadn't seen each other for almost a month. Only after both of them were satiated, they spoke to each other. "Your talk was great. You are such a good speaker, although I can't say that I followed all that chemistry."

"Thanks for coming to my talk. You were great there pretending that we are just seeing each other after so many years! You should have been an actress instead of a scientist!"

"All that was for Dave's sake. Dave doesn't know about us. All he knows is that you are an old friend from college. And we should keep it that way. Nobody has to know that we are this close."

"That's fine by me. I don't know anything about the way you kiss or touch or make love. In public we are platonic friends!"

She laughed and said, "I really don't know how fast you recover for another session," and got on top of him. The next morning she got up and left, but not before they made love one more time.

The tour with the realtor was useful, and Anant got a general idea of the area and the house prices. The realtor dropped him off at his hotel in the evening, and Meena was waiting for him. They spent time in the room, making love, talking, drinking beer, and eating pizza. Meena asked him, "So how do you like our company?"

"It is great, you guys are really doing good work. If they offer me the job, I will take it."

"Great! I am so happy that you like the company. It will be so nice to have you close to me. I will try to see you every day. What do you think of the real estate market here? Did you like any of the neighborhoods?"

"I have seen whatever the realtor showed me. If I want to find a house similar to the one I have now at Kansas, I may have to spend double the money. I think it is probably best if I rent an apartment for a few months, and then decide about a house slowly."

"That's a good idea. There is no need to rush into buying a house. I am sure there are some nice apartment complexes in the area."

They reluctantly parted, as it was getting late and Meena had to go home.

The next morning, Anant flew back to Kansas City, to the wicked world of chairman Fong. He came to know of Anant's grant and called him into his office for a chat.

Fong said, "I hear that your grant was not renewed. Are you going to resubmit it?"

"I don't think that resubmitting this proposal is going to do any good. The reviews were not encouraging. Essentially, they told me that they are no longer interested in funding this area."

"You know our departmental policy. If you don't have grant money, you don't get laboratory space. You can keep your laboratory space until your students complete their research work. Once they graduate, I will need the space because we are going to hire new people soon."

With that, Anant was dismissed from the presence of the dictator. Anant felt really bad that he was going to lose his laboratory space, the laboratory where he and his students had worked long hours for the past eight years. Along with the laboratory space, he was sure to lose his office, as they were adjacent. That meant he would be pushed to the dungeon of the department, in the basement. That was where the old faculty members without grants parked themselves. Once he went to the basement, he might as well forget about doing any more research. He was shunned by the faculty members hired by Fong and most of the older faculty members who belonged to the pre-Williams era. His only friend in the department was Petra Sokoloff. She was in a similar situation to Anant's. She was successful in getting a reasonably good-sized grant funded for about eight years, and was now struggling to get it renewed for the third time. They met often for lunch to discuss their plight.

Petra was from Ukraine and got her undergraduate and graduate degrees from universities in Kiev and Moscow. She spoke English with a strong accent, and sometimes her syntax was garbled. She did her postdoctoral work in the U.S. and published in prestigious journals. She was a good scientist and a first-rate teacher, and she worked hard. Her ex-husband was a brilliant fellow with a Ph.D. in Astronomy but one day decided to quit science and work in a department store. Petra was bitterly disappointed with him for wasting his education and begged him repeatedly not to quit his job. But he was adamant and would not listen to her. Petra got custody of their six-year-old daughter, Misha. Petra and her husband were frequent visitors at Anant's house, and Sheila enjoyed playing with Misha. When she came to know about Petra's divorce, Sheila was supportive of Petra. Petra would pour her heart out to Anant and Sheila. Neither Sheila nor Anant told Petra about their own marital problems, and when Petra learned about their divorce she was taken aback. As long as he was married to Sheila, Anant rarely had lunch at the university cafeteria, as Sheila insisted that he eat healthy home-cooked food. But after she left, Anant had no choice but to eat his lunch at the cafeteria, and that was when he started meeting Petra almost every day. Also, their problems with Fong brought them closer, and they could vent their frustrations.

Petra was an attractive, long-legged, buxom blonde. Since she was quite tall, she could carry her weight well and did not appear fat. In spite of her personal and professional problems, she took care of her appearance and was always well-dressed. During summertime, she wore sleeveless diaphanous skirts with no slip, and one could see the outline of her bra and panties and her well-shaped legs. She was oblivious to the stares of men around her and went about her business nonchalantly. Sheila teased Anant. "Sweetie, Petra looks at you so adoringly, I am beginning to think she has a crush on you. All you have to do is give her a signal, and she would be in your arms fast." Anant was embarrassed by Sheila's talk and would tell her that there was nothing but a professional relationship between him and Petra. But after Sheila left town, Anant couldn't help but wonder how Petra might react if he asked her out. Then he would sober up quickly and tell himself that a relationship with Petra was out of the question as long as they both worked in the same department. Petra might agree to have a fling with him, but it would only be a brief and unsatisfactory affair, as she was still hopeful that her ex-husband would come to his senses, and Anant was looking for a solid and long lasting relationship.

Dave called Anant to offer the job and said, "Let me know your decision soon, so that I can arrange with the personnel to mail you the contract."

"Thank you. I will call you back as soon as I decide."

There was not much to think about, and he really had no choice but to accept the job. He sent an e-mail to Meena about the job offer, and she called him in the evening from a pay phone. She was glad to know about the offer, although she would have been surprised if he didn't get the job. She volunteered to find him an apartment.

Anant met with his students the next day to inform them of his move to New Jersey. He told them that he made sure that they would have all the facilities and supplies they needed to complete their Ph.D. And then he met with Petra to let her know about the job offer. She knew that he was going to New Jersey for an interview, and was happy that he got the job. She kissed him on the cheek and congratulated him.

"So, Anant, you move to New Jersey when?"

"Maybe in a couple of months."

"So soon! I will miss you, Anant."

"I will miss you too, Petra. But we can keep in touch and maybe meet at the American Chemical Society meetings. I hope you get your grant renewed and keep that S.O.B. Mao off your back."

"I don't know. I am doing my best. We are sending to *Journal of American Chemical Society* another manuscript, and I hope they will accept it."

"I am sure they will. You are an excellent chemist, Petra. I wish I had some of your knowledge and intelligence."

"Oh! Anant, you make fun of me always."

"No, Petra, I really mean it."

After he went home that evening, Anant took stock of the situation. He could remain where he was, and nobody would fire him, not even that bastard Mao. He was a damn good teacher, and the students loved him. And he had tenure, which meant that he could work for as many years as he wanted to; some of the old bandicoots in the department were over seventy and still teaching. But to be thrown into the dungeons of the department without any means to continue his research would be unbearable. If he was in his seventies, like those old bastards, it might have been different. But he was still quite young. Was it his fault that he couldn't get his research grant funded? Generally, very few tenured faculty members got any grant money to do research. Once they got tenure, either they slowed down, or the granting agencies did not find their proposals exciting. However, not all the approved research proposals were either exciting or earth-shaking. Some proposals got funded because the peer review group determined that they were worth funding. This group was comprised of about fifteen or twenty scientists selected from around the country who had made significant contributions to a particular area of science. All of these people were respectable, sincere, and dedicated. When faced with a limited budget and many applicants, the committee had to reject a majority of proposals. The applications of the leading scientists and their groups were funded due to their track records. In addition, the reviewers' own proposals had to be funded. All this favoritism left very little money for a grant submitted by an "outsider" without connections. The peer review group looked for flaws in the proposals so that they could reject them outright, rather than trying to help a scientist to get funding. If someone looked hard enough, even a grant submitted by a Nobel Laureate might be rejected.

Anant called Dave and told him that he would accept the job in a couple of months, at the end of the semester, so that he could fulfill his teaching obligations. Dave was happy that Anant was coming on board, and promised any help that he might need in moving. Meena found a two-bedroom apartment, not too far from the company. She asked him to go to New Jersey to look at the apartment. As the company would pay for a second visit, he agreed to fly there on a Friday, and return on Sunday evening. This made Meena happy because it meant they could see each other. He arrived at the Newark airport in the evening, rented a car, and drove to the hotel where the company booked him a room. Driving for the first time on New Jersey roads was stressful, as it appeared that everybody was in a hurry and going too fast. In Kansas, people were courteous and didn't drive like maniacs. In New Jersey, nobody paid attention to the speed limit, and when Anant was going at thirty-miles-per-hour in a zone marked thirty, many people honked at him. When he didn't turn left fast enough after a light turned green, he got more honks. This made him very jittery and his nerves were frayed by the time he got to the hotel. Meena was waiting for him in the lobby, and after they went to the room, they kissed each other hungrily and made love. All his fatigue and irritability disappeared when she came to him with love and passion. She was completely uninhibited and always knew how best to please him. Afterwards, they began to make plans for the evening.

She said, "I can spend the night and the weekend with you. My husband thinks I am out of town on business. Only thing is you need to drive wherever we go, and I hope we don't run into anyone I know."

Anant groaned. "Oh! My God, driving on these roads gives me high blood pressure. They are maniacs on the roads here, how do you drive without getting mad at these crazy people?"

"Not everyone is bad, there are some who drive too fast, but most drivers are okay. You can't compare the sleepy drivers of Kansas to these people. Here everybody is more dynamic, and life is fast-paced, unlike the laid-back life style of Kansas. I guess you have to adjust to a lot of things here. Don't worry, you will be fine within a few months."

"I hope so. I almost got an ulcer driving from the airport."

"Honey, I am getting hungry. Shall we go out to eat at a nice Mexican place that I know?"

"Sure, as long as you agree to be the navigator. But why do you want to go to Mexican when there are so many Indian restaurants in this area?"

"Because at Indian restaurants, there may be people

that I know, and if they see me with a strange man, they will talk."

Anant wondered how long they could live in fear of what other people might think and say. But he didn't want to say anything, as it might lead to unpleasantness. He told himself to be patient with her. She proved to be a good navigator, and they arrived at the restaurant without anybody honking at them. After a good meal, they both relaxed and discussed his move.

"My dear, are you going to miss Kansas when you move here?"

"Not really. I don't have anything there that I really miss. I might miss teaching and dealing with students for a while, but I will get over it. Compared to Kansas, the winters and summers here are probably milder."

"Did you get in touch with the movers and fix a date for the pick up? What are you going to do about your old car? I hope you are going to ship it and not drive it all the way."

"There is plenty of time to arrange the movers. I am not sure what I should do about my car. It is still in a good shape and runs well, and I hate to give it away. You know I had it for about sixteen years and it has only seventy thousand miles. Also, that was my first car that I bought with my own money, and I am sort of attached to it."

"Dear, I heard about your car so many times that I know everything about it. How you bought it, where you bought it, what kind of advice your boss gave you and all that. It is only a car, and you shouldn't get so attached to a piece of metal that takes you from point A to B."

"Meena, I know you buy a new car every four or five years. But with a teacher's salary, I could not do that."

"I don't buy my cars; when my husband decides that I need a new car, he goes off and gets me a new one. One time when I got home from work, I saw this shining, brand-new Lexus in the driveway. I will still admiring the car when my husband walked out of the front door and gave me the car keys and told me to take it out for a spin. I was shocked when he told me that it was mine."

"I am sorry that you have to go around in the cheap rental car now. Maybe I should also buy a nice Lexus or a Mercedes to take you out in style."

"Don't be silly, my dear. I don't care what you drive as long as you love me and take good care of me."

The next day, they went to see the apartment that Meena found. The complex was relatively new, situated quite close to a strip mall that had a grocery store, a couple of restaurants, and a liquor store. Although the area was full of hustle and bustle, once they entered the apartment complex, it was serene, clean, and well-maintained, with nice landscaping and manicured lawns. The apartment was quite spacious, with a large living/dining area opening into a balcony overlooking the woods. The bedrooms were next to each other, each with a bathroom attached to it. There was also a laundry room with a washer and dryer. Anant was impressed. "You have such marvelous taste. This is nice, we can sit on a couch here and look at the woods and sip wine. Shall we take it?"

Meena was pleased with Anant's reaction. "I thought that you will like it. If you don't mind, I can keep some clothes in the spare bedroom so that when I spend the night here I can change in the morning, and go to work from here."

"You don't need my permission to use the apartment. Actually, it will be great if you simply move in with me and not go back and forth. We will get an extra key for you so that you can come here whenever you want."

The weekend went by fast, and before he knew it, it was time to fly back to Kansas. The next few months were going to be hectic for Anant: organizing his affairs in Kansas; going through a bunch of old files in his office and home, deciding what to discard, what to keep; meeting with his students every day and helping them with their experiments; and his own teaching and grading. He met with Fong and told him about his move, and Fong could not hide his glee at the prospect of filling another vacancy with his choice. He promised to let Anant's students work in the laboratory until they completed their experimental work. But Anant never trusted the fellow and made arrangements with Petra in case Fong gave his students any trouble. She was more than willing to help, and told him that his students could work in her laboratory if Fong caused any problems. He was grateful to Petra for all her moral support during the past year or so, after his divorce and during the beginning of the Fong-era in the department. He thought that the least he could do was to take her out to dinner.

"Petra, shall we go out for dinner next Friday?"

She asked, "Are you going to date me?"

Although Anant was amused at the way Petra expressed herself, he didn't show it because Petra felt bad if someone was critical of her English. But he understood what she meant, and knew he was in trouble. If he said no, he might be hurting her pride, and if he said yes, she might think there was more to it than just dinner.

So he was diplomatic. "It all depends on how you define a date. We have known each other for about eight years. We joined this department at the same time, and went through a lot in this period. After my divorce, we never met socially, and I thought that it will be nice if we spend some time and talk about different things, anything but science."

She smiled. "Anant, you are too complicated and talk too much. Let's just go out and have fun!"

Anant picked Petra up one Friday evening, and they went to Jarred's. This was an exclusive restaurant owned and operated by a couple. The husband was the chef, and the wife handled all the other affairs. Anant took care to reserve a table that he knew was in a quiet and secluded corner; he remembered it from going to the restaurant a few times with Sheila. This time, he and Petra started off with a nice bottle of Cabernet Sauvignon and delicious crab cakes. For their entrée, Petra had salmon cooked in a special mustard sauce, and Anant had spicy jambalaya. Since they were already full, they decided to share a dessert called "Death by Chocolate," a rich and creamy chocolate cake in a chocolate and strawberry sauce. It was a delectable dinner, and they both had fun. After dessert, Anant looked at his watch and said, "Petra, is it getting late for you? What time does your babysitter go home?"

"This evening I have no babysitter. My neighbor took her girls and Misha to St. Louis for the weekend."

They left the restaurant, and Anant asked if Petra would like to come to his house for a drink. She said yes. As usual, he had forgotten to turn on the front porch lights, and the house was dark. He was embarrassed. "I am sorry everything is so dark. Before I left to pick you up, I wanted to turn on the lights, but in the last minute, I forgot."

"It's no big deal. I do it all the time, and when I get back it is dark at home. I wanted to put the porch lights on a timer. But I never did it."

Anant opened the garage door with the automatic opener, and the light came on in the garage. He led Petra into the house through the kitchen door, and turned on some lights in the kitchen and den. When Sheila was around, Petra always entered his house through the front door after parking in the driveway. It felt funny to bring her into the house through the garage door. All the windows in the house were open; since it was a warm October day, he opened them in the morning and forgot to close them in the evening in his hurry to get ready and pick up Petra. But the night was chilly, and he was sure that Petra was cold in her thin cotton dress and light jacket. He started the fireplace in the den and closed all the windows. Petra squatted near the fireplace and placed her hands in front of the fire, and when her hands got warm, she placed them on her cheeks. While fixing a whiskey sour and watching Petra, Anant thought, *She is such a beautiful woman. Why didn't I ask her out all these months?* He brought the drinks and set them on the coffee table, and sat next to Petra on the hardwood floor. Petra put her warm hands on Anant's face, and kissed him on the mouth. All those years they saw each other and desired each other, but due to one reason or another, they could not consummate their wish. Now there was nothing to hold them back, like water gushing out of the floodgates of a dam. Their feelings for each other were set free, and they came together with passion and lust. Afterwards, holding each other, they talked.

"Anant, I can't believe it! After all these years, we are together, and now to New Jersey you are leaving."

"Do I really have a choice, Petra?"

"Yes, you do. You did not resign yet officially, and Mao can't kick you out."

"That may be true. But I committed to the people in New Jersey, and if I change my mind now in the last minute it will look bad."

"I always loved you, but never wanted any trouble caused between you and Sheila."

"But you were also married, Petra. How can you love me, and also love your husband?"

"Why not? There is no such rule that one woman can love only one man. I love you for what you are, a generous, decent, and sincere man. I loved my ex-husband for what he was in those days, dashing and full of joi, what is the word I want? I think it is French."

"You mean *joie de vivre?*"

"Yeah, you know all the words, English and French."

"I barely know English. I know just a few French words. As for my English, it needs a lot of work, at least that is the opinion of the reviewers of my last manuscript."

"Anant, you know how nasty some reviewers can be. They never liked my English, always corrected everything I wrote. I know my English is not great, but I write grammatically correct English. When I was married to Paul, he used to correct my manuscripts."

"Do you see him often, after your divorce?"

"Not anymore. He used to drop in whenever he wanted a good home-cooked meal. The last time he came, few months back, he told me that he met a twenty-year-old bimbo. He was so clever that he waited until he ate a good dinner, and after putting Misha to bed, he made love to me, and afterwards, he told me as though it was of no big deal, that he was seeing this young thing. I got so mad and felt so used, I kicked him out, and told him to never come back."

Anant was so relieved that she finally got that hopeless chap out of her system. Everyone except Petra knew that Sokoloff was a philanderer, and once he even hit on Sheila. She got really mad and gave him a piece of her mind, and after that he never bothered her. But she never told Petra about the incident because she did not want to upset her.

In the morning, Anant and Petra woke up late, after a night filled with lust. Both of them felt like they had just discovered sex and couldn't get enough of it. Maybe all those pent-up feelings for each other finally got unleashed and they wanted to enjoy each other to the fullest extent possible. Petra had to go and attend to her weekend chores. Before leaving she asked, "Darling, please stay here, don't leave me." After she was gone, Anant was perplexed at this new development in his life. He had never even considered Petra as a potential mate, as he was fixated on finding a suitable Indian woman. The only Indian woman he found was still very much married, and he was not sure when she might decide to divorce her husband. Until then, he would need to meet her only surreptitiously. How long could he and Meena keep their affair under wraps? Sometime, somewhere, someone would surely spot them together, and it would be only a matter of time before her husband knew about them. He did not want to think of Meena as a manipulative person, but the thought crossed his mind, that perhaps she wanted the best of both worlds: a husband to keep her family together and maintain a veneer of respectability, and a boyfriend to fulfill her carnal desires. After Petra left, he went for a long walk to ponder the situation. He could call Dave and tell him that he changed his mind and had decided to stay in Kansas. Dave might not like it, and Meena's reputation in the company might be damaged; she would be mad at him for this last-minute change of the plans. Suddenly an idea occurred to him. He was eligible for one year's sabbatical leave, and he could use it to go to New Jersey and work in the company for a year. This would serve three purposes. One, if he didn't like the job, he could always get back to his teaching in Kansas. Second, he could give Meena one year to divorce Ramana Rau. If she didn't divorce him even after one year, she might never do it. Third, he and Petra could sort out their feelings for each other in a year. Because of his students' work and thesis-writing, he needed to make frequent trips to Kansas, and that would give him opportunities to get together with Petra. The plan appeared sound, but first he had to call Dave to find out if a trial period of one year would be acceptable to him and the company. Because of a severe shortage of experienced organic chemists, Dave might be forced to accept his proposal.

When he called Petra to tell her about his idea, she was thrilled with the plan, and asked him to come to her house for dinner. He wore a nice jacket and a tie and got her a bunch of red roses and a bottle of Merlot. When he rang her doorbell, she opened the door and ushered him inside. He was astounded at the way she looked, as he never, in all those eight years, saw her so sexy and desirable. She was wearing a white halter dress. The revealing, plunge neckline exposed a lot, leaving little to his imagination. Her straight back was bare except for the sash tie at the neck. She was barefoot, and her toenails were painted bright red. Her hair was freshly shampooed and still a little wet, her luscious lips were pink, and her beautiful face had very little makeup. She kissed him. "Come in, my darling, I am happy that you have decided not to permanently leave this place."

"I hope that the people in New Jersey will be agreeable. In the beginning, the plan was that I move there for good. I have to call that guy on Monday and explain to him my new plan."

"Don't worry about all that now. Come and have a drink and relax with your Petra. I spent a lot of time today cooking a good meal for you."

On the way to the kitchen, Petra asked him, "Do you like my dress, my darling? I got it from Ukraine when I went there last Christmas."

"You look gorgeous, Petra. I've never seen you wearing such a nice dress before."

"My dear Anant, I wear this only for you. If I wear it outside it will make the men go crazy."

"You may be right, Petra. Thanks for giving me this opportunity to enjoy your pulchritude."

"You use very big words, darling. Whatever they mean, I hope it is a compliment."

"Petra, it means that I have the honor and privilege to admire your dazzling beauty."

"You are such a flatterer. Are you always like this with all of your women?"

"I rarely get the opportunity to be with such a special woman like yourself, my dear."

"You make me feel good, my darling. I have prepared a special dish for you today, and I hope you will like it."

"What did you cook?"

"It is a casserole with mixed vegetables and small pieces of salmon and shrimp. I mix them all in jalapeno cheese sauce, cream of celery soup and bake it. It will be ready in a few minutes. Pour some wine first, my darling."

Anant opened a bottle, and they sat on the couch, and sipped their wine and had crab-stuffed mushrooms. He had eaten at her house a few times before, during those days when both of them were married, and he knew Petra's culinary skills. She took the trouble to prepare tasty and simple dishes, she never made too many items, and whatever she cooked turned out delicious.

Petra said, "Everything happened so suddenly. I don't know how fast we came to this stage. I never imagined that we could be together like this, this close and intimate."

"I guess it is luck, Petra. You are a very sexy and beautiful woman, and I would be lying if I say that I didn't find you desirable. When I got divorced, I didn't think of asking you out because I knew that you were still hoping that your ex would return to you. I was not interested in starting a relationship that might not go anywhere. Even if I approached you at that time, you might have said no to me. I am glad that you finally got over your ex. You know I have always admired you in many ways; your knowledge, your intellect, and your professionalism. Now I am fortunate to admire another facet of your personality."

"Please don't make me blush, my darling. Stop saying

all those nice things about me. I will start crying and ruin my makeup."

The casserole was delectable and surprisingly spicy, maybe due to the jalapeno cheese sauce.

Petra said, "I don't use the jalapeno cheese a lot as Misha can't eat spicy food. But today I used it to please you as I know you like spicy food."

"Thanks, Petra. You didn't have to do it for my sake. It is true that I like spicy food, but I don't have to eat spicy food all the time. Only when I eat Indian food I want it spicy, as bland Indian food is tasteless, at least for me."

"Whenever I eat at the Indian restaurants, my eyes start watering because of the hot food. But I enjoy eating Indian food. When I was studying in Moscow, we sometimes ate at an Indian restaurant. They always made the food less spicy for us as they knew we couldn't tolerate too much spice."

"I didn't know that they had Indian restaurants in Moscow."

"We have a lot of Indian stuff in Russia. We import cigarettes from India. Some of my friends smoked Charminar cigarettes, those had filter tips and came in King size."

"Really? When I was a teenager I smoked Charminar cigarettes, but they were regular size and had no filter tips. I think they are produced in my hometown. I wonder if they made the king size ones especially for export."

"We all like Raj Kapoor movies in Russia, they are a big hit and the songs are great. We don't know the meaning, but the tunes are catchy." She hummed a tune, and Anant recognized the song and sang a couple of lines, "*Mera jhoota hai japany.*"

She was thrilled. "Oh, you know the song, you sang it just like the fellow in the movie!"

"I don't know all the words."

"After I moved to the U.S., I didn't see any Indian movies. Shall we go an Indian movie one day?"

"Sure, we can go. I think the Indian association screens movies in a theater on a Saturday or a Sunday. I get the information on my e-mail and usually never bother. I haven't seen a Hindi movie in ages. Sheila and I used to watch a lot of Hollywood movies or sometimes French or Chinese. Hindi movies are too long and too many song-and-dance sequences, and invariably the heroine has a belly and it hangs out when she jumps up and down. Very few of those actresses are in a good shape. And the heroes never age. It is crazy to watch a seventy-year-old guy playing the role of a thirty-year-old, and the girl that plays opposite him may only be twenty."

"That's nothing new. They do the same thing also in Hollywood movies. The women are pushed into retirement when they lose their looks, but the men keep on going forever."

They finished dinner, and Anant volunteered to clean up the kitchen and put the plates and tumblers in the dishwasher. But Petra wouldn't let him. "I can't have you doing a woman's work. You must sit in the living room and let me do the cleaning. I will be there in a few minutes."

"Please, Petra, don't be so old-fashioned. Men can also do cleaning and cooking, although I can't say that I cook. But I am pretty good at washing dishes and cleaning. Besides, I don't want your beautiful dress to get spoiled. Just for today, take it easy, Petra. You can stay here and supervise me, if you like."

Petra gave in, and they finished the work quickly, and went into the living room with the remaining bottle of wine. The living room was cozy, with a smoldering fireplace and the drapes drawn to keep out the draft. Petra sat on Anant's lap, kissed him seductively, and said, "You are a real gentleman. All evening, you didn't even try to touch me. Most men in my country are not this patient. If there was a Russian man in your place, he would have made love to me first, and then eaten his dinner. I love you because you are so decent and considerate. So far in my life, no man has ever offered to help me in the kitchen. When I was in Ukraine, my mother, me, and my sister would work hard and get the food ready. My father and my two brothers would come in, eat, and leave. Sometimes when my father was in a good mood, he would compliment my mother on the tasty food, but none of them offered to help in washing dishes or cleaning the kitchen. When I came to this country, Paul was the first man that I dated. He was a very lazy man and never got up from his chair even to get a cup of coffee. I had to wait on him all the time."

"Petra, thank you for the compliment. As soon as I saw you, I wanted to make love to you, but I figured I could wait until after dinner. I enjoyed watching you in your new dress, and I liked the way you moved around the house in this outfit. Also I thought we must do justice to the food you prepared. There is a saying that the way to a man's heart is through his stomach. I found that the way to a woman's heart is to first eat whatever she cooks, compliment her on the excellent food, and then slowly take her into the bedroom."

"How many times did your recipe work?"

"Are you asking me how many women liked my method?"

He knew he was in trouble, as he didn't want her to know his affair with Heather. He thought that it was best if he told her only about Sheila.

"Yes, my darling, please tell me."

"Only one before you, Petra."

"I thought that with your looks and patience, you must have had a lot of women."

"No, you are wrong there. Sheila was my first love in this country, and we got married after dating for a few months."

"Do you still love her, Anant?"

"I will be lying to you if I said no. Yes, there are times I do think of her, and wonder what she is up to. But I lost touch with her, and it is better that way."

"I am sorry I asked you that question. I know exactly how you feel because I felt the same way about Paul. Even after our divorce, I still loved him and welcomed him into my house. Now he has completely broken my heart, and I feel better now that he is out of my life forever."

He gently asked her, "What's for dessert?"

She was embarrassed. "I didn't make anything, I am sorry. But we can have some ice cream if you like."

He laughed. "You are my dessert, baby."

She blushed, and her face became red as a beet root.

She hugged him tightly and kissed him. "You are very bad!"

In the morning, Anant woke up in Petra's bed, and she was still sleeping with her head on his chest and her body intertwined with his. It was delightful to wake up next to such a lascivious woman. She was most energetic, and willing to do anything that gave them pleasure. Most importantly, he liked it very much that she trusted him and let him into her life with such passion and delight. He kissed her on her forehead, and she woke up immediately.

He said, "I am sorry if I woke you up. I just couldn't help kissing you. You looked so beautiful and helpless when you were asleep. It was a pleasure watching you sleep. You breathe so softly."

"You talk too much, my darling. Come inside me."

Afterwards, she told him to rest a bit while she went downstairs. She called him to come downstairs after coffee was ready. She was quite thoughtful in providing him with a toothbrush and a fresh robe. He brushed his teeth, and wearing the robe, he went downstairs, thinking, *I must drink whatever she has, even if it is regular coffee. If I ask for decaf and if she doesn't have it in the house, she will feel bad.*

But he didn't have to worry. She gave him a steaming cup of coffee, saying, "This is decaf."

He was surprised. "I didn't know you also drank decaf."

"My darling Anant, I never touch that stuff. I keep some decaf for people like you. For me, coffee should be strong, hot, and full of caffeine. Otherwise, I don't wake up properly. I know you drink decaf only."

"How come you know so much about my likes and dislikes, Petra?"

"My darling, I have been around you for many years. I know a lot about you, more than you know about yourself." While he was drinking his coffee, she whipped up a quick breakfast of eggs, bacon, ham and toast. He was surprised at her agility in the kitchen. They finished breakfast and went for a long walk.

After they returned, Anant said, "Petra, I have to go home and do laundry."

"Are you going to come this evening? We will eat dinner and watch a movie."

"Okay, can I bring something?"

"No, I am going to make something simple."

Again, they spent another blissful night in each other's arms.

The next morning, after breakfast, Anant said, "I better go home, shower and wear a fresh shirt. I have a lot of unpleasant things to do this morning. Luckily, I don't have to teach today. I will meet you for lunch. Will you wait for me?"

"Of course, I will be waiting for you in my office. I should be back around noon from my class. Good luck with New Jersey and Mao."

He went home, had a quick shower, dressed in his usual well-pressed pants, a starched shirt, a tie, and a jacket, and went off to his office. He first called Meena at her office, and was lucky to find her there. He told her, "Meena, I had second thoughts about accepting the job. I got worried about what will happen if I don't like the job. And if I quit this teaching position, I can never get another one like this. So I thought I will go to New Jersey on a sabbatical, give it a shot for a year, and then see how things shape up."

Meena was upset. "After all I and Dave have done to get you on board, how can you do this to us? And what about us? I was so looking forward to having you near me forever. I can't bear to be away from you, even for a day. If you decide after a year that you don't like it here, you will go back to Kansas, but what about me, Anant? Are you going to leave me too? You know I don't want to live in Kansas. Everything is so boring there." She went on and on in this vein for a few more minutes.

Anant kept quiet, and when she finished said, "You know that I have job security here even though I don't make much money. In the industry, the jobs are never secure and they can fire me any time. I don't want to be jobless. But right now, all I am saying is I want to try it for a year, and then make the final decision at the end of the year. Please try to understand." In the end, she relented and agreed to keep quiet about his plans and not say anything to Dave. She told him to call Dave and discuss the matter. She felt that Dave would most probably agree, as he was desperate for somebody to join the group to move some projects forward. As she predicted, after some initial resistance, Dave consented to the plan, and asked him join the group as soon as possible. Next step was to meet Fong, and get his approval for his sabbatical. This might be a tough one.

Anant never went on sabbatical leave due to Sheila's job. She couldn't very well go away for a year and leave her patients up the creek. He never even considered going on a sabbatical without Sheila. Some of his colleagues went to

Europe for a year, leaving their families behind, but Anant couldn't bear the thought of living all by himself for a whole year without Sheila. How could he live for an entire year without her when he couldn't even sleep alone when she was on a night call? Her night calls were busy, with her beeper constantly going off. She told him, "Neither I nor you can sleep with all this noise. When I am on call, I will sleep in the guest bedroom."

He was upset. "Baby, I can't sleep unless I touch you before I sleep, and sometimes in the middle of the night you know I reach for you. If you are not with me, I can't sleep."

"Sweetie, it is only for one or two nights. Just try to sleep by yourself. If you want, I will come in and kiss you good night."

He reluctantly agreed, but he could never get a good night's sleep when she was on call. It was more difficult for him when she was doing a Friday and Saturday call. She would work all day Friday, and then the call would start in the evening and end on Sunday morning. She had to work for about forty-eight hours without any sleep or rest, and some days if she was lucky, she would come home for lunch or dinner. Most of the time her beeper would beep non-stop, and she was obliged to return all those calls. Those days or nights she was on call, she was tense and didn't eat properly, relying on a lot of coffee to stay alert.

Eventually, those night calls took their toll on her physical as well as mental health. She frequently complained of belly pains and headaches, and she would yell and scream at Anant for the simplest things. Because of lack of time, she couldn't exercise and consequently gained some weight. When they got married, she had had a svelte figure, with perky breasts, a flat stomach, toned arms and thighs. Now, after a few years, her breasts became bigger and pendulous, and her belly, thighs, and arms became flabby. In spite of the weight gain, she still remained attractive and sexy. During those days, Anant wished she listened to him and took the VA job. Most of the time, he kept quiet, and let her do or say whatever she wanted. But every once in a while, he lost his temper. "You would have been better off with the VA job. What is point of working so hard and ruining your health? Your whole system is out of whack with this heavy workload. No wonder you can't get pregnant with so much stress."

Another bone of contention was his name. She chided him at every opportunity for not changing it. Among the Indians in the town, Sheila was more well known than Anant, and some people even called him Mr. Puri. When someone wanted to send them an invitation, they would call home and ask Sheila, "What is your husband's last name?" She replied, "He goes by Prasad, but his actual last name is Durvasula." Then she would turn to him and say, "Why don't you simplify your name? It gets confusing to everybody. I have to go through it all the time. Simply change your name to Anant Puri or Anant D. Vasula. It will make everybody's life easier, particularly mine."

This topic of his name change was always contentious, and he never liked to discuss it. When he happened to be in a good mood, he didn't react to her comments but brushed it off. "Leave it alone. I lived with my name for more than thirty years, and I can live for another thirty or forty years with it. Nobody has to know my surname, anyway it is in the beginning of my name, and if people think Prasad is my last name, what's the harm in it?"

"But that's exactly what I am saying. Your last name is not Prasad, it's Durvasula."

"I know that. I explained to you many times about my name and why I couldn't do anything about it. Please leave it alone."

When she repeated the same thing again and again at different times, it bothered him and he would lash out at her. "Don't bother me. My great-grandfather, my grandfather, and my father wrote their names in the same manner, and now why should I change it? It is our custom, and just because I am in USA, I need not do everything like the Americans do. If my name is so difficult for you, you should have married someone with a name like Smith or Brown. Go to hell." And he would walk out of the room.

She would get very mad and scold him loudly. "You are so pig-headed, always wanting to do everything your way. You never listen to me." And she would go into the spare bedroom and cry herself to sleep.

Since Anant never used his sabbatical, the administration couldn't really object, and in the end, after trying to put some obstacles in his way, Fong had no choice but to approve. Anant was prepared to take his case to the dean if the situation warranted. He put his request in writing and took the letter to Fong, and spoke to him for a few minutes about his change of plans. Fong was livid and said that it was most inconsiderate of Anant to tell him about his new plans at the last minute, as he was already planning to hire another faculty member in Anant's position. Anant gently pointed out that he had not given his resignation, and that the chairman needed to wait until he submitted his resignation letter. Fong knew he was beaten but still tried to browbeat Anant. "You are making a big mistake trying to stay here. You can't get your grant renewed next year, and that means you will lose your laboratory space. After that, you can only teach, and your life will be miserable without the opportunity to do any research. I want you to think about it carefully. The offer you got in New Jersey is pretty good. If I were in your position, I would take it and make it work in a big way."

For Fong, everything had to be big. He had a big grant (at least for another four years), a big car, and a big, fat wife. Anant thanked him for his advice, but told him that he was taking his sabbatical as soon as the semester ended. Since most of his teaching assignments were in the fall semester, he was actually giving Fong almost a year to find a temporary replacement to teach his courses. In the spring semester, he taught only one course along with Petra, and she had already agreed to teach his portion of the course. Fong was boxed in and couldn't object to the time frame, and in the end, Anant didn't have to go the dean after all.

Anant went into Petra's office, closed the door, and kissed her passionately. After what seemed like a long time, they released each other, and Petra said, "I think you got it. I could see it in your face when you came in. I am so happy for us. But you must promise every month to come back so that we can spend some time together. I will miss you so much you can't even imagine. I got so used to seeing you every morning in the department, and now our new love makes it all the more difficult."

He hugged her. "Petra, don't be sad. I will come back once every month to be with you. Don't lose that white halter dress. Maybe I should buy you the same dress in a couple of different colors just in case. Come on, let's go to lunch. I am starving, all that talking to people made me hungry. By the way, what are you doing this evening?"

"Nothing, I do my work-out and take a walk, cook, eat, put Misha to bed, and watch TV and go to bed. Do you want to come over to eat with us?"

"Sure, but you shouldn't make anything special for me. Just whatever you eat. Maybe I can get us all a pizza. What do you think?"

"No pizza tonight. I already have cooking in the slow cooker a beef stew, and all I have to do is prepare some mashed potatoes. It will be a simple and healthy meal."

"That's fine, then." They didn't talk about anything important in the cafeteria, as there were other people around. They had their lunch quickly, and got back to their offices, as they had to catch up with their work.

Anant got an e-mail from Meena asking him to call her at home in the evening between six and eight. He wouldn't be able to call her because he had to go to Petra's house. So he wrote to Meena saying that he had to go to a friend's house for dinner in the evening, and he promised to call her the next morning at her office. He felt bad about disappointing Meena. When she asked him to call her at home, that meant that her husband and son would be away and she could talk to him about all kinds of intimate things. He began to think how he could deal with the two women, keeping them both happy and at the same time keeping each woman unaware of the other. He had to walk this tightrope for the next year, and hopefully at the end of this period, he should be in a position to decide which one to settle down with. He was not happy doing this, but at this point in his life, he had no other choice. If he got married again, it better last forever. He couldn't go through another gut-wrenching divorce. After all, life was all about choice, and he should choose the best of the two women. This might be selfish, but what else could a man in his position do? Here were two beautiful women, in love with him and ready to spend the rest of their lives with him. The only glitch was one of them was still married, and although she promised to get a divorce from her husband next fall, he was not sure if she would do it. On the other hand, Petra was completely free of any such encumbrance, and he was sure that she would marry him immediately if he proposed to her. He and Petra had known each other for about eight years, whereas he had known Meena for only a few months. That he knew her many years ago didn't really mean anything, as he never got to know her well during his stay in Delhi. So what made Meena so special that he should wait for her a full year before she was free? His affair with Petra didn't start until last week, and before that he never even considered her as a potential partner. Before last week, he was prepared to wait for Meena, and that was why he decided to take the job in New Jersey. His affair with two women in two different states was definitely advantageous to him, but if one of them found out about the other, he would be in trouble and lose both of them. So Anant had to be careful in his dealing with the women, and should not betray his secret. But if he proposed to Petra and got married to her and lived happily ever after in Kansas, all this subterfuge could be avoided and he should be at peace with himself.

Some ten years ago, Anant had made the mistake of dumping Heather in favor of Sheila, and it ended in a divorce. A few days after he slept with Sheila, he had spent some time with Heather at her place. He left early, telling her that he had to work on a manuscript. If Heather thought that he was acting strange, she didn't say anything, as it was unusual for Anant to leave without making love to her. He was wrestling with his feelings for Sheila and Heather. He cared for Heather and was grateful for her friendship when he needed it most. In his mind, it was immoral to continue to see two women at the same time. Notwithstanding his qualms, he knew that if one of them found out about his dalliance with the other, all hell would break loose and he was sure to lose both women. He didn't want to lose Heather's friendship, but at the same he was unable to determine if their relationship would be long-lasting. Because she was a kind and considerate person and was always good to him, he hated the idea of dumping her. They had reached a certain stage in their relationship where it was difficult to take it down to a platonic level. He fervently wished to have Heather as his friend and Sheila as his lover, but he knew only too well that it was an impossible dream. Even if Heather agreed to maintain their friendship without the intimacy, he was certain that Sheila wouldn't want him to be friendly with any other woman. Sheila was capricious, and it would be difficult to make her see his point of view. He knew that he really liked Sheila and enjoyed being with her. Also, he was sure that she felt the same way about him. He asked himself why he preferred Sheila's companionship to that of Heather. Both were American girls, one white and the other of Indian descent. Apart from her Indian heritage, Sheila was as American as Heather. In many aspects they resembled each other, the way they talked, conducted themselves, and dressed. Heather was from a much lower socio-economic class than Sheila, who grew up with money and a life of privilege owing to her parents' exalted occupations. The most important distinction between them was Sheila's higher education and knowledge. He could speak to Sheila about almost any topic and she would not only understand what he was saying, but had something intelligent to contribute to the conversation. He felt that he had finally met someone who shared his passion for discussing world events and politics. With Heather, it was really difficult to carry on an intelligent conversation because she had no opinion of her own on most topics but simply repeated what she heard on TV or what her racist preacher said in their church. Anant also felt that when she spoke to him, Heather was cautious not to reveal her true feelings about some issues lest it offend him. She was aware that her right-wing beliefs clashed with his moderate view of the world. After a lot of soul-searching, he decided to confide in Heather and tell her about his feelings for Sheila. He met Heather the following day and informed her that he was seeing Sheila and that he intended to ask her to marry him.

She was shocked. "How come you never even told me that you are seeing someone else? I thought we are good friends."

"I am sorry, this happened quite suddenly. I was meaning to tell you, but I didn't want to hurt your feelings."

"I thought that we were getting very close, that's the reason why I took you to see my mama." She started crying.

Anant was helpless. "I am sorry."

She said, "Leave me alone. I don't want to see you again."

He felt terribly sad to end their relationship.

Another hasty decision on Anant's part might lead to another tragedy, and in the end nobody would be happy. As things stood, Petra was happy that they had finally come together, and the future looked bright. As far as Meena was concerned, he would have married her if she was free, and the affair with Petra would never have begun. So, it was Meena who made him wait for her, and unfortunately

Petra was paying the price. All this thinking gave him a big headache and he went home early, changed into his shorts and T-shirt, and went for a jog to clear his head. He got back after an hour, had a long, hot shower, changed into fresh clothes and went to a toy store to get a small gift for Misha. She called him Dr. Anant at her mother's behest. The kid was friendly, and came to him readily and played with him. Anant reached Petra's house at about six. Petra was dressed in her usual jeans and T-shirt. Misha was happy with her remote-control car and started to pester her mom to open the package and assemble the car. But Petra told the little girl that she would have to eat her dinner first, and then she could play with the car. Misha was obedient, and they all had their dinner. Unlike many children, Misha never made a fuss about eating. Whatever her mom put on her plate, she ate with her fork cleanly without spilling. The food was delicious, and after they ate, Petra sent Misha and Anant into the living room to play with the car. Anant removed the car from the box, inserted the batteries in the car and the remote, and showed Misha how to use the remote. She was thrilled with it, and started to play. He went back into the kitchen to see if Petra needed help. She was almost done with the dishes, and he took the sponge and wiped the counter and the stovetop. After they both washed their hands, she came to him. "Thanks for taking such trouble to get Misha that toy. You are always bringing her something or other. You mustn't do it all the time, she will be spoiled. I buy her presents on her birthday and Christmas only."

"It is no big deal, I know the kid enjoys playing with cars. So I try to get her a different car each time."

They went into the living room to find Misha still

playing with her new toy. Petra told Misha she could play for another few minutes, and then to bed. They watched her play, and sat close to each other. Petra hugged Anant, but he wasn't sure how to behave in the presence of Misha. Although she was only six, she was aware of things, and if he touched her mom in an intimate manner, he didn't know how Misha might react. Then Petra took Misha upstairs to her room, and came down after some time. "She is sleeping. I guess she was tired with all that running around with her new car. I stand next to her while she brushes her teeth and help her change into her pajamas. Then we have to read her favorite book for a few minutes, and before I finish the first page she is deep asleep." Anant took her into his arms and held her tightly and kissed her long and passionately. She kissed him back equally zealously, and they sat like that for quite some time, without moving, just letting their lips and tongues do all the work. Finally, they had to release each other in order to breath.

"I guess we must have missed each other."

He said, "I sure did, baby. I wanted to kiss you all evening, but I didn't want to upset Misha."

"That's quite considerate of you. I talked to her about us and explained to her that you are my boyfriend. She knows you well, and I am sure she will get used to seeing us together more often. I told her that her father and I are no longer seeing each other. And she knows that boyfriends kiss their girlfriends. So you can kiss me any time you want in this house, and Misha will be fine with it."

"You are great. I wouldn't know how to bring up a child."

"My darling Anant, nobody is born with a talent to raise a child. We learn as we go along. I am sure I made a lot of mistakes with Misha, but they were not terrible ones. Many times the kids get confused at our lack of consistency. Sometimes I let her do some things, but other times I forbid her to do the same exact thing. She is a smart girl, but she is only a small baby, and gets confused at the mixed signals that I give her."

"It's all part of life, and in the end she will grow up fine."

"I guess I spoil her a bit, as I feel bad that she is growing up without a father's love. Even when we were married, Paul never cared to take responsibility for Misha and left everything to me. He was one of those men who thought their duty was over after he made me pregnant. He was utterly selfish, never cared for anybody but himself. When Misha was little she used to go to him, but he never picked her up and petted her. For him, she was a nuisance, as he looked at her as someone he had to put with."

"That's really bad. Poor kid, she must be traumatized, her own father so indifferent."

"Actually, he never wanted children, but I desperately wanted at least one child and begged him to change his mind. After a lot of arguments and tears, he agreed to just one kid only. After Misha was born, he wanted me to get my tubes tied. When I refused, he went ahead and got a vasectomy. I wasn't happy with his decision, as I was hoping that he would get to love Misha and then agree to have one more baby. I guess that was when our marriage began to fall apart." Talking about the past was too emotional for Petra, and she started to cry. Anant hugged her and did his best to console her. Slowly, she recovered, went to the bathroom to wash her face, and joined him back on the couch and snuggled with him.

Anant said, "I better go home, Petra. Will you be okay?"

She didn't say anything, just got up, smiled, and took him up to her bedroom and closed the door.

6

Anant had to teach at nine, and after his class, he called Meena, but she was not in her office. So he sent her an e-mail instead. Then he met with his students to discuss a project they were working on, and by the time they solved some of the problems, it was lunchtime. Petra came in, and they went for lunch and sat with a bunch of other faculty members. The talk was all about the new science building. A few years back, the university received a donation of several million dollars, and the administration decided to build a new science building because most of the existing facilities were old and obsolete. Using the decrepit facilities, the faculty members in the science departments were doing their best to conduct their research and publish in good journals. The administration's plan was to construct a new building with state-of-the-art facilities and use it to attract well-funded scientists. There was an ongoing struggle between the administration and the science faculty about this issue. The faculty felt that, if they were allowed to move into the new building, it would give them a better chance at getting federal funds for their research. But the administration did not believe that even with better facilities the existing faculty could compete successfully for the limited federal funds. They were of the opinion that they needed to bring in fresh blood in order to attract more funds. The new science building was completed, and was named after the donor. The Doyle building was exclusive, and one had to have an access card to enter the building. At the cost of many millions of dollars, it was equipped with liquid scintillation counters, tissue culture hoods, centrifuges, spectrophotometers, mass spectrometers, fluorimeters, electron microscopes, imaging equipment, high-speed computers, and much more. In addition to the shared equipment rooms, there were four floors of laboratory space, enough to accommodate at least twenty investigators and their personnel. The building was all glass and steel and nicely furnished. There was a lot of space where the scholars could sit down and chat, and each floor had a break room equipped with a microwave and a refrigerator. The building had its own auditorium capable of accommodating a hundred people. It was inaugurated with a lot of hoopla, and the local media covered the event. The president, the provost, the dean and a lot of other administrators, local politicians, and Mr. Doyle and his family were present. There were speeches by the dignitaries extolling the philanthropy of the Doyle family and the various gifts that the family gave to the university during the past decades. The dean spoke about the high-quality research that would be conducted in the new building, and about the world-class talent that would be attracted by the state-of-the-art-facilities. The speeches were followed by a wine and cheese reception and a keynote address by a prominent cancer researcher who was flown in from California. After the lecture, selected guests were invited to a grand gala evening, filled with jazz and gourmet food and drink.

Once the dust settled, when the building was still empty almost three years after the inauguration, the authorities began to worry. It would be a public relations disaster if people found out that the university was not able to attract good scientists. Many young scientists with good grant money interviewed for the positions, but no one was interested in joining. Some of them didn't find the salary attractive enough, and others felt that Kansas was too isolated without top-class scientists to interact and collaborate with. Finally, the dean and his henchmen got a brilliant idea (at least they thought it was) to lure an aging and well-respected scientist from one of the Ivy League universities. They brought in professor Peter Stienhart, wined and dined him, and promised to give him whatever he wanted to start an Institute of Biotechnology in the Doyle building. They gave him complete freedom to hire anybody he wanted, and all the money he needed to attract young scientists. The premise was that with his reputation he would be able to entice good people from all over the country to join the new institute. In theory, it was a great idea, but Steinhart lacked vision and filled all the positions with his students and post-docs.

During the first couple of years after its establishment, the Institute of Biotechnology got a lot of publicity in the local and national press, and there was great hope that the university would at last be the hub of top-notch biotechnology research. But, alas, like all great-sounding ideas without a proper foundation, all those hopes were shattered and not even one of the scientists appointed by the great Steinhart managed to get federal grants for their research. They all were given a princely sum to start their research endeavors with the understanding that when they got grant money, they would not be dependent on the limited intramural funds. Steinhart drove a hard bargain in the beginning and consequently all his people were the fat cats of the campus, enjoying all the benefits of generous funding without getting a single penny from outside the university. Although Steinhart was untouchable at first, slowly a movement started among the faculty of other departments to censure Steinhart and his gang for their extravagant budget. The money that was given to the institute came out of the general budget of the university, at the expense of other departments. Every other department in the campus had to tighten its belt in order to support Steinhart's group, and right from the start, this led to a lot of resentment among the faculty. Now after a few years, when it was very clear that Steinhart and company were incompetent scientists incapable of supporting their research with extramural funds, all of those disgruntled faculty members began to make a lot of noise, and the dean found himself in a difficult situation. Some of the faculty members were well-established in the university, and they had a good rapport with the senior members of the university administration. They argued that the resources of the university were being drained and that something should be done to stem the hemorrhage. The university couldn't fire Steinhart, as he was hired at the full professor's rank with tenure. On the other hand, all his devotees were still on tenure track, and none of them would get tenure unless they got at least one major grant. As things stood, none of them had a chance to get money from any agency because they weren't even able to publish in top-class journals. It took almost four years for the dean to realize that Steinhart was a has-been, and that his ideas, while once popular, did not withstand the test of time. After spending millions of dollars on this futile undertaking, the dean was embarrassed and had to find another job at a different university. Nobody knew how he managed to get another position with his lousy record in Kansas. Then the president of the university had a meeting with the senior faculty members, and appointed one of them as an interim dean.

The new dean was given a clear mandate by the president to clean up the mess in the Institute of Biotechnology. First, he stripped Steinhart of all administrative powers and dismantled the Institute of Biotechnology. All the faculty in the Doyle building were attached to different departments, depending upon their background. When they were members of the Institute of Biotechnology, their teaching duties were minimal, as Steinhart argued that his people couldn't possibly waste time on teaching. Now all of them had to teach, and the money they could spend on their laboratory supplies was severely curtailed. As Steinhart didn't have any grant money, he was moved to the department of Biology to teach undergraduate courses. The Steinhart followers could see the writing on the wall, and they knew that the honeymoon was over. They all scrambled and soon found jobs either in the industry or at smaller community colleges. It took almost two years for the interim dean to undo the damage caused by his predecessor. Unfortunately, the Doyle building was again empty, and this time the dean met with the senior faculty members to formulate a realistic plan to make use of the Doyle building. They decided to bring into the building well-funded faculty members from various departments. These faculty members would still be answerable to their respective departmental chairmen and continue to fulfill their allotted teaching duties. In spite of this effort, the top floor of the building was still unused, as some faculty members decided to stay where they were in their old laboratory space. Generally, this method of rewarding well-funded professors with relatively new laboratory space was applauded by most of the university faculty members, and once again the campus was back to normal.

Petra peeped into Anant's office in the evening. "I have to take Misha to her ballet class, and after that, I have to baby-sit my neighbor's daughters, as she is going out with her husband. She promised to be back by nine. Do you want to come by after eight so that we can spend some time?" He said okay and she left. He made more revisions to a manuscript and talked to his students about some of the data and whether to include more data to make the manuscript more appealing to the reviewers. One of the students, Subash Shah, was ambitious and wanted to publish as many papers as possible. The girl, Yi Han, was laid-back. Anant recognized the difference between these two early in their careers and tried nurture them as best as he could. But sometimes when they worked together, it was difficult for Subash to slow down in order to accommodate

Yi. From the very beginning there was a clash of these two personalities, and it was amusing to watch them interact with each other. They each thought that the other was inferior. Subash, because of his command of English and much better knowledge, didn't respect Yi, and she resented it. Yi was pretty good, as she had impeccable laboratory skills, and did her work cleanly and promptly, and her data were perfect. In spite of his knowledge and better approach to problem-solving, Subash was a bit sloppy and careless in the laboratory and had to repeat the same experiment a few times, and losing precious time in the process. Apart from some housekeeping chores that they shared, they both had their independent projects and there was no need for them to interact on a daily basis. But, for the past few months, Anant wanted a new project done fast and he gave each of them different experiments, and met with them almost daily to help them move forward. This project was important to Anant, as he thought that if they could prove his hypothesis, they could build on it and write a grant proposal.

Anant went home, changed into his exercise clothes, and jogged his usual three miles. After showering, he made a cup of tea, and sat in the living room listening to the songs of Talat Mahmood. Sheila had made fun of Anant's taste in music. When at home, she never cared to listen to music and preferred watching TV, whereas music was essential for Anant. Before he had left for the United States, he had gotten his favorite songs recorded on tapes. In North Carolina, he purchased a portable tape player from K-Mart and played those tapes whenever he was at his apartment. He had tapes of Abba, the Carpenters, Engelbert, and Neil Diamond, and Hindi songs by Talat,

Hemant Kumar, Kishore Kumar, Rafi, Lata, and Asha. When he and Sheila moved to Kansas, he had installed his "music system" in the living room. Sheila knew the Hindi songs as her parents also listened to those, but she never cared for that kind of slow music and said it put her to sleep. She was into rock and roll and other modern American music. She had tapes of all kinds of singers that Anant had never heard of. The music was not melodious, the lyrics were difficult to understand, and it appeared that the singers relied heavily on instruments to enhance their songs, as though their vocal skills were not sufficient to capture the interest of their listeners. But he was smart enough not to tell this to Sheila as he didn't want to start an argument. So when they were together they listened to Hindi songs, and when Sheila drove to work she played her rock and roll music. He preferred the mellifluous songs of Lata or Talat to the yelling and screaming of rock and roll. When CDs became popular, Sheila insisted that they purchase a good music system so that he could enjoy his music.

Anant didn't want to spend money on an expensive system. "Sheila, the kind of music I listen to doesn't require CDs. My tape player should be fine."

"Sweetie, the quality of music is better when you listen to CDs. My parents bought a CD player and CDs of all their favorite Hindi songs. Now every Hindi song that was ever recorded is on CDs. My parents are ecstatic about the quality. The tapes go bad with time and they screech and sometimes get cut, destroying your songs. It seems that CDs are foolproof."

"Sheila, it will be expensive to switch over to CDs. The CD players are not cheap and we may have to spend at least fifteen dollars on each CD. I have so many tapes, and if I want to replace them with CDs it will cost a few thousand dollars."

"Sweetie, you are always worried about money. Surely we can afford to buy a CD player and some CDs. Don't worry about the money." Although in the beginning he complained about the expenditure, once the system was installed in the living room he began to enjoy his favorite songs.

It was a strange feeling to be in love with two women at the same time. In the past, when Anant was involved with Heather and Sheila at the same time, once he realized that he loved Sheila, he quickly dissociated himself from Heather. It was not because he was callous or didn't respect Heather's feelings. He felt that his relationship with Heather was not going any further. But now he felt passionate about both Petra and Meena, and he had no intention of dropping either one of them. But he was sensible enough to realize that one day in the not-too-distant future, he had to decide which one of the two beautiful women to give up. He had been tussling with this puzzle for the past few days, and had no idea how he would solve it without breaking anybody's heart. It was enough that he had broken the hearts of two good women—Heather's some ten years ago and Sheila's more recently. However much he wished that he didn't have this new problem in his life, he was glad that he and Petra had, at last, consummated their feelings for each other. He decided that in the next year he would make careful note of each and every facet of Petra and Meena in an effort to help him through the process of choosing one of them to be his wife. But the very thought of relinquishing one of the beautiful damsels was distasteful, and he wished for the very first time in his life that he was either a Mormon or a Muslim. It was a strange thought for someone who abhorred all religions. Even if he were to convert into one of those religions, what was the guarantee that the two women in question would go along with it and join his harem? After all, both the ladies were well-educated and emancipated, and it was highly unlikely they would consent to polygamy. Well, he thought, there goes one more of my pipe dreams.

Anant arrived at Petra's front door a little after eight and found the house peaceful. He wondered why the kids were so quiet. Petra told him that they were all upstairs playing in Misha's room. Petra was happy that they were all occupied and out of her way.

She asked him, "Did you eat your dinner?"

"This and that, I was not all that hungry."

"So you ate some junk food?"

He looked at her sheepishly. "Yeah, I had some chips and crackers and cheese."

"I feel terrible, my darling. I asked you come at eight so that the kids would all be fed and taken care of. I thought you will eat a proper dinner and come here. Let me get you something from the kitchen."

"Petra, don't worry about me. Sometimes I don't eat much for dinner. Come, let's sit and chat."

She took him into the den and gave him a glass of wine and they sat and watched a program about global warming on PBS. After some time, the doorbell rang and

Petra delivered the girls to her neighbor, put Misha to bed, and came downstairs.

"Anant, now I am all yours. Thanks for waiting for me to finish all my work." Without waiting for his answer, she took him to her bedroom, and he spent another night in her bed.

In the morning he said to her, "This is becoming a habit to me. I am spending every night with you. I am getting so used to you, I will have a tough time being by myself in New Jersey."

"Darling, you know you don't have to go anywhere. Just stay with me. Your Petra will take good care of you."

"I know, baby, I know that I am crazy, always chasing some phantom."

"My darling, speak plain English. Why do you talk all that literary mumbo-jumbo? Sometimes I think you would have been happier as an English teacher or a writer."

"Yeah, tell that to my father. He is the one responsible for my entry into chemistry."

"You don't like your father?"

"I don't dislike him, but as for love, I don't feel much for my parents. They both are hypocrites, always worried about their public image."

"You shouldn't talk like that about your parents. They must have taken care of you when you were little, and because of them you are here today. I love my mother and father. My father was a clerk in the government office and my mother never worked, she was not educated. She raised four kids, took care of my temperamental father, and that was a full time job. Oh! Enough of all that. I will tell you my life story some other time. I better go down and fix breakfast. Misha might be up by now."

Meena sent Anant an e-mail asking him to call her the next Saturday before noon. That weekend, after a late breakfast at Petra's, he went home and called Meena.

She was all upset. "How come it is so difficult to get you to call me? You were always so prompt with your phone calls before. Here I am, all lonely and waiting for you, and literally counting the days for your arrival, and you can't even call me once a day to say that you love me."

"Meena, I did call you at work but you were not in your office and I didn't have time afterwards to call you again. You know I am trying to take care of my students, teaching, and other work before I go off on my sabbatical. There is so much to do and I have maybe two or three months to accomplish everything. I am planning to take a couple of weeks off in December and January after the semester is over and plan to join your company in the second week of January. What do you think of the idea?"

"I don't like it that you won't be here with me for another three months. I am very lonely and miss you very much."

He didn't know how to placate Meena, as she appeared to be in a bad mood that day. He didn't enjoy talking to her when she was cranky. Ever since he changed his plans to go to New Jersey for a year to try out the industry job, she was acting grouchy.

"I miss you too. But we will see each other soon. I just got an idea. Why don't you join me for a vacation in Florida after Christmas? We can spend a few days together and after our vacation you can return to New Jersey, and I can go back to Kansas and get ready for my move to New Jersey. You think about it and send me an e-mail. I am afraid that I am going be very busy in the next couple of months and may not be able to call you that much. But we can keep in touch by e-mail."

"I don't know if I can take off so many days during Christmas holidays. Let me see my calendar and get back to you. Why don't you plan to come for a weekend here so that we can see each other?"

"I am sorry, I am too busy here to leave for a weekend. My students are working day and night to finish up their work, and if I am not here to help them, they will be demoralized and slow down. I don't want to deal with their experiments and data when I am in New Jersey. I want them to complete their laboratory work while I am here. The writing part we can handle by e-mail."

"Okay, what can I do? If your work is more important than me, I can't help it."

"Meena, baby, don't talk like that. You know I love you. Please cheer up. I will see you in three months. But if you decide to meet me in Florida, it will be great. Let me know. Now I better get going as I have to see my students in the lab."

"You are always running these days. Bye then. I will send you an e-mail."

He thought that at least the conversation did not end on a sour note. But he was surprised at her behavior this time, as usually she was fun to talk to.

It became a routine that he went to Petra's house for dinner and spent the night there. Some days when she agreed to baby-sit her friends' kids she would inform him ahead of time and he would go to her house around the time the kids were picked up by the parents. This was a necessary evil for Petra, as she also depended upon her friends to baby-sit Misha every once in a while. Also, they had a regular schedule of sleepovers for the kids at different houses, and this helped the parents to have a free night to themselves. Sometimes, when none of her friends were available to baby-sit Misha, Petra would pay a student to baby-sit. Misha was getting used to Anant's presence at the dining table at dinnertime as well as breakfast. She was a quiet kid and shy with most people except her mom. Petra told Anant that when she was alone with Misha, the kid would talk incessantly and tell her about everything she did that day.

Daytime would go by quickly for Anant with his teaching, students in the laboratory, and writing manuscripts. Lately, his conversations on the phone with Meena were short and to the point; he didn't have the time to chat with her for a long time as he used to before the advent of Petra into his love life. When he called Meena in the morning, she was either at a meeting or away from her desk. Most of his nights and weekends were spent with Petra and there was no way he could call Meena when Petra was around. He would blame it all on work, and Meena would be grumpy. But they exchanged e-mails on a daily basis, and this was the best he could do under the circumstances. Meena informed him that she couldn't take time off to join him in Florida. He was not too disappointed with her decision, as he suggested the trip mainly to mollify her, and it appeared to have served the purpose. The pace of work was relentless, and some days he was really tired. Subash and Yi were making good progress, and it appeared that they would complete the experimental part of their work soon. He was putting a lot of pressure on them, and they understood the need for urgency. He also encouraged them to apply for jobs as this was the best time to look for a teaching job. Their best bet was to find either a post-doctoral fellowship or a teaching position at a small college. As neither of them had a green card, it would be difficult for them find a job in an industry. Although there was a demand for organic chemists in the private sector, the companies were reluctant to sponsor a candidate for a green card as it was a lengthy and time-consuming process.

Misha was at a sleepover, and Petra asked Anant to come to her house for dinner. He felt bad, as she always cooked for him and he never did anything for her. So he suggested that they go out, but she said that she was not in a mood to sit in a restaurant. He understood that feeling, as sometimes after a heavy day, all he wanted was to sit back, relax, sip his drink and listen to music. He got a couple of bottles of wine and arrived at her house. Petra opened the door in her bathrobe, and it appeared that she just got out of the shower as her hair was still wet and there were a few water drops on her neck. She must have hurriedly dried herself, and come out to open the door.

He said, "I hope I didn't interrupt your shower. You know I could have waited a few minutes sitting on the porch."

"Oh, no, my darling. I was about to blow-dry my hair when you rang the bell. It's all right, come in."

"You look very beautiful with your wet hair, and without any makeup."

"You don't like me using makeup, my darling?"

"No, no, I don't mean it like that. What I wanted to say was that even without makeup, you look lovely."

He took her into his arms and kissed her. She was nude under the robe and with his body pressed tightly against her, Petra couldn't help but notice that he was aroused. She gave a coquettish smile and slowly released the strings of her robe to reveal her twin charms. He didn't need any further encouragement, and they spent a blissful hour luxuriating in the sensuality of their coupling.

Drenched in sweat, Anant commented, "We have known each other for about three months now and every time it is different and great with you."

With her head on his chest, Petra replied, "My darling, our newfound love is three months old only, but we have known each other for a long time. And that's why so fast we got this close. All those years, we didn't want to admit it to ourselves that we were in love with each other."

"You may be right."

"Your Petra is always right. Are you getting hungry?"

"Yes. But I don't want you to cook anything now. Let's order a pizza."

"You must not underestimate your Petra. I have already prepared everything and it will be ready in about half-hour. Come, let's go down and open a bottle of wine, and I will turn on the oven."

She took out two dishes from the refrigerator "The broccoli casserole goes into the oven, and the crab cakes will be cooked on the stove-top."

The crab cakes were delicious with Merlot, and by the time they finished the appetizers in a leisurely manner, the casserole was ready to eat. Petra was a fantastic cook;

everything she made was tasty. They didn't bother to sit at the dining table to eat their food. They took their food into the den and laid their drinks on the coffee table and had their dinner sitting close to each other on the couch.

Anant asked, "Petra, do you want to go to Florida in December, after we finish this semester?"

"You mean around Christmas time?"

"I thought we could leave right after Christmas day and return on January fifth or sixth."

"I usually go to the Ukraine every year in the first week of January for the Ukranian Christmas, and return a week after our New Year Day, which will be a week after our Christmas. So if we return from Florida on fifth, I can catch a flight the next day to Kiev. I guess that would be fine. Where do you want to go in Florida?"

"I thought we can go to Sarasota and take it easy there for a few days. But it will be hectic for you, because as soon as you return you have to catch another flight. All those days living out of a suitcase might not be great."

"You know, my darling, I don't mind it at all. It is no big deal. Anyway, the clothes I take to Florida will be different from the ones I carry to Kiev. When we return from Florida, all I have to do is a few loads of laundry, and I will be ready. Apart from the beaches, is there anything in Sarasota to see?"

"There are a lot of art galleries in town, and I think there is a museum. The beaches are quieter than the Atlantic side, and I hope that the water won't be too cold. We may not be able to go into the water, but at least if we can put our feet in the water and walk on the beach, that will be great. I think you and Misha will enjoy it."

"I wasn't thinking of bringing Misha with us. I think

she will get bored there. You know how kids are at that age, they want constant action, and Misha gets restless if she has to sit in one place and look at the sky. You and I can do that, we can gaze into each other's eyes and make love to each other without even touching our hands, which we did for a long time."

"But where will you leave Misha?"

"I am pretty sure my neighbor will be happy to keep Misha with her, and Misha plays well with her kids."

Their trip to Sarasota was fantastic, and it was the first time they spent a whole week, day and night, in each other's company without worrying about their students, teaching, phone calls, or other problems. Every day, Petra checked on Misha and spoke to her and was assured that she was happy and enjoying herself with her friends. They walked around downtown looking at various art galleries, went to the beaches, and took long walks, and saw the spectacular sunsets from both Siesta Key and Lido Key beaches. The weather was quite decent, but the water was still cold, and when they put their feet in the water, it took their breath away at first. They gradually got used to the cold temperatures and walked hand in hand. Petra asked, "You wanted to come here because you and Sheila were here a few years back?"

"No, not really. It is true we came here for our wedding anniversary. I wanted to come here not because I felt nostalgic, but because I like this place. It is very peaceful here, and if we can ignore the crazy traffic on Tamiami trail, this is a beautiful place to spend a week. I don't want you to think that I have Sheila on my mind all the time."

"No, I don't think like that at all. I simply asked. Please

don't mind my questions. Sometimes I get selfish and want you to be with me, erasing all those old memories. I know I am asking too much, and if you ask me to do the same thing, it will be difficult for me too. I guess we can't forget the past completely. It will always be there to haunt us."

"You are right, Petra. Come, let me buy you a nice sexy dress."

"You are not buying me anything, my darling. You have a lot of expenses ahead of you, and you better save some money. This trip was quite expensive, and you didn't let me spend even a penny on anything."

"Don't worry. You know next year I will get my full salary in Kansas, and at the same time I will also get paid in New Jersey."

"But still, you promised to come back to Kansas every month for a few days. That means flying and more money on airplanes."

"You are a worry-wart, Petra. I want to buy you a dress for purely selfish reasons. I know after we get it, you will model it for me and we will have a lovely evening."

"Anant, we don't need a new dress to have a great evening, but if it makes you happy, let's go get it."

They returned to Kansas to find gray and gloomy weather, and the temperatures in the twenties, and the bitter cold wind made it feel like they were in Siberia. Petra insisted that he spend the night with her.

He protested, "Petra, you must get some rest. If I sleep in your house, you won't get much rest in the night, and you have a long flight ahead of you tomorrow."

"My darling, I don't care for rest. I want you in my bed next to me so that I can touch you and sleep in your arms.

Don't worry, I will get a lot of rest once I reach my parents' house. My mother will spoil me and feed me all kinds of good stuff, and I will return to Kansas a lot heavier. When I come back I will have to starve and workout on my Nordic Track and lose all that weight."

He went to her house in the evening and helped her with laundry and packing, and for once Petra permitted him get a pizza delivered. Misha was happy with the pizza, and after eating she was put to bed, and Petra came downstairs to the den where Anant was relaxing with a glass of wine. She got her a glass, and they sat in companionable silence. He drew her close to him, and stroked her and kissed her. He could see that she was tired with all the work in preparation for her trip the next day. Luckily, she did all her shopping right after Christmas just before they left for Sarasota. But packing three suitcases loaded with all the gifts to her folks in Ukraine was time-consuming, and it took its toll on her.

Anant said, "Take care of yourself while you are there, and send me e-mails regularly. You know I would call you, but I hate to bother you when you are having fun there."

"No, my darling, to talk to you I will stop anything. I enjoy spending time with my people, but you are important to me. Please call me whenever you can. I will try to call you too, but I don't know whether you will have your cell phone with you. Most of the time it is either on your desk or in your car. But I will send you e-mails."

"That's settled, then. I will call you when I can, and you can send me e-mails."

"You promised that you will come back here every month to be with me. So you will be here in February?"

"Sure, I will be here. I can't wait to see you."

"Good, then let's go upstairs and make love all night. I have to be without you for almost two months. Do you think I can survive, my darling? I got so used to you in my bed at night time, it will be difficult again to sleep alone."

"I will miss you too, Petra. But I am sure we will manage."

The next day, he dropped them off at the airport and came back to his house. At the airport, Petra's eyes were red, and she hugged and kissed Anant. "Take care of yourself. Call me as soon you get to New Jersey. I will miss you."

Misha rolled her eyes at her mom's antics, and smiled at Anant. "Bye, Dr. Anant. We will see you soon." She gave him a big hug and a peck on his cheek. Petra gave him another big kiss and clung to him until the flight was announced. Then, reluctantly, she got hold of Misha and they went into the vestibule to board the aircraft.

Anant left a set of house keys with Petra and another with Kevin so that between them they could periodically check on the house to make sure the heating and plumbing were in good shape. He arranged with the electric and water company to forward the monthly bills to his New Jersey address. The mortgage payments would be automatically deducted from his checking account every month. He decided to disconnect his landline, as there was no point in keeping the telephone connection in the house when no one lived there. Actually, he should have gotten it disconnected right after Sheila left, as she was the one who used the phone most of the time. He was not sure what he should with his old car. He could leave it in the garage or simply sell it. When he checked the price that he would get by selling it himself, he found that it was worth almost nothing. He hated to sell it for such a small amount, assuming he found somebody to buy it.

During the past few weeks, communication with Meena had become rather sporadic as both of them were quite busy, she with her year-end stuff, and he with his usual struggle to get his manuscripts published in good journals. In spite of including the exciting data that Subash and Yi had produced, the manuscripts they submitted were not received enthusiastically by the reviewers, and Anant had no idea how to convince the skeptical reviewers that his paper was worth publishing. He knew that it was an uphill battle, but he was determined not to give up the fight. Last time, he had fought the mafia with professor Martin's help, but this time he had to do it all by himself. He and Petra discussed the project several times, and Petra was convinced that it was an important finding. He involved her in this venture because he felt that she would be able to take care of the day-to-day problems that his students might face in his absence, and this move turned out to be beneficial to everyone. Petra was a sentimental individual when it came to love, but she was sharp and critical at work. She was convinced that the compounds Anant's laboratory had produced might be useful in cancer chemotherapy. As soon as she saw the data, she suggested that Anant patent the compounds. This involved talking to the university officials and lawyers, and a lot of time was spent in convincing the bureaucrats, but in the end it was done. As most of the drugs that were currently in the market had unwanted side effects, Anant hoped to produce a series of compounds that were more active with fewer side effects. This was not a new idea, and many other laboratories were working on this concept, but Anant's approach was unconventional and seemed to work, as evidenced by the chemical and biophysical testing.

But the most crucial evidence that the compounds would work in animals was lacking. Since Anant's team was neither equipped nor knowledgeable enough to do biological testing, they approached Kevin. While the biological testing was being done in Kevin's laboratory, Anant wanted to publish the initial results with the synthesis of the new compounds, and he was running into difficulties with the reviewers. Since he would be leaving for New Jersey in less than a week, he went to Kevin's office for a chat. Kevin put two of his graduate students to work on the project, and Anant found that any experiment dealing with a biological system took a long time, compared to their work in the chemistry laboratory. Kevin explained patiently, "First, we tested your compounds in a series of cancer cells. These cells were obtained from human cancers such as breast, prostate or ovarian. By a special procedure, we made these cells grow in cell culture flasks, and when we had sufficient quantities of each type, we froze them in small aliquots and kept them in liquid nitrogen tanks for future use. This helps us ensure that we use the same cell type each time we test a particular compound. We grew these cells in Petri dishes and then hit them with your compounds. Some of your compounds were very active in these cell cultures. By active, I mean that extremely low concentrations of your compounds killed the tumor cells. This is encouraging. Next we will move on to experiments in mice. We have to induce tumors in mice and make sure that the tumors are malignant by biopsy, and this can easily take a few more months. Then we will inject your compounds to those mice tumors, and see the effect on tumor growth. Of course, we also have the control compounds that you gave us, and these should not interfere with the tumor growth, and the mice will eventually die. But we hope that the test compounds will arrest the tumor growth, and the mice will be back to their merry selves and have fun and games and produce little ones. We will periodically test the offspring to make sure they are healthy, and if everything is normal we are home free and you can get millions of dollars from the National Institute of Health." Anant then told him of his difficulties of getting the initial observations published. Kevin suggested, "Why don't you hold off until we have completed our biological experiments in the mice. If we succeed, then you can publish the whole thing in one big paper in a really first-class journal like *Nature* or *Science*."

It was every scientist's dream to publish in one of those two journals. For every manuscript that these journals accepted, there were probably thousands that were summarily rejected. Anant agreed, "Yeah, I think you have good point there. I am in a hurry to publish because my students are about to graduate and they will need publications in order to find good jobs. They have a few papers already but those are run-of-the-mill type. I was hoping this paper describing the various chemical steps in the synthesis of the compounds will give their job search a boost."

"I applaud your concern for your students. But you maybe fighting a losing battle with those reviewers. You must understand that those bastards are trying to delay your publication because they are probably trying the same thing that you have already done. Because you have already applied for a patent, I think you are safe. Let them delay the publication, but they can't steal your idea. Don't worry. Go to New Jersey and have some fun. We will keep in touch. I will let you know as soon as there is some progress. In fact, I am thinking of putting a third student on this project. I am sure Subash and Yi will give us more of those compounds when we need them."

Anant flew into the Newark airport on a Friday afternoon, and Meena was there to receive him. He hadn't seen her for almost three months, and it appeared that she had lost some weight.

He commented, "Are you dieting or what? I see your face is appearing drawn and you look thinner."

She looked at him accusingly. "What do you expect? You hardly talk to me anymore, and I am worried to death about you. Now that you are here, first thing you tell me is that I am looking ugly." She looked like she was about to cry.

He took her into his arms and kissed her firmly on her lips. "I am very sorry for neglecting you these few months, but we have been very busy in the laboratory."

He was glad to see her at the gate, and his heart was racing just like it did when he first received her in Kansas City. He held her gently and led her out of the terminal to her car. She was somewhat pacified and drove him to the apartment. She had gone to the trouble of furnishing the living room with a simple but elegant couch, a matching chair, a coffee table, and an adjustable floor lamp. Also in the living room was a Bose CD player. In the master bedroom there was a mahogany sleigh bed, matching side tables with reading lamps, and a chest of drawers. A cherry-wood desk and a swivel executive chair were placed in the spare bedroom. He told her in one of his e-mails not to spend a lot of money on the furniture, as he would go to the apartment only to sleep. It appeared that she had spent a bundle on furnishing the apartment with all brand-new stuff. He felt bad that she spent all that money on him.

He said, "Please let me know how much you spent. I would like to give you a check."

"Forget about the money. Do you like the furniture?"

"Yes, my dear, everything is terrific. But first tell me what's wrong with you. Is your health OK? Why do you look as though you haven't slept in weeks?"

"It is because I haven't slept in weeks."

"But why?"

"You are a *buddhu*, that's why."

She didn't let him talk anymore as she pushed him on to the bed, disrobed herself quickly, and stood in front of him. "Do you still think I lost weight?"

He also took his clothes off, then took her into his arms and said, "In order to answer your question, I have to examine you thoroughly." She was as sexy as ever, and when, as usual, she got on top and made love to him vigorously, all his worries about her health were dispelled.

In the evening she cooked a nice meal for them. She bought pots and pans, crockery and cutlery, and stocked the refrigerator and pantry with food, white and red wine, his favorite beer and whiskey. He was embarrassed at her generosity and thoughtfulness.

"Meena, you shouldn't have gotten all this stuff. It is my

job to get everything for us. You have already done enough by finding this apartment. Thank you for everything. Please let me give you a check for the money you spent."

"I don't like to talk about money. Keep quiet and enjoy it. You are crazy to think I will take your money."

She knew that he didn't like the way rice came out in a rice cooker, and that he preferred his rice somewhat firm and not like a paste. She made sambar and mixed vegetable curry and salmon in a ginger-garlic sauce. The food was delicious. While they were cleaning up, Meena said, "I will spend the weekend with you. My husband thinks that I am out of town on company work. So what do you want to do tomorrow and the day after?"

"I need to buy a car this weekend. I hope to find a good deal. If not, I may rent a car for a couple of weeks until I find a car that I can afford."

"Honey, I can pick you up every day and take you to work and drop you back here. You need not rent a car. As for buying one, take your time and don't hurry. If the car salesman knows you are desperate, he won't give you a deal."

"Shall we go to a car dealership tomorrow?"

"Sure, we can. What kind of car are you planning on buying?"

"I think I will go for a Japanese car. They are reliable and last a long time, like my old car."

"What did you do with that old car?"

"It is in my garage. I gave the car keys to my friend Kevin, and he promised to drive it every now and then to keep the battery charged."

"So what kind of Japanese car do you want now?"

"I am thinking of Toyota or Honda, something small that will give good gas mileage."

"Good, I thought you said that you will get a Lexus so that you can take me out in style."

"Yes, I did think of Lexus. But that was before I got this idea of sabbatical leave. Now that I have to go back to Kansas City often, I will be spending some money on travel. I am not sure if I can afford to buy a Lexus."

"I still don't understand why you suddenly changed your mind and started this sabbatical thing."

"I told you, Meena. I am scared of being jobless. The industry jobs are insecure. I know so many of my friends who go on switching jobs from one company to another every now and then. I am afraid that I can't do that."

"Honey, I am in the same company for the past fifteen years and I hope to work here for another twenty years or so."

"Well, let's see how I do here for the next few months, and then we will decide about the future. Dave may find me so useless, he may be glad to get rid of me after one year."

"No, honey, you underestimate yourself. Dave and his group think highly of your credentials and your publication record. They have high hopes for your success here."

Anant unpacked and put his clothes in the closet and set up his laptop on the desk in the spare bedroom. Meena told him, "You can connect your computer to Internet. I got a high speed Internet connection installed so that you can do your work from here. Also, I got CDs of all your favorite Hindi songs."

"I got some CDs too. Actually, I was planning to buy a small CD player after I settle down, but you beat me to it. You are too good to me. I don't think that I deserve so much generosity. You constantly amaze me with your thoughtfulness. I can never thank you enough for everything you have done for me."

She just smiled and kissed him. "I will make you pay for everything this weekend."

The next day, they went to a Toyota dealer and Anant test drove a Camry and a Corolla. He didn't care for all the bells and whistles, just a bare-bones model (he still remembered Martin's advice). Meena stood by his side patiently, and played the role of an obedient wife. Anant asked her if she wanted to test drive the car, and she declined. He found the Camry more to his liking, as it had more power and better pickup. Once he knew that he would buy a Camry, he started to negotiate the price. The salesman offered the car for a certain amount and Anant made a counter offer, and this went on for a while. Then the salesman brought the manager into the picture, and he gave Anant a new "rock-bottom price," which was still a little higher than what Anant had in mind. He was sure he could get the car for less, and so he told them he was going elsewhere and walked out.

Meena asked him "I thought that you liked the Camry. What is a couple of thousand when you are spending almost thirty-thousand dollars?"

"You are right. But why give them the money if we can get it for less?"

They were at the dealership for so long that they missed their lunch. Meena proposed, "Let's have a light snack now so that we can eat a good dinner." So they had a slice of pizza, and then drove home. Meena wanted to rest for a while, and went into the bedroom.

Anant said that he would catch up on his e-mails to his students. It appeared that his students were doing fine, as he didn't have any e-mails from them.

He did have a message from Petra:

My dear Anant:

Why are you not calling me or writing to me?
Did you reach safely to New Jersey?
Misha is having a good time here with her cousins. They can't speak much English and Misha's Ukrainian is not all that good, so it is fun to watch them trying speak to her. My parents are fine and they are happy to see me and Misha. But they worry too much that I am single. They think I need a man to take care of me and Misha. I didn't tell them about you. Maybe I will tell them once you are back from your sabbatical.
I love you, my darling and I miss you in my bed. Every night I think of your loving touch and remember our romps in the bed. I need you very badly.
Please come to Kansas as soon as we return.
Love Petra

First he wanted to call her, but was afraid to wake her up as it would be the middle of the night in the Ukraine. So he sent her an e-mail.

My dear Petra:

It was so sweet of you write to me in spite of your busy life there with your folks. I love you very much. But I was busy, what with packing and all that. I got here on Friday, and am getting set up in the apartment. I will write whenever I can. It is going be too hectic in the company, as I have to start some new projects here. I will try to call you also but the time difference may make it difficult for us. Please bear with me. Once you get back to Kansas we should be able to talk.

Take care and say hi to Misha.

Love,

A

Then he worked for an hour or so on the manuscript Subash had given him before he left Kansas. Meena came over in her robe and hugged him. "Are you busy, honey?"

"No, not much. I am trying to work on this manuscript that my student gave me before I left. It is in a pretty good shape. I can work on it tomorrow, there is no big hurry. Come to me, baby."

He took her onto his lap and kissed her neck and stroked her hair.

"I love it when you do that."

By the time she said it, one of his hands was inside her robe.

He teased her. "Do what, this or that?"

She shuddered at his touch. "Both, you horny bastard!"

"Does it mean you are horny too?"

"You are always asking me dumb questions."

The entire Sunday they didn't do anything but laze around the apartment, making love whenever they felt like it and eating when they were hungry. Somehow Meena found time to cook mouth-watering food and offered the delectable dishes and herself at regular intervals. Anant paid homage to her opulent charms as well as to her culinary skills. She slept with him on Sunday night, and they went to work together on Monday morning.

Dave introduced Anant to everyone in the group. He had already met some of them when he came for his interview, and some were new to him. They all welcomed him aboard and offered to help him get adjusted. Dave showed him a small office with a computer, a filing cabinet, and a bookshelf. "This is your office. I hope it is adequate. Unlike in the universities, here we have a space crunch. When I was a post-doc at Princeton, our laboratory was huge. We also had nice office space for all the post-docs. We even had big windows in the lab and our office. Here, everything is so cramped, and very few offices have windows. You should have your e-mail account set up today." Then Dave met with Anant and a couple of senior scientists for an hour or so, mainly to acquaint Anant with their projects and also to give him a chance to learn about the way they approached problems in the industry. Dave told Anant, "I see your role in our group as a trouble-shooter. You are too experienced to waste your time doing experiments in the lab. All I want is for you to talk to all the senior people regularly and get to know what they are doing, and give them advice when they need it." Anant was fine with the idea, plunged himself into work, and within a few weeks became knowledgeable of all the projects. The company's focus was development of AIDS and cancer drugs, and they were constantly looking to improve the existing formulations. The research work at the company was pretty routine, mainly designing, synthesizing and screening thousands of compounds using biochemical, biophysical and biological assays. Dave's group produced the compounds, or sometimes modified the chemical structure of commercially available compounds, and then used molecular modeling to predict which of them might be active. Then the compounds were sent to various divisions for testing, and the division heads met once a month to compare notes. It was a time-consuming job, and sometimes after months of hard work they got nothing. But once in a while they found an active compound, which would give them the impetus to go on searching for more active compounds. Most of Anant's time was spent in meetings and planning new strategies to design compounds that might eventually be useful.

When they found the time, Anant and Meena went to another Toyota dealer, and this time since he already knew what he wanted, it was less time-consuming and he found a Camry that was fully loaded with all kinds of options he didn't need. Since the car was a demonstrator and had a couple thousand miles on it, the salesman agreed to give Anant a decent discount, and Anant became the proud owner of a new car. After buying the car, he went grocery shopping. It was an entirely different experience, going to the grocery store in New Jersey. The first time he went to the store with Meena, he was shocked that one had to put a quarter in the cart stand to release the shopping cart; after the shopping was done, the quarter was returned when the cart was placed back where it belonged. He had never had to do that in North Carolina or Kansas. From this he concluded that the people in New Jersey were so unruly that this was the only way to make them behave. Meena was particular which supermarket he should go to, and she gave him a list of items that she needed for her weekend cooking. Since he ate a big lunch in the company cafeteria, he didn't really care to eat dinner; most nights, he had a snack and hot chocolate before going to bed. Meena didn't approve of his eating habits and would give him lectures about eating small portions three or four times a day. She was a health freak, and read all kinds of magazines about fitness and diet. So she made it a point to cook for him during the weekend. He felt bad that she had to cook at two households during the weekend. He knew that she came to the apartment after cooking for her son and husband. He told her many times that when she came to the apartment she should simply relax and shouldn't worry about cooking. But she would say, "Honey, I want to keep you healthy for the next forty years at least. Please cooperate with me. I love to cook for you, and when you enjoy my food it gives me great satisfaction." Some days, Meena came to the apartment in the evening after work and they spent some time together. But most often she went home, and after finishing her evening workout and dinner, she dropped in for a few hours, and went back to her house at midnight. Her husband was under the impression that she went back to her office to catch up with her work. Most weekends, she arrived at the apartment around noon on Saturday, left in the evening, and returned Sunday morning. Sometimes she spent the entire weekend with him starting Friday evening, and went to work on Monday morning directly from the apartment. She did this frequently, and Anant would wonder why her husband didn't suspect something was amiss. But as long she was happy, he didn't bother about it. Meena was kind and considerate and never intruded on his space. She respected his privacy and never came into his study without knocking. Likewise, although she slept with him in the same bedroom, she always kept her toiletries in the guest bathroom. At dinnertime, she had a quaint habit of serving him first and then helping herself. He knew that this was the custom in India where men were always served first. To observe those old-fashioned customs in this enlightened country where women were completely emancipated was baffling to Anant, but he never criticized her actions.

The manner in which Meena treated him was such a contrast to Sheila's behavior, particularly during the latter part of their marriage. The busier Sheila had gotten at her office and hospital, the more she expected Anant to be responsible for the household chores such as laundry, washing dishes, paying bills, and balancing bank accounts. All these jobs took time to complete, and it invariably cut into his free time. If he didn't keep her favorite bath towel in the bathroom, she would raise hell. "Why can't you do such a simple thing like putting my towel where it belongs? I work so hard and come home, and you expect me to look through the linen closet?" Sometimes, she would come home in the evening and demand tea, and he had to prepare the tea and place it by her chair. Most often she never acknowledged his help, and went on reading her journals. At dinnertime, it was he who took the soup out of the refrigerator, heated it, and placed it on the table. It was he who heated the bread rolls and applied butter. When he called her for dinner, she would come and, instead of thanking him, make remarks such as, "The soup is cold, you put too much butter on my bread." Sometimes, when he was working on a manuscript or a grant proposal, he would ask her to clear the dishes after dinner, and she would go crazy and make a mess in the kitchen, bang the dishes and mutter to herself. She behaved as though he was there just to wait on her. Many times he was sorely tempted to leave her and get an apartment and file for a divorce. But he somehow controlled himself and put up with her inconsiderate behavior until he finally decided to leave for good. That she worked hard and did her best for her patients was undeniable. But this hard work took its toll on their marital life, and led to a lot of rift and resentment.

Whenever Meena was with Anant in the apartment, she conducted herself as though she was his wife. He had no doubt in his mind that she loved him completely, without any reservations. But his feelings towards her were ambivalent because of her reluctance to move away from her husband. He couldn't understand why she should stay in that house with her husband and son, and not move in with him permanently, pending the divorce. Her son was almost eighteen and was capable of taking care of himself. She always said that she would file for a divorce as soon as her son entered college, which should be in the fall. Anant was impatient at this strict adherence to a set time frame, since he felt that even after she moved in with him, she could still visit her son and make sure he was doing okay. Whenever he brought up the topic of her divorce, there was a certain amount of reluctance on her part to discuss the matter, and invariably he lost his temper and would say things like, "If you really love me, you will move in with me completely and not live this kind of life, partly here and partly there and no one is satisfied with this arrangement." At this she would burst into tears and sob loudly, and her eyes would become swollen and red. He hated to see her cry and would go into his study and do his work. After one of those outbursts, she left the apartment and he didn't see her for a few days. She returned after a few days and apologized for her behavior, and they embraced and made up.

Anant did his best to go to Kansas as frequently as he could. The purpose, ostensibly, was to follow the progress of his two students. But there was really no need for him to go there in person, as he could very well get their data by e-mail and speak to them by telephone. Petra and Kevin kept him abreast of the progress in that project as well. Petra kept pestering him to come to Kansas in every e-mail she sent, and when they spoke on the phone, she was insistent that he join her soon. She was lonely and missed him a lot. So, after working for two months, Anant took a few days off to spend some time with Petra. She told him that he better stay with her at her house; there was no point in his going to his house, as it had to be cleaned, and all the dust covers removed from the furniture. He agreed to her proposal and was glad to see her at the airport gate with a smile on her beautiful face. She kissed him repeatedly. "Oh, my darling, You don't know how much I missed you all this time. I thought that you would be back here as soon as I returned from Kiev, but you couldn't, and I was so disappointed that I cried all night thinking of you. I am so glad you are back." She got so emotional that her eyes were red and full of tears.

He took her into his arms and kissed her passionately. "Baby, I too missed you, but you know how it is, I couldn't take leave so soon after joining, and they are really making use of me there. I never thought that I can be of any use in the industry."

She took him home, and they had lunch and talked. She said, "I am not going to the lab for the next few days, and I want to be with you during these few days that you are here. I have to teach on Monday and Wednesday, and those two days I will give my lectures and come back home. My students know how to get hold of me."

Anant was glad to be with her and to be back in the familiar surroundings. He asked Petra, "Can you take me to my house? I want to get my car out so that I can drive to the university by myself."

"So soon! You love your old car more than your Petra. I will take you wherever you want. But first relax with your Petra, come upstairs with me."

She took him to his house in the evening and he got his car out of the garage and was glad to see that it still drove well. Petra told him, "Why don't you go to your lab and meet the students and come back home in a couple of hours for dinner."

Subash and Yi were happy to see Anant, and they discussed the pending manuscripts and the *in vivo* project with Kevin. Anant told them that he would meet with Kevin the next week. He told them that they must start writing their dissertation in the next month or so and also begin to apply for jobs. It was good to see them and be back in his office.

He went to a liquor shop and got a case of Petra's favorite wines, and then drove to her house. She was almost done with her cooking and was going upstairs for a shower.

She asked, "Are you going to have a shower before dinner?"

"Are you inviting me to have a romantic shower with you?"

She blushed. "Of course, I welcome you everywhere, my shower, my bed. You know I am yours completely."

They had a nice evening together, with good food, wine, and lots of cuddling and kissing. It was so good to be with Petra, without worrying whether she would spend the entire night with him. Petra gave him her undivided attention, and he felt secure knowing that he would see her in the morning next to him in the bed. They both got up late, ate a leisurely breakfast, and went for a long walk all bundled up to ward off the biting cold wind. When they got back home, they were cold and Petra's face was flushed and almost red. He started the fireplace, and they sat down in front of it and drank hot chocolate.

Petra asked, "Are you going to stay in New Jersey for the complete year, or is there any chance of your returning sooner?"

"I think I should stay the full year as I promised Dave that I would. I think they are getting their money's worth by keeping me in the company. Also, I am beginning to enjoy the challenge of making commercially useful compounds. Here we always plan our experiments in such a way as to get data for a good manuscript. There in the industry they don't care about papers. They always worry about the economic impact of their discovery."

"I hope you are not falling in love with the industry, Anant. I will be miserable if you decide to stay there permanently."

"Don't worry, Petra. I was just telling you how it is there compared to the academia."

Kevin, Petra, and Anant met for lunch on Monday. They all discussed the progress of the *in vivo* work. Kevin told them, "I think we made some progress in the past few months. We can now induce tumors in mice, and once the tumor reaches a particular size, the mice succumb to the tumor and eventually die. The next step is to decide when to give the test compounds and monitor the tumor growth. We are thinking of testing the most active compounds first. The plan is to administer the compounds to mice at different stages of tumor development. We also have to play with the dose of the compounds and test them in mice with different sizes of tumors. There is a lot of work to be done, and I am glad that you both are helping me with money from your grants to purchase mice. My grant is going to end by next year this time. I submitted a renewal application last month, I don't know what will happen."

Petra told him, "You are doing interesting work. I think you have a good chance at getting your grant renewed."

Anant said, "It is tough, but you can only do so much. After that, why bother?"

Kevin said, "Enough of all this. Tell me how it is in New Jersey. Do you like it there? Are the natives friendly? Did you meet any sexy women?"

Anant said, "I like working in the industry. It is an entirely different ball game. But I really don't like living in

New Jersey. The only thing good there is the weather. People there are in a perpetual hurry, always running red lights and going at breakneck speeds. Whenever I drive, I am sure to get at least two or three honks from irate drivers. They don't like my driving, as I always drive at the speed limit. Even the expensive restaurants are not all that great, the food barely edible and the service terrible. Can you believe it, they serve bread pudding cold, they take it out of a refrigerator? I never had cold bread pudding here or in North Carolina."

Petra looked at him. "You won't be happy there, Anant. I think it's too crowded for you."

Kevin interjected, "I think Petra is absolutely right, Anant. Do you know that in Kansas there are only thirty people for every square mile, and in New Jersey there are eleven-hundred people for square mile? You are seeing for yourself what happens when you have too many people in a small area. They are anxious, angry, and always in a hurry to get nowhere. It's no different from the mice in the cages. When we keep two per cage they are happy, and when we keep four or more per cage, they fight all the time and scratch each other."

Anant said, "You know, Kevin, I want to agree with your hypothesis, but when I think about my hometown, Hyderabad, it's more crowded than New Jersey, and people there don't behave so badly. I am not sure if it is population density alone. In Hyderabad, in some areas it's so dense you can't even walk without brushing against another person."

Kevin said, "You don't have so many cars in India. If it is only people, they just avoid each other and go their way. But if they are in cars, it's different. When you put a nice human being in an automobile, he or she has the potential to become a demon."

Anant returned to Kansas in late April for a few days and stayed with Petra and Misha. Misha was getting used to Anant, and looked forward to his visits, as he asked her about her activities and always got her a small gift. In the beginning, Misha wasn't sure how to conduct herself with Anant. But slowly she warmed up to him and talked to him about her school, and her hobbies, and many other things. Petra liked that Anant was nice to Misha.

"I enjoy spending time with her, Petra. She is a smart kid, and I like talking to her."

When they went for walks, Anant would ask Misha to join them, and the kid liked to hold Anant's hand. When they went out to eat, Anant made sure that they took Misha, and the little girl enjoyed the outing and was always well behaved. All in all, she was a happy child.

Petra picked Anant up at the airport, and took him to his house first to get his car out of his garage. They went to Petra's house, and after spending some time with her, Anant went to his lab to meet with Subash and Yi. The students were working hard and were almost through with their experiments, and were now spending more time on writing their dissertation. They talked about their job applications and possible dates for their thesis defense.

Anant said, "It looks like both of you should be ready to defend your thesis by this summer, what do you think?"

Subash agreed. "I think I can do it, Dr. Prasad. But if I graduate in summer and have no job by that time, how can I survive? You know, once I graduate my teaching assistantship will come to an end."

Anant didn't want him to worry. "I thought about it. I have kept some money from our grant for paying you and

Yi until you guys find a job. I am sure that both of you will get good jobs soon."

Yi said, "I am slow in writing. I don't know if I can complete my thesis by this summer."

Anant knew her problem. "I think you will be fine. Write what you can, and I will do my best to help you. Both of you should e-mail me whatever you write every week, and I will do the corrections and send it back to you. But in the meantime, apply to as many jobs as you can. You must remember that it is very competitive out there, and unless you try hard it will be difficult to find a good position. Try for all kinds of jobs—teaching jobs in small colleges, post-doctoral positions, and industry jobs. I want both of you to give me your resumes so that I can circulate them in the New Jersey company. But you know it will be difficult to find a job in the industry due to your visa status. As both of you are on a student visa now, your prospective employer should agree to sponsor you for a H1 visa, and many industry people are not willing to go out of their way to hire foreigners. But we will see."

In the evening, Anant returned to Petra's house, and after dinner, Petra put Misha to bed and came downstairs.

Petra said, "We will meet with Kevin tomorrow at lunch. I am sure he e-mailed you about the new data they got last week."

"Yeah, it is very exciting. Our compounds seem to stop the growth of the tumors in mice. But I think we should all look at the data carefully, and decide the next step."

"I teach tomorrow until noon, and after that I am completely free. Enough of all this talk about work. My darling, I missed you very much these few months. It is getting more difficult without you by my side. Last time you came it was for such a short time, and now you are leaving also after a few days with me."

"Petra, even if I am away, I still think about you and Misha. You know I love you very much. I wish I could stay a little longer with you, but I can't get that much vacation time. But I will be back in the summer for the defense of Subash and Yi."

Anant woke up first in the morning, and saw Petra asleep with her back to him. He admired her straight back, the curve of her waist, and the ample but firm hips and thighs. It was a pleasure just to watch her sensuous body, a pleasure that he was not ready to give up. He remembered fondly how difficult it was in the beginning of their relationship to convince Petra to take off her pajamas. She would insist on coming to bed with her night clothes on and remove them only after she was under the covers. After they made love, she went to the bathroom, washed herself, brought a warm washcloth, cleaned him, and then promptly put on her pajamas and slept.

Anant had told Petra, "Baby, please don't wear anything when we sleep together. I like to sleep nude, and when I touch you in the middle of the night, I hate to feel all those clothes instead of your silky skin."

"But my darling, I got used to wearing pajamas to bed ever since I was little. I don't think I can sleep nude."

"Please try to sleep for a few nights without your pajamas, and if you can't get used to it, you can go back to wearing them, okay?"

Petra did her best to please him and in this instance he was glad that she listened to him. In the middle of the night,

Anant would touch her and stroke her, and this would lead to some interesting romantic interludes. He slept on his back, and didn't normally move in his sleep, whereas Petra always slept on her side, either facing him or with her back turned towards him. When he woke up in the morning, he would gently massage her hips, thighs and other strategic areas with his right hand. She would then wake up and stretch languorously and snuggle up to him. Invariably this led to a marvelous quickie. This morning too, his touch had the desired effect on this gorgeous woman.

Afterwards she said, "My darling, with your love you are spoiling me. I hate it when you leave me all lonely and cold in my bed."

"I will be back. I will still be here for a few more days. Why don't we enjoy the time instead of worrying about the future?"

"You always talk about the present, and I think about the future constantly. I better go down and make breakfast. Why don't you sleep for a little while and come down?"

She got out of bed, wore her robe and went downstairs. Lying on the bed, Anant thought about his early mornings with Sheila.

In the beginning of their relationship, Anant and Sheila rarely got out of bed in the morning without having a quickie. One Sunday morning, after a relatively longer session, he explained, "You know, baby, the morning time is the best for me as the testosterone levels are still high. The nocturnal peak of luteinizing hormone drives the production of testosterone in the testis, and leads to some interesting consequences as you just experienced."

She playfully chided him, "You and your goddamn lectures, stop it. I know all about it. God only can save me, all this experimenting on my body with your nocturnal peaks. Since when you have become an expert in the male reproductive system?"

"My roommate in Bangalore was a reproductive biologist, and he told me about stuff like that."

"Why did you even talk about such things? Didn't you have more interesting stuff to talk about, like girls?"

"Yeah, we talked about girls. But reproductive biology was also an interesting topic. He was always going to the lab at five in the morning, and when he got up I also would be up, as I couldn't sleep anymore once I was awake. So one day I asked him why he went to the lab so early. He took me to his lab and told me all that stuff about testosterone peaks and said that he had to check on the female mice every morning to identify those that might be pregnant."

"How could he tell that the females were pregnant?"

"You see, he would go to the lab every evening and keep one male mouse with two female mice in each of some twenty cages. In the morning when he looked at the females he could determine which ones might get pregnant."

"How could he tell just by looking?"

"That's interesting. He would hold the female in one hand and using blunt forceps open up its vagina, and looked for what he called a vaginal plug. When they had some white stuff in and around the vagina that meant that they had had intercourse. All those mice with plugs would be kept separately, and by day eight or so one could tell whether they really got pregnant because they will be much bigger. You must understand that the gestation period of a mouse is around twenty days. Generally most females with plugs do get pregnant, and if some didn't, they would be removed from the pregnant group and rebred."

"Where is your friend now?"

"He went to California to do his post-doc, and last I heard he was working for some pharmaceutical company there. I lost touch with him."

Sheila and Anant had such wonderful times, playing with each other, teasing each other, and making love. The thought of those joyous days brought tears to his eyes. He never understood why Sheila became so refractory, and stopped reciprocating to his overtures. Whereas in the first few years she was always receptive and never said no to anything he did or suggested, towards the end of their marriage she became difficult to deal with. Even when he simply touched her shoulder or back, she would recoil and shun him. There were a lot of couples without children, and not all of them ended up in getting a divorce. He suspected that Sheila's behavior had a lot to do with some chemical imbalance in her brain rather than her disappointment with her inability to have children. Whenever he suggested that she see a psychiatrist, she got angry and said, "You have never understood me. All you care is about sex, sex, sex."

Petra and Anant went to Kevin's office after lunch and looked at the data. Kevin showed them the pictures of mice with tumors, and pictures of animals after treatment with the test compound. There was a dramatic reduction in tumor size in those mice treated with the compound. The animals were then sacrificed, and their kidneys and livers were examined by histopathology. Anant asked him how they did this testing. Kevin replied, "At the dose we gave, the mice showed remarkable progress. Their tumors disappeared completely, and for all practical purposes they seemed healthy. But we asked a question: Did the drug cause any damage to these their kidneys and livers? Unfortunately, in order to answer the question, we had to sacrifice the animals. We then took out the kidneys and livers out of the mice and sent them to a pathologist for an examination. The compound, at the dose we administered, had no effect on the cellular structures of either kidney or liver. We have some more drug-treated mice in our colony, and these are being constantly monitored for their kidney and liver function. We draw blood from these mice, and send it for biochemical testing of various proteins and enzymes which are important in kidney and liver function. We will do this testing for about a month or so, and if all the tests are negative, that means that both the organs are functioning well. We have another batch of drug-treated mice that are housed with normal female mice, and we are monitoring the ability of the drug-treated male mice to impregnate the females. Once the pups are delivered, we will keep the mother and pups in a separate cage and monitor their health as well. This will take a few more months."

Petra asked, "Why are you testing the compound in male mice only, and not in female mice?"

Kevin smiled. "The male system is simpler than the female body. When we work with females, we have to take into consideration their estrous cycle and the concomitant hormone surges. This can sometimes confound our drug trials, and that's why we chose to work with males. Eventually, the drug has to be tested in female mice. But first if we succeed in the male mice, we can report that the compounds are efficacious in cancer treatment."

Anant asked, "So, do you think with this new data we can rewrite our manuscript and submit it to a good journal?"

Kevin said, "Absolutely, just give me another two or three months. I will make sure all the data is reproducible, and meanwhile, we will monitor how the new pups and their mothers are doing. This is going to be an exciting manuscript to write. Where do you want to send it, Anant?"

Anant looked at Petra. "What is your idea?"

"This is a very important finding. I don't know of any other active compound that can fight cancer in such a dramatic manner. The data is convincing. I think we should write first a short manuscript, and send it to *Nature*, and then immediately follow it up with a detailed manuscript to *Journal of Experimental Medicine*. I think we should also use this data to submit a grant proposal to National Institute of Health. The next deadline is June and now it is April. That means we have roughly a month to put together a proposal. I think that if the three of us work hard, we can do it."

Kevin said, "Boy, if we get money, we can move into

the Doyle building. I will be surprised if they don't give us space in that building."

Petra shrugged, "I like where I am right now. I know that our building sometimes leaks when it rains heavily and the plumbing needs constant attention, but I got used to it for the past eight years. I am not sure that I want to move everything and go to the Doyle building."

Anant understood her concern. "Well, we don't have to think about lab space right now. First we have to do a lot of work and submit the grant and the manuscripts."

The next day was his birthday, and he was leaving for New Jersey by the afternoon flight. Petra got up in the morning and came to him. "Happy birthday, my darling."

"Thanks."

"Today, you are not going anywhere near the department. I want you all to myself. After breakfast, I will send Misha off to her school and then we can spend a few hours together before I take you to the airport." She made a lot of fuss, baking him a cake and cooking a nice lunch, and cried when he was going to board the airplane. That's typical of Petra, he thought. On the flight to Newark, his thoughts were on the birthdays that he was with Sheila.

Sheila and Anant had been sleeping in separate bedrooms for the past few years. Their divorce was supposed to be finalized in a few days. Anant told his attorney that he didn't want to subject Sheila to any courtroom nonsense. The attorney assured him that Sheila didn't have to appear before the judge, as the divorce was not contested. Anant would meet the judge in a conference room and answer a few questions, and it would be over in a few minutes. A week before his divorce, he woke up one morning in April and realized that it was his birthday. They never did anything for their birthdays, as neither of them really cared. In the first few years, they had given each other funny cards, but they never made a big deal about it. Most of the time, their birthdays happened to be on a weekday, and it was difficult to do anything or even to go out to eat on a weekday due to Sheila's busy schedule. So they postponed the birthday celebrations to the weekend and went to a nice place on a Saturday evening for a relaxed lunch or dinner. As usual, he got up and did his exercise, and he woke her up and went downstairs. She always left for work a lot earlier than he did, and this day was no exception. He went to work, taught his classes, took care of business in the lab, and went home in the evening. He was surprised to find Sheila's car in the garage, as she never got home before seven. When he went in, she was working furiously, mixing flour, sliced apples, cinnamon, nutmeg, oil and sugar in a dish.

He asked, "How come you are home so early?"

"I took the afternoon off and came home early to bake a cake for your birthday."

"That's sweet of you. There is no need for you take the trouble."

"I never did anything for all your birthdays all those years. I thought that this is the least I can do." Saying that, she rushed into the powder room and closed the door. He could hear her crying and felt sad for her.

Once Anant returned to New Jersey, everything became hectic, his own work on the grant proposal, the two manuscripts, his students' thesis, and his work at the company. Most of his day was taken up by looking at chemical structures designed by the chemists, and the data obtained with those compounds. He had to go through the information and give his input so that they could improve the chemical structures, to make them more active. Sometimes his suggestions yielded good results, but in many cases it didn't help. They all understood that it was the nature of the business they were in. But even if one compound made it to the final stage, that would make a lot of money for the company. Consequently, Anant was overworked and had very little time for himself. However, he still managed to jog his usual three miles every day and sleep at least five hours at night. Meena came whenever she could, and they spent some time together. But more often than not, he was tied up with his writing and she left him alone. When she spent the night at the apartment, she waited for him to come to bed, and they made love and went to sleep. It was a mechanical act to fulfill each other's needs and lacked the intensity they felt at the beginning of their relationship. But they still cared for each other.

After a lot of editing, innumerable e-mails, and telephone calls, Anant, Petra and Kevin completed the grant proposal. They were almost ready to submit the grant proposal, and were all doing the final revision when Petra called Anant. He was concerned as she was calling him late at night. "Hi, Petra, what's happening, are you okay?"

"I am fine. Did I wake you up?"

"No, I am still working on the final draft of the grant. I am almost done. I think it looks good."

"Anant, I called about the grant. I think you should not include my name as a co-investigator in the grant. It is your idea, and most of the work was done by your students, and the biological testing was done by Kevin's group. My contribution is really nothing."

Anant was upset at this last-minute decision by Petra. "Petra, you are helpful to the project. I don't think that we would have made this much progress without your input. At every stage, you have given such good advice, and your critical analysis of data helped us to see the pitfalls. Please don't drop out. I need you to participate in this project."

"You know I am always available to you, and I will do my best for the project. Can't you put me down as a consultant instead of an investigator?"

Anant was vehement in his opposition to her idea. "Petra, please understand. I need you as an investigator. The budget we have written is for running three labs, not two. If you back out now, we have to change everything, and it's going to take a lot of time, and we don't have the luxury of time at this eleventh hour."

"I know that. But I don't want you to include my name as an investigator because of our personal relationship."

Only then did it occur to him that Petra was concerned that their affair could be a factor in his decision to give a third of the grant money to her lab. His respect for Petra increased by a thousand times right at that instant.

He was decisive and swift. "Petra, I love you very deeply.

But that's not the reason for involving you in this grant. I know you are more valuable to me than a grant proposal. What we have between us is more important than any of these papers in *Nature* and grants. I honestly believe that your scientific knowledge and input will be very useful in conducting the work when, and if the grant proposal is approved and funded. Petra, without your advice, there was no way we could have designed a compound that is so active. Most of the chemistry was your idea, not mine. I only got the broad idea, but you have contributed in an enormous way by deciphering the chemical structures, and without your encyclopedic knowledge we couldn't have synthesized these compounds. Petra, if you drop out, there will be no grant. I refuse to submit it without you as a full-fledged investigator."

When he put it so strongly, Petra couldn't do anything but agree. "I am sorry if I upset you. I don't want you to worry about it. Let's submit it as it is. I want to thank you for your decency. You are one in a million. But I still think my contribution is not all that significant."

He was glad that Petra was on board, and that they completed the work on time, and all that was left was getting the administrative officials to sign off on the proposal, prior to its submission to the National Institute of Health.

The next day, just before lunch time, Petra called Anant all angry and upset. She said, "Mao is blocking our grant. He is refusing to sign it, and unless he signs off on it we can't take it to the grants office for the approval by the vice president for research."

Anant was surprised at this news. "But why is he doing

that? He has no business to block the grant. It is surprising that he is acting so crazy."

"Oh, he is saying that he doesn't want trashy proposals submitted from his department. He says that he made a new policy that all grant proposals going out of the department should be peer-reviewed by two faculty members in the department, and only after we incorporate their suggestions will he sign."

"I am not sure anybody in our department is competent to review our grant. They all are either analytical chemists or material science people."

"That's what I told him, but he is sticking to his guns. I called Kevin, but he is teaching and will only be back after an hour or so. I thought that in the meantime I can ask your advice. There is no time at all for any peer-review. I never heard of such a crazy idea. The chairman can't impose such restrictions on faculty members. I think he is doing this out of spite and jealousy. Once he saw the dollar amount that we are requesting, his eyes popped, and I can imagine what's going through his puny little brain."

Anant thought very hard about the new problem. Unfortunately, he couldn't fly to Kansas at the drop of a hat due to his commitments at the company. Dave had been quite decent to him and let him take time off whenever he needed to go back to Kansas. But to ask him for leave now would be abusing his generosity.

He told her, "Petra, wait until Kevin is out of his class, and tell him about this new development. Kevin and the dean are fishing buddies, and maybe the dean can make Mao behave himself."

Anant was now more glad than ever that Kevin was

part of the team. Kevin had a lot to lose if the grant was not submitted to National Institute of Health on time. Because, if they missed the June deadline, the next one was in October and that meant that everything–the review process, the budget review, and the final approval–would all be delayed by almost six months. The three of them were managing to stretch the money they had to fund this new project. If the grant was submitted on time, the money should start coming in about eight or nine months.

Anant had a quick lunch, and went back to his office to finish a report that he was writing for Dave. The report took him almost four days to write, as there were so many aspects that he had to review. Finally at about three he was done, sent it off to Dave by e-mail, and went to the cafeteria for a cup of coffee, where he ran into Meena.

She said, "Hi stranger. How are things with you?"

He felt guilty that he wasn't spending time with her these past few weeks. "It has been hectic. I am hoping the next week I should be more relaxed. I must have told you about the grant that we are submitting to the National Institute of Health, and that is taking a lot of my free time."

"I know, my dear. Whenever I came into the apartment, you are working away. But I understand. I think I can spend the entire weekend with you. Will you be free this Friday evening? We can go out to a nice French restaurant. It is new, and I heard good things about it."

"Yeah, I guess I can use some relaxation. I will wait for you in the apartment, okay?"

Anant returned to his office. His cell phone rang, and Kevin was at the other end. "Hi buddy, how are you doing?"

Anant asked, "Did Petra speak to you?"

"Yeah, she told me about the problem with your chairman. Boy, what an asshole! I spoke to the dean, and told him about the project and its importance and the amount of money the university would lose if Fong blocked the grant. The dean was sympathetic but said that Fong was within his rights to institute a new policy of a prior review of grants before they are submitted to a granting agency. But he said that this should not be required of a faculty member at the last minute. The dean felt that Fong should have called a faculty meeting to discuss the issue, and let the faculty reach a consensus. Anyway, to cut a long story short, the dean spoke to the vice president of research, and they talked. I don't know what transpired between them, but the dean told us to send a copy of our grant to the grants office so they can look at it. In the meantime, he will talk to Fong and persuade him to sign off on our grant. I will know more about it tomorrow morning. I think the chances are that we can swing it. Don't worry. From what I gather, the administration is not too happy at the way Fong is managing his department. He is filling all the faculty slots with people in his field, and that is only going to hinder the department's ability to teach diverse topics. In the long run, the department's reputation will suffer, and the university's rating will also go down."

"Great, I am so glad that you are handling the mess. If I were there, I would have strangled that bastard's neck."

"I know how you feel. One day, Fong will get his share of misery. It will only be a matter of time. Take it easy. I will call you tomorrow morning. In the meantime, let's not lose any time about the manuscript to *Nature*. I have written my part, and will send it to you and Petra. You guys have to fill in the chemistry part. We should submit that next week. I am glad that no one needs to sign off on that one!"

"No problem. Petra and I can do it quickly and submit it to the editorial office next week. It's exciting, this is the first time I am submitting a paper to *Nature*."

"This is the first time for me too, man. Let's hope it will fly."

Anant called Petra and brought her up to date about the situation. She was still mad at Fong and was ready to have it out with him if he didn't sign off on the grant. Petra was calm and quiet most of the time, but when she saw someone being unfair, it got her really mad, and she could be undiplomatic. Anant asked her to take it easy, and let Kevin handle the situation. She agreed but still felt as though she failed him. He told her that it was not her fault, as it was Fong's doing.

Anant went home and fixed himself a whiskey sour and listened to his favorite Hindi songs. The drink and the melodious music relaxed him, and he dozed off on the couch. He didn't hear Meena walk into the apartment. She came in and gently woke him up. "Honey, did you eat your dinner?"

He woke up and saw that it was after nine. He asked her, "When did you come in?"

"Just a few minutes ago. I was worried about you and thought I would drop in to check on you. I am really glad that I came in. Did you drink a lot, honey?"

"I made a whiskey sour and had a few sips, you can see that most of the drink is still there in the glass. I must have been really tired for me to sleep like that on the couch. This never happened to me before; I must be getting old. Come to me, baby."

She was upset with him. "No 'come to me, baby' business. First, I want to make sure you eat some food and then you go to sleep properly on the bed. And tomorrow you will not go to work. Sleep or relax or do anything. But don't come to work. All employees are entitled to sick leave, and you must take a day or two off."

When she spoke in that severe tone, he knew that she meant business. He kept quiet and let her whip up a nice fluffy cheese omelet and buttered wheat toast. She brought the food to him and watched him tenderly while he ate voraciously. After finishing the meal, he said, "I didn't know I was this hungry. Thanks for the food. Are you going to spend the night with me?"

"I told Ramana that I am going to the office, and that I should be back by midnight. I guess I can call him and say that I will spend the night at a girlfriend's house."

She went into the study, and called her house. He couldn't hear what she said. But she came out smiling and said, "Now I am all yours, my dear." She kissed him warmly on his lips. He got up from the couch and took hold of her, and gently led her into the bedroom.

She got up early, fixed coffee, and brought him a cup to his bedside. "Don't even think of going out today. Call Dave and tell him that you are sick. I will drop by at lunchtime and bring you some food. I am sorry I don't have the time to cook something for you. I need to be at a meeting at eight sharp."

Anant got out of bed, brushed his teeth, and went for his jog. After he got back, he called Dave and told him that he was under the weather and couldn't come to the office. Once that was out of the way, he fixed himself cereal, toast, and decaf tea. He didn't care for coffee; all the women he had ever been with drank coffee in the morning and imposed their taste on him. But he never told any of them that he preferred tea in the morning.

He had exactly six months to decide whether to go back to Kansas or stay permanently in New Jersey. This decision was not dependent upon Meena's divorce; it was an entirely separate issue, to be dealt with after he thought about his job. As per his habit, he made a list of the pros and cons.

Why go back to Kansas	Why stay in NJ
Tenure	Lot more money
Job security	No need to write grants
Independence	Work with smart scientists
Enjoy teaching	Don't have to deal with Mao
Laid-back life style	Meena
No honking irate motorists	
Petra	

It was difficult to decide whether to go or stay, and no matter which way he looked at the issue, he couldn't decide. While he was still pondering the future, Kevin called to tell him that the forces of evil were defeated, and Fong had beat a hasty retreat. The dean prevailed upon Fong to sign off on the grant, and the man had no choice but to obey the higher authority. The dean told Fong that the idea of a prior peer review of grant proposals by in-house faculty members was fantastic and would eventually lead to better proposals. But he said that this should be done in a democratic manner with the input of all the faculty from all the departments.

He proposed to form a faculty sub-committee to look into the matter. In effect, the issue was buried and everyone was happy; even Fong had a face-saving solution to the crisis that he created in the first place.

It was almost noon, and Anant went into the bathroom to have a shave and a shower. Just when he came out of the shower, Meena came in with boxes containing delicious-smelling food. "I went to an Indian restaurant and got us some fish curry, *nans*, and lamb biryani. I think you will like the food. Get dressed and come. We will eat."

"Thank you. You shouldn't have gone to all this trouble, driving up and down to feed me. I am fine, there is nothing wrong with me. Do you have to go back soon?"

"Not immediately, but I need to take care of a few things before the end of the day. I will go for a couple of hours and be back here for the night. I think I want to be with you tonight, my dear." The way she said it indicated that she was troubled about something. After lunch, she cleared the dishes and ran out. Late in the evening she came back, had a shower, and changed into her jeans and a tank top. When she was at home she never wore a bra, and when she walked around the apartment her breasts bounced up and down. She knew that he was watching her chest and smiled at him. "Honey, do you like what you see?" She came to him and sat next to him on the couch. He put the manuscript that he was reviewing aside and hugged her, saying, "I like what I see, and I like what I don't see, and I also like what I can't see."

"Shut up and hold me, my dear."

"What's the matter?"

She put her head on his shoulder and started to cry. He was shocked at the sudden change in her mood. Just a few minutes ago she had been joking with him. He patted her and tried to console her. But not knowing why she was in such a miserable shape, it was difficult for him to cheer her up. Finally, after what seemed like an eternity, she stopped the waterworks, went to the bathroom, and came out after washing her face and eyes. He again hugged her and asked, "Tell me why you are feeling so bad. I feel sad when you cry like that."

"It's my husband."

"What happened to him?"

"Nothing. I told him that I wanted a divorce. He went crazy and threatened to commit suicide if I file for a divorce."

"Did he tell you how he will do it?"

"What does it matter? How he will do it is not important. If he kills himself, how can I live with myself and be happy with you?"

"I think he is bluffing. Why don't you simply leave him, and move in with me? If he kills himself when you are not at home, you are not responsible."

"Dear, you don't know him. He will do it if I leave him. It doesn't matter whether I am at home or not. I will know that he killed himself because I left him, and that will be enough to make me miserable."

"So what is the solution?"

"I am helpless. I will continue to live in the same house with him and be miserable. It is unfair of me to ask you to wait for me indefinitely. Please go ahead and look for another woman, and get married. I know many people in this area, and I can find you a nice girl." After saying this, she started to cry again. He found the whole thing so surreal, he was at a loss for words. He went into the kitchen and fixed whiskey sours for both of them, then brought the drinks to the living room, and placed them on the coffee table. He got a Kleenex and gently wiped her eyes and face and said, "Meena, have this drink. It will calm you down, and you will feel better. Please try to forget it for today, and let's try to relax. No matter what, I love you, Meena." He felt so bad for her that he too had tears in his eyes.

When she saw him become so emotional, she stopped crying and hugged him and said, "You are the only man who ever shed tears for me. I am really sorry that I am troubling you with my problems."

"Life is a mess. Let's drink and relax."

"Anant, I am telling you one more time. Please forget me and move on with your life."

"Okay, I will do that. But first go and fix your face. Let's go out to eat. I am hungry."

"No, we are not going anywhere after having such a stiff drink. You must have dumped half a bottle in our drinks. I am already feeling woozy. I am going to make something quick and we will eat at home tonight."

"I am not sure you are in a position to cook tonight. I think it is better to call in a pizza or Chinese."

"Okay, my dear. Call in whatever you want."

They had a pizza delivered, and after eating, they had another of Anant's stiff drinks and went to bed. Meena was asleep almost immediately, but Anant couldn't sleep and thought about Sheila.

A few weeks after she left Kansas, Sheila had sent Anant an e-mail:

Dear Anant:

I am sorry for everything. I know you did your best to cope with a bad situation, but even you couldn't, with all your patience, handle it. I know the past few years have been bad for you. It was my inability to come to terms with my disappointment that ruined everything between us. It may sound funny, but I still love you, and most probably will always love you. You have so much good in you, and you are capable of giving so much love that I hated myself every day for putting you through those agonizing days, weeks and years. I know you are hurting too, but I sincerely hope that eventually you will recover and move on with your life.

Take care and if you feel like it, write to me.

I am seeing a psychiatrist on a regular basis.

Sheila

Sheila's parents knew about all the trouble she went through to get pregnant, and that she was disappointed by the many unsuccessful attempts. But they were unaware of the deep depression she slipped into after everything failed. They didn't know about her bouts of irrational anger, crying, and suicidal tendencies.

She used ask Anant, "You must have some cyanide in your laboratory. Why don't you give me some? I want to end my miserable life."

During those times, he was very supportive and used to say, "Sheila, you shouldn't talk like that. We don't keep poisons like cyanide in the laboratory. I want you to relax, exercise, and start going to your yoga classes again. You have to cut back your hours at work, and find time for yourself. You are very young, you have at least another fifty years to live. I am sure, once you get over this, you will be fine and have a happy and productive life."

In spite of his pleading with her many times, she never tried to reduce her workload and never made time for exercise, not even a simple walk around the neighborhood. She would come home late and plop down on her couch in front the TV, and watch meaningless shows, and many nights she fell asleep right there in the TV room. In the beginning, he used to wake her up and take her to bed, but when she complained bitterly that he was disturbing her sleep, he gave up and let her sleep on the couch. She claimed that the noise from the TV put her to sleep. But then the next day she would complain about pain in the back or neck due to the uncomfortable position while sleeping on the couch.

There were many such instances that made Anant feel that he was squandering his love on an ungrateful, cantankerous, and capricious woman. While he felt bad for her condition and tried to help her in every possible way that he could think of, she rebuffed his advice and shunned all discourse. It was true that, compared to him, she made a lot more money, which was useful for their vacations and other luxuries. But he could live without all those things and return to a simple life in a one-bedroom apartment. Most of the clothes that he had purchased in North Carolina were still in good shape. Thanks to his regular jogging and careful habits, Anant never put on any weight, and his old clothes still fit him perfectly. But every couple of years he bought a few good quality cotton shirts and underwear from J.C. Penny. In contrast, Sheila spent her money like water, buying anything and everything that she saw in the mall. Whenever she could find some time, she went off all by herself on her shopping sprees, and got all kinds of gizmos for the kitchen, shoes, clothes, and cosmetics. Some of the clothes in her closet, which she had purchased a few years back, still had the tags on them and she never wore them, not even once. It seemed as though she got some kind of weird satisfaction from acquiring things that she never used. She would bring all this stuff into the house and dump it on the floor in the living room, and never bothered to keep the purchases in their respective places. It was left to Anant to take care of those useless and horribly expensive items. He thought of returning them to the shops without her knowledge but restrained himself because he knew that she would throw temper tantrums when she couldn't find the stuff, because despite all her craziness, she had an extremely sharp memory. She was careless about everything in the house, her clothes and shoes lying all over the place in either the TV room or their bedroom. She never placed used dishes in the dishwasher. She never did laundry. Towards the last few years of their marriage, she didn't care about anything, took him for granted, and let him do all the work. He had to take her pantsuits and silk blouses to the dry cleaners and pick them up and hang them in her closet. He routinely washed her underwear, bras and casual clothes, and white coats. Her office had a contract with a cleaning company to wash all the white coats; they picked up the coats once every week and brought them back clean. As they were not properly cleaned to Sheila's satisfaction, she brought them home for washing and ironing, and of course Anant ended up doing this job also. Whenever he washed her coats, he had to empty the pockets of several Kleenexes, dollar bills, candy, and all kinds of small pieces of paper with notes in her incomprehensible handwriting. Whenever he was doing laundry or taking care of the house, he used to wonder, "I wouldn't have to do so many loads of laundry if I lived by myself, and I wouldn't have to constantly put the stuff back where it belonged. I think I will be better off if I divorce this unbearable harridan."

The next day morning, Meena looked horrible with her puffy red eyes and pinched face. One look at her told Anant that she was not in a position to go to work. First, he made coffee the way she liked it. He took out Mocha Java beans from the freezer, ground them, added the exact amount of water, and turned on the coffee machine. Then he went into the bedroom and stood by her side and looked at her. She opened her eyes and said, "My dear, thanks for putting on the coffee. I will get up in a minute. Why don't you come into the bed and hold me?" He did what he was told, but he was feeling terribly sad for her. She came to him and hugged him, and they both knew that their relationship was coming to an end. But neither of them dared to bring up the subject, as it was a painful topic. He told her to call in sick, and she agreed to do so. He had to go to work, as it wouldn't look good if he was absent two days in a row.

He asked her, "Meena, can I fix you some breakfast before I go to work?"

"No, my dear. I am not hungry. I will just lie down and take a rest. Maybe I will listen to some of your sad songs."

"Okay, I am going to call you every hour or so. You better keep your cell phone nearby."

"Don't worry about me. I don't have the guts to commit suicide."

Luckily, the day wasn't crazy, and he didn't have to deal with too many problems. He had a meeting with scientists from the immunology division. The meeting was interesting in that the immunologists wanted his input on a compound that they were trying measure in the blood. They were trying to develop antibodies to a small molecule and were running into difficulties. They wanted to know if Anant had any ideas to modify the molecule so that the new structure might elicit better response. Anant suggested a couple of ideas, and told them that he could get a scientist in the medicinal chemistry division to work on the problem.

Then he had lunch with a candidate interviewing for a scientist position in the medicinal chemistry division. Dave was busy with some meetings, and he wanted

Anant to take care of the fellow. The fellow was fresh out of graduate school from Princeton University. His name was Matt Malone, and he didn't look older than twenty-six. Anant was pleasant to him, and asked him about his Ph.D. thesis project, and they talked about organic synthesis and some of the other problems the company was handling. Matt appeared to be bright, intelligent, and curious about the way the people in industry functioned. He had gotten his undergraduate education at Duke, and gone to Princeton for his Ph.D. Anant thought that with education at two such top-class universities, the boy would have no problem finding a job at some of the better-known pharmaceutical companies, and wondered why he was interviewing at this relatively small company. If the company could get such good candidates, they might not be interested in either Subash or Yi, who didn't have such stellar schools on their resume. Before they went to lunch, Anant excused himself and called Meena and spoke to her for a minute. "Hi, Meena, how are you feeling?"

"I am fine, don't worry about me. I am lying down and listening to your Hindi songs."

"Did you eat some breakfast?"

"No, I am not hungry. When you get home, we will go out to eat."

"Okay, I got to go now and take a candidate for lunch. See you in the evening."

After lunch, he delivered Matt to the next person on the list and came back to his office to do some work designing compounds for the people in immunology.

Anant left work a little early and went straight to the apartment. Meena was still in her pajamas, looking haggard and sick. He had never seen her in such a state and was worried about her health. "Maybe I should take you to a doctor. Would you like that?"

"There is nothing wrong with me. I am a little tired and unhappy. It will pass. Don't make a fuss. Go for your jog and come back. I will get ready by the time you are back. Then if you feel like it, we will go out to eat."

It was quite hot and muggy outside, and when he finished his jog, Anant was sweating profusely. He cooled off and then had a quick shower and got dressed.

He asked, "Where do you want to eat?"

"Anywhere but Indian. We had Indian yesterday."

"How about Chinese?"

"Fine."

They went to an upscale Chinese restaurant where the food and service were tolerable. Meena wanted a glass of white wine, and Anant ordered a cold beer. They had shrimp egg rolls, house special soft rice noodles with beef, pork and shrimp, and chicken lo mein. After eating, they went into the adjacent mall just to stretch their legs, as it was still quite muggy outside. Then he took her back to the apartment. She said, "I am sorry I was not great company this evening. Thanks for putting up with me and my lousy mood."

"We all have those days. You will get over it. Why don't we go to sleep, and tomorrow let's not be up too early. It is a Saturday and we can relax."

"I think I will go home now."

"I thought that you were going to be with me this weekend."

"Yeah, I wanted to but now I feel that if I stay here I will spoil your weekend."

He was hurt that she thought that he was so selfish as to think only of himself. "What will you do going home? Your son is away visiting his friends, and your husband is probably busy with his Internet browsing. Why don't you stay here? If you want, we can go to Cape May or Atlantic City tomorrow and get back Sunday evening. What do you think?"

"Do you really know what I want?"

"Of course, you know I will do whatever it takes to make you happy. I want to see a smile on your beautiful face again."

"All I want is to spend the entire weekend in your arms. Please make love to me and drive out all my demons. Hold me tightly and never let me go."

Anant thought that she must be in a really bad shape to talk like that. "I am here for you. Come to bed."

8

Anant received the *Nature* manuscript from Kevin and Petra, and it was well-written. Anant integrated the chemistry part into it, made sure it read well, and sent it off to the editorial office. At lunchtime, he went over to Meena's office to see if she was free for lunch. Even though she was still depressed, she came to work every day. Meena was talking to somebody. She told Anant that she would join him later at the cafeteria. So he went ahead and got his food and sat at a small table. In a few minutes she came with her tray. She looked pale and unhealthy.

Anant took a sip of water. "How are you feeling today?"

"Same as before. I know I have to get better and move on with things."

"I know, but you have to take care of your health. Are you going to come to the apartment this evening?"

"No. I can't. My son is back from his trip. I want to spend time with him now before he goes off to college."

"Where is he going?"

"He is going to Brown to do M.D. They have a program where they can get an M.D. in eight years. It's neat, and once they get admitted into this program they are all set and don't have to do MCAT."

"That's great. But what if the boy decides after a couple of years that he doesn't want to become a doctor?"

"That's okay too. He will get a B.S. and then go to any other course he wants."

"I am sure you will miss him once he goes off to Rhode Island."

"I know I will be more lonely than before at home. At least he was there for me to talk to, and sometimes go to movies and eat out."

"I am sorry."

"Did you decide about staying here full time after you are done with the sabbatical?"

"I am still thinking about it. I am not sure if I told you about our grant proposal. I will know whether it will be funded or not by late fall, depending on the score given by the review committee. If we get the money, that will be a strong incentive for me stay back in Kansas. We have requested about five million dollars spread over a period of five years. It may look like a lot of money, but when we figure in the cost of mice and the salaries for technicians and graduate students, it is not really that much. Also, the money will be shared by three laboratories."

"That means that you will decide about staying here when you hear about the score."

"Yeah, I guess so."

"If you get the funds, will your salary go up?"

"Yes, but not by a whole lot. I think I will get about ten thousand dollars more per year."

"You can make much more here if you decide to stay back. I heard that Dave maybe promoted to a vice-president's position, and if he takes it, they will need somebody to head the division. You will be the most attractive candidate because you are already working in the company, and know how the system works."

"I didn't know about Dave's promotion."

"No one knows but the division heads, and what I am telling you is confidential. I think they will offer you Dave's job, and at that time you can easily negotiate a salary of at least two hundred thousand per year."

"I didn't know that I can be worth that much to the company."

"That's a chronic problem of yours, Anant. You always underestimate yourself. But I am curious about one thing. Why is it that you are so fond of living in Kansas?"

"I am not really fond of Kansas. But that's where I got a teaching job, and then I got lucky and got tenure, and now I am trapped there until I retire. Actually, I would like to live in North Carolina. I came to North Carolina for my post-doc right after I completed my Ph.D. in Bangalore and lived there for few years. I love the place, people, food, beaches. Maybe I will retire in North Carolina."

"That's at least another thirty years from now."

"I know, right now I have to think about the next few months. I guess I better get back to my office and see if someone needs me. Today is kind of slow. I'm getting bored without work."

"You can afford to take it easy for a day or two. No

one works hard all the time. I guess I will see you at the apartment in a couple of days."

The more he understood Meena's predicament, the less he felt attracted to her. He didn't comprehend why she was so worried about her husband's threats. If he was foolish enough to commit suicide if she left him, so be it. Anant felt that Meena should simply leave that house, and move in with him, and file for a divorce. But Meena's ambivalence was driving him crazy and ruining their relationship. Although Meena didn't tell him in so many words that she would not leave her husband, he knew from the way she acted that she would never divorce that man. At least this would make his decision a little easier. After he was done in New Jersey by the end of the year, he should return to his job in Kansas, and get married to Petra, and live there until they both retired. But in the meantime, he should support Meena and be there for her.

The next day he got an e-mail from Petra:

My dear Anant:

I have some news. I missed my period and am wondering if I am pregnant. I will watch it for some more time, and then if I don't get my period in another week or two, I will make an appointment with my gynecologist. I will keep you posted. Don't worry. I love you very much and wish you were coming to me sooner than the end of July.

Your Petra.

Anant wasn't sure how to take the news about Petra's period. Just because she missed one period, it didn't mean she was pregnant. If she didn't get her period in the next few weeks, her gynecologist would do a pregnancy test, and that should be more definitive. If Petra was really pregnant, he was sure that the baby was his, as he knew that Petra would never think of sleeping with anyone else. Her love for him was unconditional, and she was absolutely faithful to him. He was thrilled at the possibility of Petra carrying his child. But he told himself not to jump to a hasty conclusion and just to wait and see. He replied to Petra:

My dear Petra:

Let's hope for the best. I will come to Kansas as soon as I hear from you, even if it is only for a day or two. I will constantly think of you for the next few weeks. I will call you tonight.
Take care of yourself and say hi to Misha.

A

Anant called Petra that evening. She was thrilled to hear his voice. "My darling, how are you? I miss you all the time. I am so glad that you wrote that you will come to me if I am pregnant. So you are not mad that I may be pregnant?"

"Petra, how can you even think like that? Why should I be mad if you get pregnant?"

"Because we never talked about having children. You know that we made love many times without protection because I thought it was safe those days as it was right after my period. Also, the last time you were here, we were careless during our early morning sessions in the bed. That's why I am suspecting that I may be pregnant. I want you to know that you are the father, if I am really pregnant."

"Petra, you don't have to say it. I know that."

"I will wait for another two weeks and then see the gynecologist. But I am so relieved that you are not mad at me."

"Petra, I am never mad at you. But if you are pregnant, we should get married soon. Are you willing to marry me at short notice?"

"Anant, you know I love you with all my heart, and of course I will marry you. But I don't want you to think that you should marry me just because I may be pregnant. Let's continue to go about our lives as before, and do at the right time what's best. Let's not make any plans until we know for sure. My darling, nothing will make me more happy than to be your wife. Would you have asked me to marry you if this pregnancy thing didn't come up suddenly?"

She had asked a difficult question, and Anant replied quickly, "Well, to be frank with you, this new development hastened my decision. Otherwise, I was planning to ask you to marry me in December after I am back from my sabbatical."

"I am glad that you were thinking about our marriage also. I was also thinking that we can get married in December, and then go with you to Ukraine to visit my parents. They will be happy to see that I got a man to take care of me. They will also be glad to meet you."

"Great, I will talk to you later. Go and get some sleep."

"Okay, my darling, goodnight."

Petra's plan to take Anant to Ukraine evoked memories of his trip with Sheila to Hyderabad to visit his parents. Although his parents had not come to his wedding, Anant felt that he should try to keep the channels of communication with them open, as he hoped that one day they would come to terms with his marriage. So immediately after his wedding, he selected a bunch of photographs from their wedding pictures and sent them to his parents in Hyderabad. After a couple of weeks, he called and asked his father, "Did you get our pictures?"

"Yes."

"Do you like them?"

"Yes, they are nice. Some of them were overexposed and some were too dark. I think your photographer didn't know how to use the flash."

Anant wondered why his father started to give him a lecture on the use of the flash. But he was happy that at least his father was talking to him instead of hanging up. He was a little disappointed that his father did not congratulate him on his marriage, and didn't even say that Sheila was pretty. Then his mother came on line, and she too was laconic. After they exchanged a few pleasantries, his mother gave the phone to his sister. Her name was Swathi, but all the family members called her by her nick name—Chitti. She was Anant's favorite in that house.

He asked her, "Chitti, how do you like your sister-in-law?"

"She is gorgeous, she looks like a movie star in that

sari. When are you going to visit us? You know that we all miss you, and want see you and meet Sheila."

"Thanks, I know you want to see Sheila, but what about father and mother? Are they still angry at me?"

"You know how they are, one has to learn to ignore them and do what you want to do. Once you come here with her, they will be all right. Actually, grandfather wants to meet Sheila too. He saw all the photographs that you sent us, and he is very proud that she is a doctor. Now he is telling everybody in the village that he has two lady doctors in his family."

"With you, it will be three."

"Yeah, I am still in my final year. It will be a few more years before I become a full-fledged doctor."

"I am very proud of you, Chitti. I am sure you will be a good doctor."

"We will see. Now don't side track. When are you coming to Hyderabad? Everybody is waiting for you and Sheila. You must come soon."

"You say everybody, but father and mother didn't say anything. I think they are still mad at me."

"Yes, they are, but not as much as before you got married. After grandfather came and talked to them, they are much better now. You know how they are, always proud and worried about family name and stuff like that. If grandfather is happy with Sheila, how can our parents remain aloof? I think you must come soon. Let me know the date of your arrival, and I will ask grandfather to be here so that he can patch things up between you and our parents. You know father doesn't like to displease grandfather."

"How come our grandfather has become such an

easygoing man? I never thought that he would be happy with my marriage to Sheila."

"I think he still feels bad about our uncle Ganesh, and all that happened after grandfather prevented him from marrying that Reddy girl. It appears that grandfather has realized his mistakes, and probably this is his way of atoning for them. Don't worry about our parents. When are you coming here?"

"I am glad that the old man will be on our side. I can't come immediately, as we already took a lot of time off for the wedding. Now I started to look for a job, and I may get interview calls in the winter months. I am thinking that we can probably go there during Christmas holidays. Do you want to talk to Sheila? She is here by my side."

He let Sheila and Chitti talk to each other. After she hung up, Sheila said, "You have an affectionate sister. She loves you very much. She is calling me *bhabi*, and spoke to me in Hindi all the time. Her Hindi is very good."

"Thanks for speaking to her. She is adorable. She is five years younger than I am, and we have always been close. Even though I haven't seen her for about five years, we keep in touch by writing to each other."

"Now we have to go to Hyderabad, as it seems your parents are slowly coming to terms with our marriage."

"Let's plan to go this December."

"How long should we stay there?"

"Ten days should be enough. We will lose three days traveling, and the rest of the time we can spend in Hyderabad and my grandfather's village."

"Aren't you forgetting something?"

"What?"

"What about my grandparents in Delhi? Don't you think we should see them too?"

"I am sorry, I wasn't thinking about Delhi. Of course, we should see them and pay our respects. I know they couldn't come to our wedding due to their poor health."

"If we are going to Delhi, Hyderabad, and your village, I think we need more than ten days."

"Okay, let's plan on taking two weeks off."

So they booked their tickets to India, going in the third week of December and returning by the second week of January. Before they left, they did a lot of shopping, purchasing gifts for their relatives. Although they decided to take gifts only to a select few, the list became rather long, and Anant wasn't all that happy at the amount of money they had to spend. He complained bitterly, "This trip is going to cost us a lot of money. All these gifts, our tickets, and expenses in India will add up to at least six thousand dollars. All our savings are gone in just two weeks. When you convert this amount into Indian rupees, it is about two hundred thousand. Do you know that a common man in India does not make this much money even if he works for five years?"

But Sheila was happy to do all the shopping in her spare time, and she dragged Anant along with her to the shopping malls. She told him, "Sweetie, you are going to your hometown after almost five years. It doesn't hurt to spend some money on gifts for our relatives. What is the point of making money if we can't spend it on our people?" They bought a lot of candy, pen and pencil sets, wrist watches, shaving razors and blades, aftershave lotion for men and perfume for women, small gold ornaments, fancy earrings, remote-control cars, rock-and-roll music tapes, and a lot of other knick-knacks. They packed four large suitcases, and Anant was worried about their weight as he thought that they might have to pay for the excess baggage.

First they landed in Delhi and stayed with Sheila's grandparents for four days. Her grandparents were glad to meet him, and although their health was not great, they went out of their way to arrange a party so that all the relatives could meet the newlyweds. It was great visiting with Sheila's cousins, aunts and uncles, and they had a great time. From Delhi, they hopped on a plane to go to Hyderabad and were received at the airport by Swathi and his grandfather. Conspicuously absent from the reception committee were his parents, but Anant didn't let it bother him. Swathi had blossomed into a radiant beauty. As soon as she spotted them, Swathi came running to him and hugged him. "It is so good see you after so many years."

Then she turned to Sheila and greeted her affectionately. Sheila playfully asked her, "Don't I get a hug too?"

Swathi blushed and hugged her sister-in-law, saying in Hindi, "*Bhabi*, when I see my brother, I forget everything else." Even though he was in his late sixties, Mr. Swamy was vigorous and handsome in his starched white dhoti and kurta. He was tall and muscular, with a clean-shaven face and sparkling eyes adorned with gold-rimmed spectacles. As a mark of respect, Anant and Sheila bent down and touched his grandfather's feet. After receiving his blessing, they all got into the family car and drove to Banjara Hills.

Mr. Swamy asked them, "So how was your flight from Delhi?"

Sheila replied, "It was good, sir, and not too long."

"I am glad that both of you at last found time to visit all of us. Your grandmother has come from the village especially to see you, Puttu. For the past few years, she never stepped out of the village and stopped coming to Hyderabad. Your parents are at home waiting for us. They also wanted to come to the airport, but I told them stay at home as the car can't take so many people. As it is, we got two cars, one for us and the other for your luggage. I am glad that you informed Chitti that you are bringing four large suitcases. If we didn't know about this luggage, we would have brought only one car."

They reached home and were welcomed by his parents and the rest of his grandparents. It was a grand reunion of all the family members, and Sheila was overwhelmed with all the attention she got from everybody. All through the journey and during their stay in Delhi, she wore nothing but jeans and a T-shirt, but when they left Delhi, she wore a simple conservative sari, gold earrings, and a gold chain with *mangala sutra*. And she didn't forget to apply *bindi* on her forehead. All this preparation really paid off, and all the relatives were happy and relieved to see that Puttu's wife looked like any other Andhra girl. The only drawback was that she couldn't speak Telugu. Professor Bala and Lalitha spoke to Sheila in English or Hindi, but the grandmothers knew only Telugu and needed somebody to interpret for them. Swathi did an admirable job translating from Telugu to Hindi and vice-versa. They all settled down in the large living room and chatted about Puttu when he was a baby, Puttu when he was a boy, and Puttu when he was a man studying at far-off places such as Agra, Delhi and Bangalore. He was embarrassed and hoped that his people would stop talking about his childhood, although he knew they were doing it for Sheila's benefit. He managed to escape into the kitchen, where the old cook was busy supervising two other cooks. The lady had been with his family for almost twenty-five years, and the only life she had was cooking and cleaning. She was widowed when she was only twenty, her husband dead in an accident in the village. Anant's grandmother had felt bad for the penniless widow and sent her to Hyderabad to help in her son's house. In those days, a widow from a lower-class family had no prospects whatsoever and had to survive by working in some rich man's household.

As soon as she saw Anant, she came to him and hugged him. "Puttu, how are you? I know you have arrived, but I didn't want to come out and intrude in the family reunion. I know that eventually you will find your way here." The cook had never had any kids, and she treated Anant and Swathi like her own. She told Anant, "We are making a lot of special dishes today, and I hope you haven't lost the taste for our Andhra food."

Anant was glad that everything was going well and that his parents were happy. They were nice to Sheila, and his mother hugged her and welcomed her into the family. The next day, the newlyweds were persuaded to sit through a Satyanarayana pooja, a ceremony conducted to ensure abundance of everything—riches, children, happiness. On this occasion, Lalitha presented Sheila with expensive saris and jewelry; she got diamond earrings, gold necklaces, a heavy gold waistband, and silver anklets. Lalitha and Swathi helped Sheila put on all these things and made her sit next to Anant in front of the pundits who conducted the ceremony. Professor Bala arranged a grand gala reception at the Secunderabad club, to celebrate the marriage of his eldest son. The guest list of about five hundred people, comprised the elite of the twin cities, and professor Bala's and Lalitha's colleagues, friends, and relatives. After a few days in Hyderabad, they went to his grandfather's village, and there was another party to meet all the important people in the village. At the end of the trip, Sheila and Anant were very tired but happy that his parents got over their initial reluctance to accept their marriage.

Now that Anant had decided to marry Petra, he faced a moral dilemma about his relationship with Meena. In spite of Meena's ambivalence regarding her marriage, divorce, and her relationship to Anant, he still cared for her deeply and wanted to spare her further agony. His first thought was to inform Meena about his relationship with Petra and his intention to marry her. If he told Meena about Petra now, it might hurt Meena's feelings, and she might never want to speak to him again. But it was Meena who told him to marry someone else because she was unable to file for a divorce. Even if Meena felt bad at first, she was sensible enough to understand the reason for his decision. He should tell her the truth, but not the whole truth. Meena should never know that he was seeing both of them simultaneously. So the best thing now was do nothing, and say nothing. Just carry on as before. Once he found out whether or not Petra was pregnant, he could decide his further course of action. If she was pregnant, he would simply give Dave a month's notice and leave for Kansas for good. If, on the other hand, it turned out that Petra was not pregnant, he would go to Kansas in July, according to his previous plan, and inform Meena of his decision to marry Petra. Timing was everything, he told himself. He could pull it off with a little bit of luck.

The next couple of weeks had Anant on tenterhooks, not able to focus on anything. He managed to take care of work at the company, and in the evenings he worked on their second manuscript that Kevin and Petra sent. He integrated the chemistry part with the biological testing of the compounds, and rewrote certain sections of the manuscript. When he was satisfied with the final version, he sent it to the editorial office. Meena came to the apartment a few times, but she was not herself. She was trying to spend as much time as possible with her son before he went off to Rhode Island. Anant understood her need to be with her son and felt bad for the poor woman, as she was about to lose the only person she dearly loved in that house. Whenever her son was away for a couple of days, spending time with his friends or cousins, Meena spent the night with Anant. But it was not the same for either of them. She was constantly aware that their relationship was about to end, and he felt guilty for being with her and was unable to be attentive to her. She interpreted his indifference as dismay at her unwillingness to file for a divorce. But mutual respect still remained, and they treated each other with tenderness and care. The embers of love between them had definitely cooled, and there was no way they could be rekindled.

Finally, after what seemed like a long wait, he got a call from Petra:

"I did not get my period even after two weeks. So I went to see my gynecologist, and they did a test on my urine and found that I am definitely pregnant. I am so glad."

"Great news. We will enjoy our baby."

"You said that you will come immediately if I am pregnant. When are you coming?"

"I will call the travel agent to find out about a flight. I will call you once I know the flight details."

His travel agent got him a flight at an exorbitant price, as it was very short notice. But he had made a promise to Petra, and now that she was carrying his child, he felt that he should see her at any cost. He took off a little early on Friday and caught an evening flight to Kansas City. It was quite late when he got there. Petra was waiting for him, and they hugged and kissed. Petra was overjoyed at seeing Anant. "You are looking good, my darling. I really missed you."

"I missed you too. You are looking radiant, Petra. Pregnancy suits you."

"Thank you, my darling."

She drove them home. As they went in, Anant asked, "Is Misha sleeping upstairs?"

"No, the girls are having a sleep over at my neighbor's house tonight. It worked out fine, as I didn't want her sleeping in the house all by herself when I went to the airport to pick you up. I knew it will be quite late by the time we got back from the airport."

"I guess I will see her tomorrow."

"Sure, she should be back here in the morning. Now, what do you want to eat? You must be hungry."

"I had a hamburger at the Newark airport just before we took off. But I could have some hot chocolate, if you don't mind."

"Anything you want, my darling."

After they had the drink, they went upstairs and made love. Petra was ecstatic to be with him, and Anant felt elated to hold her in his arms. To be with the mother of his child was something he could never experience before, and he knew that this was the beginning of a new chapter in his life. Afterwards, when they were drenched with sweat and holding each other, he said, "How can I ever thank you for giving me this great gift of fatherhood, my dear?"

"No, my darling, it is I who should thank you for giving me your child. You know that I have always wanted another kid, and I am glad that you are the father."

"Petra, I think you should get a lot of rest now that you are pregnant. And no more wine for you until you deliver. Do you know when the baby is due?"

"In December, I guess."

"Great, that will give us plenty of time to get married before the baby is born."

Anant took Petra and Misha out for a nice lunch at a seafood place, and they walked around the plaza and did a little window shopping. Anant took them into Tivol, an upscale jewelry shop, and asked Petra to pick out a ring. As this was not expected so soon, Petra was pleasantly surprised but agreed to look at the rings. She said, "I don't think I want two rings, one for the engagement and another for the wedding. I just want one nice ring that symbolizes our love for each other."

The salesgirl showed her many rings of various shapes and sizes, diamond rings set in platinum, yellow gold, or white gold. Petra spotted one ring and asked the girl about it. The girl told her, "This is an eternity-style engagement ring. It's called 'Endless Love,' and this has three round Bezel-set diamonds." She gave the ring to Petra to put on her finger. The ring looked good on her finger, and Anant asked Petra, "It looks elegant on you. Do you like it?"

"Yes, my darling, it looks very pretty."

"Great, then, it's settled. Let's get it."

Petra said, "Don't we have to find out first the price?"

The sales girl looked at them "With tax the price will come to $10,120.45."

Anant told her, "Fine, let's make sure it fits her finger properly."

"Don't worry sir, I will take the measurements and get her the exact fit in about a week."

Petra took Anant aside and said, "My darling, you must not spend so much money on that ring. Just because I like it, it doesn't mean we should buy it."

"Petra, you must have the ring. This my gift to you, and you should not say no to it."

After they went home, Petra admonished him. "My darling, if you spend money like that, we won't have anything left for other things. You don't need to buy me such expensive gifts to show your love to me."

"Petra, this is once-in-a-lifetime thing. I want us to

celebrate our love, our baby, and our life together for many, many years to come."

Sunday evening, she came to the airport to see him off. "So are you planning to return to Kansas for good in the next month or so? You know I need you here more than ever."

"Yes, my dear. I will talk to Dave about it. I only hope he won't get mad at me."

Anant reached Newark quite late and drove to the apartment. He fixed himself a whiskey sour, ate some chips, and went to bed. The next day, he got up a little late and was getting ready to go to his office. His cell phone rang. It was Meena.

She sounded extremely distraught. "My dear, something bad happened. My husband is dead."

Anant was shocked. "How did he die, when this happened?"

"Just this morning. He is usually up quite early, but this morning when he didn't show up for his morning coffee, my son went into his room to wake him up, and found him deep asleep, at least that's what my son thought. But I had a premonition and went in to check on him myself. He was not breathing. Immediately, we called 911 and the paramedics tried to revive him but it was too late. They took the body to the hospital anyway, and there the doctors pronounced him dead."

Anant was at a loss for words. "I am sorry, Meena."

Meena was crying, "He swallowed a lot pills and killed himself."

"Meena, is there anything you want me to do? Shall I go to your house now?"

"No, Anant, don't come here. I have already informed his sister who lives in Virginia, and his parents are coming from India. We will keep the body until everybody arrives, and then have the funeral. I won't be coming to the office for a couple of weeks."

"Meena, call me if you need anything. If you can manage to spare some time, try to come to our apartment. Take care of your health."

He went to his office and did some work, but his mind was not functioning properly. Somehow, he got through the day, but he was preoccupied with his thoughts about Petra and Meena.

The death of Meena's husband came as a complete shock. Anant felt bad for Meena as she had to put up with the probing questions of relatives and friends. He really wanted to be with her in this hour of need, but she didn't want to involve him. Maybe she didn't want the relatives to know that she was having a relationship with Anant. Irrespective of her motivations, he felt helpless and didn't know what to do.

In view of this new development, should he still stick to his plan to move back to Kansas in a month or so? If he did, it would be very insensitive, and Meena would be without his support, right when she needed it most. On the other hand, Petra would be upset if he didn't keep his word to her. How could he tell Petra about Meena's loss without revealing the whole affair; that he was seeing Meena, while at the same time declaring his ever-lasting love to Petra. He never thought that he would be in this situation, caught between his loyalty to two women. Did he really love them so much, and if so which one did he love more? He couldn't very well tell Petra that Meena needed him, and that he must remain in New Jersey for a few more months. On the other hand, if he left now, Meena would be very unhappy. Now that the husband was out of the picture, she might even expect him to marry her, of course, after a decent interval. He thought, very naively, that he could manage the two women at the same and somehow contrive to lose one and spend the rest of his life with the other. Petra's pregnancy and Meena's husband had complicated the whole scheme. He thought, *"Birth and death, beginning and end, and I am in the middle of it."* He had no doubt in his mind that if he told Petra about Meena, she would dump him. And, surely this was not the time to burden Meena with his revelations about Petra and his impending fatherhood.

All his life, he survived with the help of other people. Although he hated that his father pushed him to get his Ph.D., without that prodding he wouldn't have achieved anything. Then there was professor Martin, who helped him secure a faculty position, and saw him through his tenure battle. And Heather, with whose help he became a man. There was Sheila who loved him and helped him get his green card and eventually his U.S. citizenship. Now, finally there were Petra and Meena, who trusted him with their love and affection and gave everything to him. In addition to their love, they also helped him professionally. Petra's help with his new project was invaluable, and without Meena's help he wouldn't have found this job in the pharmaceutical industry. He needed to talk to somebody about his predicament. He thought about calling his sister

Swathi, but decided against it as he never told her that he was seeing other women after the divorce. When he told Swathi about his divorce she was really upset and cried. At his request, she agreed not to reveal about his divorce to anyone else in the family. But there was no one in the U.S.A. that he could trust. Although he was close to Kevin, and they talked about a lot of things, he didn't want to confide in him. He told Kevin about his divorce only after Sheila left, and he never told him about his affair with Petra. Other than Kevin he had no close friends, and the only friend he had, he drove her away.

Sheila. He had to swallow his pride and call her. She was the only one who could help him out of the predicament that he got himself into. He never replied to her e-mail that she sent few months back. He was not sure how she would react when she heard about his affairs. Would she be angry, hurt or indifferent? He felt guilty that he was calling her because of his dire need. In any case, he got Sheila's number from Mrs. Puri and called her.

She was surprised. "Hi, Anant, how are you doing?"

"I am fine, Sheila, how is everything with you? What are you doing and where are you now?"

"Anant, I know you very well. I am sure you didn't call me to discuss my health and all. What's the matter?"

It was difficult for him to come to the point and reveal all his sordid dealings. But, in the end he did.

She was very mad, "What a fool you are Anant, I left you to your devices, and you land yourself in this mess. Don't you know better than to play with women's feelings. So you called me to help you make up your mind? You want me to tell you which one to dump? You should have thought about what you were getting into before unzipping your pants so quickly. I always knew that you only think one thing—sex."

He said plaintively, "Sorry Sheila, but I have no friends, you are the only one I can talk to. Please don't be mad. You know I was never unfaithful to you."

"You are a bloody jackass. At least if you had screwed around while you were married to me, you wouldn't have been in this mess."

"I need your help. I am sorry that I have hurt you."

They talked for a long time. After she got over her anger and frustration at his stupid behavior, they compared notes about their lives after divorce. He told her about his problems with Fong, his new job at the pharmaceutical company in New Jersey, and his pending NIH grant. After she moved to Maryland, she lived with her parents for a few months. Her mother pampered her and helped her regain her health. Sheila used to get up late everyday, go for long walks, and relax and reflect on her life. Also, she consulted a psychiatrist, and got herself a personal trainer. With the help of some medications and a vigorous exercise program, she regained her equilibrium and came to terms with her loss. In the meanwhile, her license to practice in Maryland came through. She knew that she was burnt out with practicing conventional medicine, taking care of patients. Although she enjoyed the challenge, she paid a heavy price in terms of her health and happiness. She wanted to find a less stressful job which let her have some time for herself. Her father was a consultant to a few pharmaceutical companies in the area, and with his help, she found a job. The company wanted someone with clinical experience to oversee their clinical trials program. She had been working for that company for over a year. This was a far cry from her previous job at Kansas City, where she used to slog day and night, see endless number of patients and argue with insurance companies. Her new job was to audit various reports of clinical trials conducted by the company and approve or send some of them back with her comments. The work was easy, and she even had a full hour for her lunch. She was out of the door at the stroke of five and was at her gym in a few minutes. Since her condominium was only a few miles from her parents' house, she spent almost every weekend with them. He wondered if she was seeing anyone.

She said, "After so much crap I went through, I don't think I want to date anybody. I am happy as I am, single, nobody to answer to. I come and go as I please. Okay, enough about me. What shall we do about your problem?"

"I don't know, I will do whatever you suggest."

"Okay, tell you what, why don't you visit me this weekend. It's only a three-hour drive from your place to mine. Come here by lunchtime on Saturday and you can leave on Sunday."

"Thanks, Sheila. I will be there. I appreciate your help."

Meena came to the apartment the next day evening. She looked very tired and sick.

He hugged her, "I am very sorry, Meena. I am glad that you came over. I was worried sick about you."

"My dear, I wanted to be with you but all those relatives and friends were in the house. My sister-in-law,

Anita, arrived yesterday and took over. That's the way she is, always taking charge, she is such a control-freak. She was close to my husband, and she always blamed me for all his troubles. She thinks that because I put so much pressure on him, he went into all those business ventures. I can't stand that bitch."

"Meena, screw her. Just ignore her and take care of your son. Are you still going to send him to college? He must be very upset, poor boy."

"Actually, my boy is taking it much better than I expected. You know, he was close to his dad, but he also knew how sick his dad was. We talked about it, and he told me that he would like to join his college this fall. There is really no need to delay his admission. There is nothing that he could do by staying here with me."

"I am glad that he will move to an entirely different atmosphere, away from all this. But you will miss him, I know."

"Yeah, but I will get over it. Anyway, he will be visiting me during the holidays. My son will be okay, and I am not worried about him. It is my in-laws that are a big concern for me. They will be here in about three days and camp out for six months."

"Why six months? After the funeral, what is it that they can do here? You will be at work, your son gone to college. There won't be anybody to talk to them. How will they spend their time?"

"You don't know what I have to put up with. My father-in-law is a real old-fashioned gentleman and expects people to wait on him. He won't even come into the kitchen to fix himself a cup of coffee. All day he is at the computer playing internet-bridge. I don't know how anyone can spend so much time sitting at the computer. He can't drive in this country, as he doesn't have a driving license. Even in India he didn't drive for the past many years. They have a driver to take them everywhere. After he retired, he stopped driving. My mother-in-law has led a really sheltered life. She is used to servants and cooks in the house, she didn't have to lift her little finger. She is absolutely incompetent, can't even cook a cup of rice. Oh, God, I don't know how I can get through the next few months." She started crying.

Anant hugged and comforted her. "It's okay Meena. I am here with you. Come here anytime you can and relax. I will be here for you."

After she recovered from her crying spell, she asked him, "What shall I do with them? I can't be rude and tell them to leave after the funeral. But I just don't want to deal with them anymore."

"Meena, tell your sister-in-law to take care of them. She can take them to Virginia."

"I guess I can do that. I hope that the female will listen to me. She never liked me. We will see. Anyway, I am not going to cook and clean for all these people. I arranged a lady to come in twice a day to cook all the meals and clean up. I am going to stay in my room and play the part of a mourning widow."

"Meena, you don't have to play the part, you are in mourning."

"Only you know, my dear, about how I really feel. You know, a part of me is feeling bad for a wasted life. He was a brilliant man, very knowledgeable and capable. He took care of everything in the house, and I will miss that. Another part of me is relieved that I don't have to put up with his bouts of depression and crazy behavior. But I feel guilty for not empathizing with him. I guess that I am too selfish."

"Just get through the next few weeks. You know I am here to support you."

"Okay, my dear. I better go now. People at home might wonder where I went. I told Anita that I needed to get out. She looked at me as though I was weird. The thing is, they all expect me to be heart-broken and wail and cry. But I am not like that."

Sheila lived in a gated community. Set adjacent to a golf course, the complex was posh, with nice mature trees, flowering plants, and lush green lawns. He thought that it must be expensive to live in such a neighborhood. Sheila was waiting for him in the parking lot. As soon as she saw him, she waved at him. After he parked his car, he came up to her and stood in front of her. He wasn't sure what to do, whether to hug her or kiss her on the cheek. Unfortunately, he never came across a manual for divorced couples—how they should greet each other after almost two years of separation. He wasn't even sure whether it was appropriate to give her a bunch of roses. During his drive from Princeton, New Jersey to Silver Springs, Maryland, he thought about the roses and their color, because he remembered vaguely reading somewhere that a certain color denoted a specific emotion. Since he forgot all about it, he stopped at a florist and consulted the girl at the counter. She showed him a small chart indicating each color and what it signified. So he chose yellow for friendship.

She said, "Hi Anant, you look cool in this summer

heat, why are you standing so far away, come on, give me a hug."

He hugged her, "I wasn't sure whether I should hug you or kiss you on the cheek."

"For God's sake, there are no bloody rules, just be yourself. Don't behave as though you committed some great sin. We just got divorced, and that's that. Come on in. Bring your bag inside, you don't want to leave it the car in this heat."

"There is not much in it. Just my toothbrush and a change of clothes. I thought that I will put up in a hotel for the night."

"Anant, don't be silly. We lived together for about ten years and there is nothing we don't know about each other. You are staying with me."

He knew there was no point in arguing about it. He picked up his bag and the bunch of roses.

She was pleased with the roses, "That's sweet of you, Anant. You didn't have to do it."

She led the way into the building. She lived on the second floor. It was a spacious condominium, facing the golf course. The view from the living room was spectacular, with all those lush green links. The living room was sparsely furnished with a couch and a chair, and a TV in the corner. The dining area was contiguous and led into a small kitchen. There was a small dining table with four chairs. The carpet was lily white, and the walls were painted ivory white with a few nice paintings hanging. He set his bag in a corner and stood admiring the view, the paintings, and Sheila. She looked stunning in a simple T-shirt and jeans and high-heeled sandals. The dark circles under her eyes were gone and her face, devoid of any make-up, had a happy glow about it. Her glistening black hair was long, almost down to her shoulders.

He told her, "You look happy and healthy."

"Thank you Anant, you don't look bad yourself. I see that you are taking care of yourself. Still jogging, drinking decaf, and all that?"

"Yeah, I can't stop exercising. That's what keeps me going."

"Anant, I cooked some simple food, shall we eat? I am starving."

"Oh, Sheila, you didn't have to cook for me. We could have gone out for lunch."

"It's too hot to go out during the day. For the past few days it has been very hot and muggy."

"Yeah, the weather is pretty much same in New Jersey also."

They had white rice, sambar, a curry with potatoes and red bell peppers, and a piece of grilled salmon.

Anant complimented Sheila, "The lunch was delicious, Sheila. You haven't lost your touch."

After clearing the dishes they sat in the living room, looking at each other and wondering about the vagaries of life that brought them together again.

"Anant, I never thought that we would see each other again after we parted ways on that April morning."

"It was a difficult time for both of us. I don't know what else we could have done."

"After all the therapy I had after I left Kansas, I now realize that I was not easy to live with. I know you tried your best to put up with me, but in the end you gave up."

"I am sorry too. Maybe if you had gone to a psychiatrist in Kansas, we might have saved our marriage."

"It's all water under the bridge now. Anyway, you didn't come here to rehash our past. I was thinking about your problem for the past few days. I think the best course of action would be to confess your stupid behavior to Petra and Meena."

"That will be hard, they will hate me for the rest of their lives. You know, I even gave a ring to Petra when I went to Kansas City last week."

"You mean you proposed to her?"

"What else could I do, she is pregnant with my child."

She was shocked. "Pregnant? You never told me about any pregnancy. How sure are you that she is with your baby?"

"Because she told me so, and I have to believe her."

"You are naïve, Anant. I know for sure that Petra is promiscuous. Even while she was married to Paul, she was screwing around. I know this for a fact because she used confide in me. You know we were good friends, but apart from our friendship, she was my patient as well. She was involved with Kevin for a very long time. She once told me that she would divorce Paul and marry Kevin. I don't know why that plan didn't work out after Paul left her. Maybe she got tired of Kevin."

Anant was shocked at these revelations about Petra. "I didn't have any idea. How come you never told me about all this when were together. You used to tell me everything."

"Anant, whatever Petra told me in my office was confidential, and you know I never discussed my patients with you or anyone else. But now that you are in trouble, I don't feel bad to reveal the information about Petra. Also, I don't want you to be miserable for the rest of your life."

Anant was mollified. "The way she came across was that she knew only Paul after she moved to the U.S.A., and after dating for some time, they got married."

"Anant, don't be a fool. Is there any woman or a man in this world who is completely truthful about their past liaisons? Were you honest with me? When I met you in that bar in Chapel Hill, dancing with that blonde, I guessed right away that you were fucking her. I didn't care about it as long as you didn't see her after we started our affair."

Anant got up and went into the kitchen to get a glass of water. "You know, Sheila, if Petra is such a nympho, why she never hit on me before our divorce?"

"Oh poor Anant, you have such a bizarre image of a nymphomaniac in your mind. They don't run around and jump on any male they can lay their hands on. Also, remember, you were working in the same department. Petra was careful in choosing her men. She got close to you after our divorce because she felt that you were a good catch. You would have made a good husband, and a caring step-father to Misha."

"After marrying me, do you think she would be faithful to me?"

"I can't answer that question. But knowing about Petra's condition, I doubt very much if she could control her urges."

"Oh, God, What should I do with Petra?"

"Here is the acid test. Who do you love more, Petra or Meena?"

"Neither, I love only you and no one else. You know, I was seeing those women only because I was so lonely after you left. I missed you and used to cry in my bed. I never wanted that divorce, but I was pushed into a corner."

"That's a very touching speech, Anant. I am sure you didn't come here to revive our relationship."

"What's wrong with it, Sheila? Didn't Elizabeth Taylor and Richard Burton got divorced and remarried?"

"Yes, that's true. But they also got re-divorced. What about that?"

"I don't care whether they got divorced again or not. That's not the point. I wouldn't have tried to find a woman if we never got divorced."

"Please don't try to make feel guilty. It's over, and let's move on. First, you deal with your women. Now that you know about Petra, do you still believe that the child could be yours?

"It's hard to answer the question without a DNA analysis. But she told me very emphatically that the child is mine."

"Anant, I want you to answer a question truthfully. Will you?"

"Sure, what do you want to know?"

"Tell me approximately how many times you were with Petra."

"Oh, may be twenty or thirty times, spread over a period of seven or eight months."

"So there were days or even weeks when you did not see Petra after you started living in your love-shack with Meena."

"You make it sound so horrible. I was only trying to find a suitable woman."

She said sarcastically, "I am sorry, I hurt your feelings. Anyway, coming to the point, there was no way Petra could have gone without sex for such a long time. She told me several times that she had to have it very frequently, otherwise she couldn't function. For her it was like an addiction. Petra is a nymphomaniac, and she deceived you with all that talk about her virtuous behavior. Of course, like a fool that you are, you fell for it."

"I guess that I should not marry her."

"I know you well, Anant. You are too sensitive, and it would be devastating if you got stuck to an unfaithful woman."

"Now that I know about Petra, I don't feel bad about dumping her."

"Good, we are making some progress with your love life. What about Meena? Do you love her?"

"I don't know, I guess I feel bad for her. But I am not sure. You see, she helped me find this job in New Jersey, and I am sort of obliged to her."

"Anant, just because she used her contacts to find you a job, you don't have to be her boyfriend for the rest of her life."

"She said that she would file for a divorce once her son went to college."

"But she didn't even start the proceedings so far, and now that the husband committed suicide, there is no need for a divorce. You see, Anant, divorce means she would get only a part of the estate. Now that the guy is dead, Meena stands to inherit the whole property. She was keeping you on the side for this eventuality. She probably knew one day that her loony husband will do something like that. You only know her side of the story. God only knows what she did, to push him over the edge. You are too gullible, Anant."

Anant got up and stretched, "Sheila, my head is spinning with all this talk. I feel like a drink. Do you have anything?"

"I have some beer and wine in the fridge. Help yourself."

He got himself a beer, "What do you like?"

"Nothing for me, I hardly drink. I got the beer and wine for you. I know you would like a drink in the evening."

He said, "Thanks. You know, I had my doubts about Meena's motives when she wanted me to join her company. But at that time I was also quite desperate about my fate in the department at Kansas City. It may look like she used me, but I also used her."

"Do you think you will be happy with her in the long run, Anant?"

"I really don't know, Sheila. If someone asked me whether you and I were going to be happy when we married, I would have told them that we would be together forever. But you know what happened. Life is very unpredictable."

She sat next to him and touched him on his shoulder. "I am sorry, Anant. I am the reason for the mess you are in. If only I listened to you in the beginning and took that VA job, things would have been very different. I guess it's too late now."

Anant put his drink down and came close to her and took her into his arms, "Sheila, it's not too late. You know I still love you. I always thought about you during these past two years. I know I am very selfish and never thought of calling you to see how you were doing. But one reason for not calling you was that I was not sure how you would respond. You see, during the last years of our marriage you would never listen to me, and I gave up on you. Now that you are back to your reasonable self, I can talk to you again."

He kissed her and was pleasantly surprised when she responded. It had been a long time since she felt this way, and she was quite amazed at herself. Neither of them had even the slightest inkling that their meeting would lead to this—a kiss which was a prelude to other things.

Afterwards, lying in his arms, she looked at him playfully. "Now what are we going to do? You made a mess of things again. I was leading a happy celibate life on the way to becoming a nun, now you have seduced me."

"Please come back to me, baby. I missed you very much. We will try again, and this time I promise you, I will do my best to keep you happy. If you still want to, we will adopt a baby. I should have agreed to adopt when we were together, and maybe we wouldn't have had the divorce."

"Anant, you are a good man. But why should we marry again? Can't we see each other without getting married?"

"No, Sheila. That won't work. I want you with me all the time. I want to live in the same house with you. I want to eat the food that you cook everyday. I want to make love to you everyday. You see, without you I am lost and make a mess of things."

"Okay, sweetie, why don't we take things slowly. But first get your affairs in order. Get rid of those women. You know, I don't care if you screwed around when I was not with you. But now that we are together again, I want you to be completely faithful to me. I don't believe in sharing you with any other woman. Is that clear?"

"Yes, Sheila. If you are with me, I don't want anyone else."

The next day, he left her place in the afternoon and reached his apartment in the evening. It was still hot and muggy with no rain in sight. He called Sheila to let her know that he reached safely. After that he sat down with a drink and thought about Petra. How could she deceive him like that with her, "My darling" business. He wondered how many other men she was darling-ing. But then again wasn't he also playing games with her, seeing Meena without Petra's knowledge? What's good for the goose is good for the gander. But in his case, he decided, once he settled down with one of them, he would be faithful. But if were to believe Sheila, and there was no reason for Sheila to tell a lie, he couldn't trust Petra to be satisfied with just one man. That would be miserable for him, and his marriage to Petra would be doomed from the beginning. After careful thought he composed a letter to Petra outlining his desire to end their relationship. He struggled with the idea of whether he should bring up the matter of her sexual promiscuity. He wrote one draft and then rewrote the whole thing. He struggled with the wording of his sentences, and in the end decided to sleep on it as he didn't strike the right chord. Unfortunately for him, it was not just a personal relationship that was going to be affected. Petra's participation was essential for their research project, and if she got upset, she might be crazy enough to pull out of the whole deal.

The next day he went to his office and saw a message from Dave, asking him to meet him at ten in the morning. Anant was surprised at this memo, as Dave was always informal, and if he needed something, he just walked into Anant's office. Anyway, he went to Dave's office at the appointed time. Dave offered him a seat and closed the office door.

"What I am going to tell you is confidential. This should not leave this room."

Anant was intrigued, "Fine."

"The fact is, I will be promoted to Vice President of Research and Development, and I need someone of your caliber to take up my position in this division. I would like to recommend your name to the president of the company. But before I speak to him I want you to think about it and get back to me as soon as you made up your mind. Your salary will go up quite significantly."

Anant was expecting this, but acted surprised. "Oh, Dave this is so unexpected. I am really glad that you are considering me for your job. I must have done something right!"

"Anant, you are very good, and we all love your work. I couldn't have found a better person to fill my shoes. So, think about it and let me know, okay."

"Fine, Dave, thanks for the vote of confidence. I will let you know in a day or two. I am concerned about the thesis defense of my two students, and I need to go to Kansas whenever the date is fixed. Once my students graduate, I can leave that place for good."

"I understand, Anant. The new job will be more stressful. You have to deal with the money men upstairs. But don't worry, I will be there to guide you in the beginning. But, if you need to make a couple of trips to Kansas to wind down your affairs there, you should be able to do it."

After he reached home in the evening he again thought

about Petra and how best to frame the e-mail. With the offer of a better job in the company, his future is reasonably secure in New Jersey, and he no longer had to worry about keeping the teaching job at Kansas City. Apart from his personal relationship with Petra, he felt that he should inform both Petra and Kevin about his decision to accept the job in New Jersey. He wanted to reassure them that he would continue to collaborate with them. Since he was still undecided about what to write to Petra, he first called Kevin. It was around nine in Kansas City, and Kevin never went to bed that early. Anant tried his landline first, and when there was no response, he tried Kevin's cell phone. After a few rings, Kevin answered.

"Hi, Kevin, this is Anant. Are you busy now, can we talk for a few minutes?"

"Sure, buddy. How are things there, man?"

"Actually, Kevin, I called to tell you about a new development here. I have been offered the position of a division head of medicinal chemistry, and I will accept it."

"Wow, that's great, buddy. Congratulations! I am really proud of you. Now you will be making mega bucks!"

"Yeah, the salary is pretty good, and I am excited about my new job and the challenges I will be facing."

"Thanks for the heads up. I appreciate your call."

"Okay, Kevin, let's keep in touch. I will let you know when I will be going to Kansas City. We can meet and have a drink."

"Fine by me, buddy, see you soon."

Just when Anant was about to hang up, he heard a high-pitched female voice with a distinctive Russian accent. "Come back to me, my darling."

Next he heard Kevin's voice. "That was Anant calling from New Jersey."

"Oh, Kevin, don't talk about work now. Just come inside me."

There was no doubt that the female was Petra. Anant didn't want to hear anymore and switched off his cell phone. He was surprised that he could hear their private conversation. Apparently, Kevin, in his hurry to be in Petra's arms, forgot to press the button to end the call and his phone was still active. Anant was furious with Petra. How could she take his diamond ring and then screw around with Kevin? That too such an expensive ring. Although he had complete faith in Sheila's words, there was a very small hope in his mind that, may be, just may be, Petra was not such a loose woman. Now he had no compunction in dumping her. This was the last straw. Given that he was no paragon of virtue, in his own mind, he decided to end his affair with Meena and settle down to a monogamous relationship with Petra when he proposed to her in Kansas City.

He sent an e-mail to Petra.

Hi Petra:

I wanted to call you but I thought it better if I sent you this e-mail. Due to reasons beyond my control, I can't marry you. I sincerely apologize for the inconvenience that my decision might cause you. I thought about this matter very carefully, and also consulted with Sheila about this. After listening to Sheila, I came to the conclusion that I will be very miserable if I chose to marry you. I think you know what I am talking about. I enjoyed your friendship and your moral support after my divorce. If the baby that you are going to have is really mine, I will provide child support. I hope that my decision will not cloud our professional relationship.

I also would like to inform you that I have accepted a permanent job here in this company. I will be the head of medicinal chemistry division, and I will take up this position in a month or two.

With best wishes to you and Misha.

A

Her reply came the next day.

Dear Anant:

I am going to have the baby and I don't need your money to raise my child. I don't really care who the father is.

I need to think about our professional relationship. It won't be easy for me to carry on as though nothing has happened. Even if you get your grant proposal funded, I am not sure that I want to be part of it.

Petra

He was relieved that he dealt with Petra swiftly and with minimal rancor. Now he had to tackle Meena, and let her know that he wouldn't be able to spend time with her anymore. He called Meena.

She answered, "Hi Anant, I can't talk now. But I will be at the apartment this evening. Will you be there?"

"Okay, see you then."

She came, and he offered her a glass of wine. She looked like she needed the drink as she gulped it down rather quickly. He refilled her glass.

She asked him, "Why did you call me? You know, at that time I was with some friends, that's why I couldn't talk."

"Oh, that's fine, Meena. I just wanted to tell you that Dave offered me the job. Thank you for all your help."

"It's my pleasure, my dear. I want you to be happy. So, are you going to accept the offer, or are you still thinking of going back to the boonies?"

"I think I will take the job."

She was thrilled. She got up from the couch and hugged and kissed him. When he didn't kiss her back, she was perturbed. "What's the matter, why are you so glum. I thought you will be happy about the new job."

He was feeling wretched to break the news to her at this moment when she was already burdened with so many problems. Whatever her motives regarding their relationship, she was always kind, gentle, and considerate, and did her best to keep him happy.

When he was silent for a long time, she asked him, "What's happening, my dear, why are you looking so sad?"

He couldn't keep quiet any longer. "Sheila wants to get back with me."

She was shocked. "What? I didn't know you kept in touch with her."

He didn't want to tell her the whole truth. "I didn't. But I got an e-mail from her."

She started crying and screamed. "But what right has she to walk into your life again, just like that? Does she think that you are still pining away for her? Now what is going to happen to us? I thought sometime next year we could get married." She looked into her wine glass and refused to make eye contact with Anant. He saw her lips tremble.

"I am sorry, Meena. I don't have any choice. Sheila is my first love, and I can't abandon her. She went through a lot, and if she needs me now, I should be with her."

She stopped crying, and wiped her eyes with a tissue, and took big swig of her wine. "Well, I guess we all have to make our choices. I know I can't stop you from doing whatever you want to do. I will get over my grief. Go to your Sheila, and make her happy."

Anant was relieved that she recovered rather quickly. "I want to talk to you about this apartment. I know we took a one-year lease. I can talk to the management and find out how I can get out of the lease. But I don't know what we should do about the furniture. Knowing Sheila, she won't be staying in this place. I need to get another apartment."

"Don't worry about the apartment and the furniture. I may vacate it and take the furniture to my house."

"But let me pay the rent until the end of the year."

"No, don't bother. I will take care of all that. You can stay here as long you need to. When you get your new place, just leave the key in the kitchen." She was gone.

The next weekend he visited Sheila. She was happy about his new job.

He asked, "So when are you going to join me in Princeton?"

"Who said anything about my going there? What gave you idea that I will leave my job and go to New Jersey?"

"But, you agreed that we will get back together."

"What I said was that we will take things slow and easy. Don't want to rush into anything. Let's see how this works out."

He was mad. "How the hell can we see how it will work out if we are three hours apart?"

"Come on, sweetie, don't be upset. Let's talk about it."

She went to the fridge, got him a beer, "Sweetie, can you open this wine bottle? I feel like having a glass."

He got her a glass of white wine, and after a few sips of their drinks, they again discussed the matter.

"Sweetie, I know what you want. I want the same thing too. But after one divorce and all that heart-ache, we need to be careful. That's all I am saying."

He cooled down. "I agree with you, Sheila. But I need to be with you. If we commute every weekend for about six hours, it won't leave us any time to relax. Please tell me what you are afraid of. In my new job I will be paid about two-hundred-thousand dollars per year, and we can afford to buy a nice house in the Princeton area. You don't have to work. I want you to stay at home, relax and take care of yourself. I am looking for an apartment, and most probably will move into it in a week or two. You can come there and help me furnish it, and we will stay in the apartment until we find a house. What do you think?"

"It's a great idea, sweetie. But I got a cushy job here.

They are paying me quite well and I hate to move again. Why don't you look for a job in this area? There are some pharmaceutical companies here, and I can ask my father to put in a word. After you work in the Princeton company for a few months in your new capacity as a division head, you can look around here for a similar job. That way you won't lose any pay or seniority."

"I see your logic. I don't mind doing that."

"Come on, sweetie, I know you will see my point of view. Let's go out for dinner and celebrate."

Epilogue

Anant received the reviewers' comments from *Nature*'s editorial office. The editor informed him that he would accept the manuscript after all the four reviewers' comments were addressed. It was unusual for a manuscript to be reviewed by four people, so Anant thought that the editor was being extra-careful. But after reading the comments, he understood why there were four reviewers. It appeared that the first two reviewers had had differing opinions about the work. One recommended it for publication, and the other rejected it. In view of those two conflicting reports, the editor had no choice but to send the manuscript to two other people. Finally, three out of four reviewers recommended that the manuscript be published. When he read all the comments carefully, the comments of the reviewer who rejected the manuscript appeared harsh and irrelevant. It appeared as though the person had made up his mind to reject the work even before writing those useless comments. In any case, the fact that the editor gave him a chance to revise the manuscript was good news.

It took some coaxing on part of Anant for Petra to help in revising the manuscript. She was still mad at Anant, but probably decided to participate as she was a co-author. Petra, Anant and Kevin worked hard to address each and every point made by the four reviewers, and revised the manuscript and sent it back to the editor. Within a week, they heard from the editor that their manuscript was accepted for publication. All the students who were co-authors on the manuscript were thrilled at the news. Since Subash and Yi did all the synthesis, they were the first authors of the manuscript. Anant took pains to indicate in the manuscript that they both had contributed equally to the work, and hence, both deserved to be first authors. It was a shot in the arm for his idea, and they all felt that their grant should be funded. As soon as he got the acceptance letter, Anant sent the final version of the manuscript to the project director in charge of processing their grant. Anant requested that the project director relay this information to the peer-review committee before they met to review the grant. The news that their work had been accepted in *Nature* spread like wildfire, and even Fong called Anant to congratulate him.

Sheila was thrilled see Anant so deliriously happy about his *Nature* paper. "Sweetie, it looks like you pulled off a very big one. Your father will be very proud of you. You must send him a reprint of your paper."

"Yeah. But you know without the help of Kevin and Petra, I couldn't have done it."

"But, sweetie, it's your idea. They were simply providing technical expertise. You are too modest."